C000108299

LONDON INTERRUPTED

THE DANNY FELIX SERIES: BOOK 1

J.A. MARLEY

First published in 2017 by Bloodhound Books
Re Published in 2023 by Spellbound Books
Copyright © J.A. Marley

The moral right of the author to be identified as the owner of this Work has
been asserted by them in accordance with the Copyright, Designs and Patents
Act, 1988.

All rights reserved. No part of this publication may be reproduced, stored in a
retrieval system, or transmitted, in any form or by any means, electronic,
mechanical, photocopying, recording or otherwise, without the prior
permission of the publisher.
This is a work of fiction. All names, characters, places, locations and events in
this publication, other than those clearly in the public domain, are fictitious,
and any resemblance to actual persons, living or dead, or any actual places,
business establishments, locations or events is purely coincidental.

Cover image and design © ARTeast 2023

To HJ...Storytellers together...

CHAPTER I
A RUDE AWAKENING

With a sound like the crack of a whip, the flat's front door exploded. The slam of the battering ram tore through, just below the dead lock.

Danny Felix was instantly reminded why this four-room wonder was his latest home, not because the rent was low and the landlord a lowlife, but because he could see the front door from his bed once he removed the bedroom door. That was a 'unique selling point' for Danny. With uninvited guests at the door he was pleased all the DIY paid off.

Four or five burly men came cramming into the apartment like a pack of crazed sale shoppers bursting into a department store on Black Friday... trying to get that eight hundred quid telly for twenty.

Danny spent the previous evening convincing the barmaid with the wicked laugh that he was a twenty-first century knight in shining armour and that she should come home with him... and she had. Any thought of some morning glory was shattered along with his front door.

Danny stayed put.

He lay there, his tall frame cool beneath the sheets, his deep set, blue-grey eyes watching, his breathing even despite the immediate threat before him.

A face pushed its way through the melee of bodies. Danny did not recognize it but assumed that it belonged to the main player.

Fuck me, he's big, Danny thought.

And then The Tall Man spoke.

"Good morning, Danny... pleased to see us? Or maybe not, eh?"

Turning to the girl. "Put something on love, I haven't had me breakfast yet. Danny here has to come with us for a chat, while we search the place. So, you might want to fucking do one... all right?"

The barmaid didn't need a second invitation, sprinting into the bathroom, gathering up her clothes as she went.

Once she was dealt with, they hauled Danny out of his bed. He stood there naked, matter of fact, all six four of him. He did not feel exposed or embarrassed. This was his home, after all, so why should he be? Danny caught sight of himself in the mirror on the wardrobe, taking in the scratch marks the recently departed young woman left on his side and back. At least she'd had a good time.

At twenty-eight, he was in his prime, a slim waist with a solid torso vee-ing up to broad shoulders and muscled, strong arms. His grey-flecked eyes were the most striking feature in an oval face with a firm jaw. All this was set off by early morning stubble with hint of auburn that matched his close-cropped hair. Last, but not least, was a small, quarter inch scar by his left eye, about where he would probably develop crows' feet in a few years. This was the only giveaway that he was taking this developing situation seriously. In times of excitement, stress, arousal, or all three, it glowed, the heat of it a constant reminder of a night when he didn't move fast enough. Right now, he could feel its burning presence without even having to study it in the mirror.

Maybe, Danny thought, *it's time to break the silence...* "Morning, officer... Shall I put the kettle on?"

The Tall Man, smiling now, took a long slow look around the room. "A brew would be most welcome... but what makes you think I'm Old Bill?" The Tall Man winked as he said it, and then nodded to his accomplices.

Suddenly, they were tearing the place apart...

Danny Felix was a thief.

He didn't feel proud of the fact, but neither was he embarrassed by it.

He also knew he was very, very good at the dark art of thievery.

Betting shops, post offices, cash in transit vans, he'd even had a crack at a bank a few times. He pulled off jobs in them all and spent not so much as a single day in the grey-barred hotel.

Still, he had always known that a day like today would roll around at some point.

The men were a blur, while he stood impassive. He knew their search wouldn't last long. His small flat didn't sport much more than the basics: Bed. TV. Small sofa and some kitchen stuff, no fuss, no paraphernalia, no excess. It was one of Danny's rules for what he did. Stick the spoils of your light-fingered fun somewhere and don't over complicate matters. Keep your outward life minimal, so that there would never be regret should you have to abandon it all at a moment's notice.

Except... after his most recent little bit of misappropriation Danny had not yet had time to do the sticking away. Not that he hadn't been clever, just that it was closer than he would have liked.

Watching the various kitchen drawers being emptied and the mattress being ripped apart was all rather amusing, but for the hunters it was unfruitful. At first, he thought he might just get away with it this time. They looked like they couldn't find their own dicks in the toilet without help. Then his heart sank. A yelp. An excited bark. A flurry of furry.

Bollocks.

A Springer Spaniel, all tail wagging, sniffing and eager to please. *If you are going to take one on the chin, losing out to a cute dog was just about bearable,* Danny mused. At least it would be fun to watch because the dog was about to get a dose of sensory overload.

"Anything you want to discuss with me before this little Hound of the Baskervilles gets going?"

The Tall Man, who Danny noted was yet to give himself a name, was standing in the living room looking down with barely concealed mirth in his eyes that soon spread to a full-on smile.

Danny thought a shrug would suffice for now. Why make their lives any easier? The Springer went to work and as Danny expected, went bananas. Like, apoplectic bananas. Barking, growling, dancing around in circles as though he was trying to chase his tail but couldn't. Next it was shooting from the kitchen to the bedroom to the living room to the bathroom, and generally looking like a kid on a sugar rush.

Everybody stopped.

The amusement on The Tall Man's face faded.

The dog's handler became flustered, repeatedly calling the dog's name, "Jiffy," in a vain attempt to gain some control.

"Fucking hell, Jim. Get furry balls down to business, will you?"

Jiffy was panicking. The poor dog didn't know which way to turn and Danny couldn't hold out any longer. He laughed.

The sound of the heavy, flat-handed slap The Tall Man delivered to Danny's face gave even Jiffy pause. Kicking out at the dog, he grabbed Danny by the hair, his face reddening, spit flying.

"Think this is a fucking joke, do you? Where is it? You know what we're looking for. Now do yourself a favour and tell me or do I have to wipe the walls with your face?"

"Guv... Guv."

The Tall Man backed away long enough to look at where the dog handler was pointing. Jiffy was licking the wallpaper like it was made of beef gravy.

"What the fuck is the bloody dog doing?"

Danny knew. He knew only too well, and as his head was swimming and his eyes watering, he couldn't do much to mask his gathering disappointment. The dog was good. Give the furry grass some credit.

The Tall Man and the dog handler were crouched at the spot where Jiffy was sniffing and licking furiously. Using a knife from Danny's own kitchen (insult to injury), they peeled away at a corner of the wallpaper. The game was up, at least for now, as it revealed a fresh and additional layer of insulation between the actual wall and the wallpaper. Made exclusively of fifty-pound notes, the new insulation was stuck there temporarily using an old-fashioned mixture of flour and water. No wonder the poor dog went nuts. Sensory overload indeed. At least two walls in each room were extravagantly decorated this way.

The Tall Man, now back to his original good humour, stood up and crossed to Danny, who braced himself for another not-so-happy slap.

"I'm Detective Inspector Harkness. You are Danny Felix and

that..." – pointing to the wall of money – "... is much, much more like it. Clear out, lads. Danny and I need a chat..."

Surprise, surprise, Danny thought, *a fucking cop, a big one at that, and now he's got what he was looking for. Jiffy got a dog treat and I'm going to get what? A chat? This'll be interesting.*

Oh, and another thing; someone else must have been chatting, too. A little too chatty, or else why was Danny standing here now with his ears ringing, sick to his stomach and nowhere to escape to before the shit hit the fan?

The flat emptied almost as rapidly as it filled up, and the newly revealed detective looked squarely at the thief before him. "Get dressed. Let's do a little redecorating before we talk, shall we?"

CHAPTER 2

CHANCE

THE YOUNG COUPLE STOOD OUTSIDE THE BOUTIQUE JEWELLERY STORE in Wheathampstead for the umpteenth time.

And it was still there, twinkling beautifully in the window; the engagement ring that had been the subject of seventy-five percent of the girl's waking thoughts since she'd first laid eyes on it.

There was no price tag, but her boyfriend had managed to find out the bad news on the quiet; just shy of £3,000. He supposed it wasn't much to ask, it was a once in a lifetime purchase. What she didn't know was that he had managed to sell his motorcycle and his old man had weighed in with a loan of sorts to tip the balance. And so, here they were at the window, looking.

Today, their adventure was to take her into the shop and buy that ring for her.

Except today was not to be a romantic day.

Not in the slightest.

As the young man gently whispered into her ear that they should go in and maybe try on that ring, as the surprise spread across her face, a huge motorbike roared up the street and all the romance in the world rushed to someplace else.

The bike, a beast of a Suzuki, with a rider and a passenger, reared up onto the pavement right by the window. The passenger wielded what looked like some kind of gun, and as that thought registered with the young man... *Bang!*

Suddenly the window was gone, and the bike passenger rifled through the shattered glass and had his hand on the ring, their fucking ring, and everything else around it.

The bike revved up in pitch and intensity, about to scream off... except now three cars had arrived, tires screeching. Acrid burnt rubber hung in the air, as cops in peaked, checked black and white caps dived out of cars, shouting, also holding guns. The driver clearly thought it was time to make an exit.

The Suzuki's big engine roared with a whopping kick when the throttle was pulled back, causing the whole bike to leap.

Leap.

Forward it went, just five feet from where the boy had pulled his girl behind him, trying his best to shelter her from this fucking craziness.

The motorcycle's front wheel met the front end of the BMW 3 series that tried to obstruct its way, the heavy engine block under the bonnet enough to send the bike up.

Up.

People talk about such events unfolding in front of them in slow motion.

Crock of shit.

He saw what happened next in a series of flashing, shiny, heart-breaking moments. The bike cartwheeled up, rear wheel over front, the two riders propelled like projectiles over the handlebars. As they did, the shotgun used so expertly to destroy the window was now spinning, first up, then with gravity playing its part, dropping right in front of him.

Asked many times after that day, he still couldn't remember the next moment. He heard his girlfriend scream her head off. He suddenly couldn't stand. The glass and gravel were digging into his face and he felt an unrelenting heat in his legs. He could smell a bitter mix of fireworks and burning flesh. And then more burning to a level of intensity he hadn't thought possible. He screamed.

Suddenly there were lots of people. A flurry of activity and the nearest, a woman with one of the checked caps, told him to take it easy, stay where he was, not to move his legs if he could at all help it.

And that was all Detective Inspector Christine Chance could say to the man… she didn't want to be the one to tell him.

If only the shotgun had landed facing the other way. If only they had not removed the trigger guard when they had sawn it down. If only the blast from the shotgun had not been close enough to blow this poor bloke's foot off at the ankle.

Christine Chance, or CC to her friends and colleagues, had experienced bad days on the job before. All coppers had. The days that really upset them were the random, meaningless ones. Ones like today. Should've, would've, could've…

So, when she had one, she couldn't help but turn the events over in her mind again and again, just as she was doing now.

In all other respects, 'the job' had gone off perfectly. They kept the would-be robbers in their sights, no Old Bill got rumbled. Textbook follow and foil.

Except for the accident, she thought. Was it that? An accident? Once the thieves pulled the gun and the shout "robbery

robbery robbery" went up, the cops had to move in. Guns out, civilians in the line of fire, game on.

For someone who considered herself a proud-to-serve, life-long, career copper, today was like a thumb in the eye. Still, the bad guys had been taken out right on the pavement . It was better than allowing these bastards another chance and another set of bystanders to crash through.

No, Christine felt proud of what she did. She understood that sometimes there were payoffs and compromises, but what she really loved was the sound of a set of cuffs biting into a pathetic suspect's wrists. CC knew in her heart that hers was a big job, a big set of responsibilities and she loved doing it, especially the action-packed stuff.

And now that she had answered all the follow-up questions from the police oversight team, signed the statements, and taken statements for her own arrests, it was time to deal with completely different stuff.

The really difficult stuff. Personal stuff.

Christine Chance got out of the car and started towards the building that contained everything in her life that she held dear but was now heartbreak made solid in brick. The weight of the walk threatened to push her under, drowning her beneath the wash of her own anxiety, but she kept going, kept walking. It was funny, in life-or-death moments, ones that involved crime, random fate, violence and, sometimes, sheer luck, she never doubted her next step. She never wavered, always propelled herself forward. How about now? How about here? Here she felt continually unsure. Off balance. Sliding towards a certainty that she would try to deny with each and every breath she took, despite the futility of the effort.

CC stood at the entrance to the hospice. She was here to spend time with her dying daughter.

CHAPTER 3

Q&A HARKNESS STYLE

THEY STRIPPED THE WALLS OF THE FIRST ROOM AND ALREADY THERE was a stack of crisp, or rather crispy, fifty-pound notes on the floor between them. Danny was giving it the broken TV treatment – all picture, fuck all sound. But as long as they were peeling money from behind the wallpaper, D.I. Harkness seemed content enough.

Now that there were only the two of them left in the room, it seemed the huge policeman had decided he had seen enough.

Time to have that chitchat.

"How much...?"

Danny looked at him with flat eyes, trying to keep all emotion from his face, trying to telegraph indifference and defiance simultaneously. The two of them measuring the size of their respective robber/detective dicks, like two boxers sharing a ring for the first time together.

"I don't know anything about anything... I only rent this flat."

Harkness cocked his head to one side, like a dog listening to the sound of his food being poured into a bowl, a smile breaking across his big flat wide face.

"Now, Danny, you don't think I'm here through simple detective work, do you? No! You're already trying to figure out who grassed up you and your little private bank. So, let's just say, let's pretend, that I'm not your run-of-the-mill 'inspector plod'. All right? Now how much did you steal from that security van?"

Danny gave him nothing back.

"It was you and two others. A driver. Someone else to do the lift work while you used the charm and guile of a pair of Glocks to convince the poor dumb dickhead in the helmet to hand over the bags. Your driver was a big Polish lad, Janusz Piesakowska. Done time once before for a botched bookie job. The heavy lifter was a sweaty jock, Nelson... Frankie, I believe. They were interesting old pros."

Were? What did he mean "were"? Danny was beginning to feel anxious about this supposed policeman. He was starting to feel like a rat that had just nibbled on the wrong bit of cheese.

"Let me see your hands."

Danny didn't quite compute first time round so the cop repeated the demand, this time grabbing Danny's wrists and flipping the palms upwards.

"Now Danny, didn't your old mum ever tell you that your hands are supposed to be used for good? These are supposed to be God's hands. To do the Lord's work. Hands can give, not just take all the time. Didn't your mother ever tell you that?"

And suddenly Harkness had one of Danny's wrists in a vice-like grip. One meaty fist twisting his palm upwards and into place, the other hand slapped down on top. But this was no handshake of peace.

Harkness had a sharpened door key between two of his fingers. The fat end was just visible between his knuckles. The toothy, business end of it was pointing downward.

Harkness started to grind.

Danny was shocked at how much pain such an everyday, seemingly innocent object could inflict. His breath caught in his chest. He held it there to show no weakness to the big cop.

The key felt like it had been stuck in a furnace, scorching hot, twisting, digging, gouging into Danny's flesh. All the while, Harkness looked straight into Danny's eyes, not smiling, not blinking... just looking. He was taking the measure of the man in front of him.

Danny could feel blood drip at his own feet. Try as he might, he could not squirm free of the grip. Just as he thought the red-hot burn of the key might make its way clear through to the bone, Harkness let go. He palmed the key away, almost as magically as he had made it appear between his fingers, and finally stood back.

"Danny, I am a very determined man. Motivated, you might say. Just give me an approximate figure for your fancy wallpaper and I will give you the lay of the land."

Staring at the bloody hole in the centre of his hand, Danny didn't look up...

"Twenty-five and change. Maybe thirty, I haven't counted."

Smiling again, a playful light in his eyes, Harkness passed Danny a dish towel for the blood on his hand and then clapped his big meaty hands together, letting out a short laugh. "Take a drive with me."

And with that, Danny was ushered out of his own flat, taken down the staircase to the front passenger seat of an Audi, and driven off into the early morning light.

The buildings of central London whipped by at seventy miles an hour. At around five in the morning, the sun, extending light and benevolence into the June sky, helped make this particular joyride almost a pleasant one.

The burning in the palm of his hand was a simple refrain anchoring Danny to the gravity of his situation. Right now, sitting in the car next to Harkness, the pull of that gravity seemed to be getting heavier by the second.

The big cop had not said a word since he fired up the car's engine and took off like he was a race car driver. And now here they were, heading towards London's West End theatre district at a hundred and illegal miles an hour.

Harkness finally broke the silence. "I love the sound of a great, dirty, big engine telling the world to fuck right off... don't you, Danny? Or are you too full of questions right now to appreciate the *Vorsprung durch Technik*? Tell you what, just sit back and enjoy the revs, Mr. Felix."

And with that, Harkness pushed the accelerator even flatter to the floor, Marylebone Road flashing past them, Harkness stealing only glances at the road while staring at the side of Danny's face. Even at that time of day, and despite the traffic on the London thoroughfares, Harkness handled the German car like a pro. To a chorus of horns and gesticulations only glimpsed in the rear-view mirror, the car blew every red light between Tottenham Court Road and Baker Street. Traffic cameras flashed like paparazzi as they went, but his driver didn't seem to mind, and as they climbed the elevated section of the road, Danny could have sworn they would take off as they crested the rise. As they did, Harkness let out what can only be described as a feral howl, filling the interior of the car with noise and his breath.

Just eight minutes later, they reached an exit off the divided highway leading to a cluttered industrial park that sat cheek by jowl with rows upon rows of housing projects, a journey that at the wrong time of day could take the guts of an hour. But now they were slowing.

The Audi found its way to the gate of a construction site where a new set of high-rise somethings were emerging from the scrabbly ground. Flashier, classier, the latest part of the city to get the gentrification treatment.

The car came to a rest.

"Out." Harkness barked like he was talking to a dog.

As they stood in front of a gate at the entrance to the site, Harkness motioned for Danny to go through first. As they walked, Harkness talked.

"Cities are amazing things aren't they, Danny? Living. Breathing. Constantly changing. Refreshing themselves in the image of some corporation or billionaire developer at the skyline, while the little man does what he can with his shop front or a window box hanging off a shitty flat at street level."

"What cities *don't* do is stand still. If you do, you might as well die, my fine young thief. Orders change, circumstance shifts and that is why we were supposed to meet. Today."

Harkness had Danny's attention. Fuck knows he had got it from the moment he had walked into his flat. This crazy bastard made Danny's intuition crackle, an alarming, static charge in his gut that could not be ignored. This copper was one player not to be ignored, underestimated, or crossed lightly.

Danny took that moment to take him in again, assessing the Tall Man who jerked his chain like the owner of a puppy in obedience school.

Harkness was big, yes, but not bulky or fat. He was just... big. He looked cut from granite, standing there, all six feet something of him, broad in the shoulders with a massive head that seemed out-of-scale for his body. He might even have been considered handsome, except at the last minute the head size robbed him of that particular gift. His wide, flat face was perhaps a touch Slavic or Eastern European, but his accent was pure London. His hair was swept back and dark. There were no signs of grey, not even at the temples. And then there were his eyes — they bothered Danny the most. The pupils wide and dark, like they were dilated, the surface almost devoid of an iris, just deep dark pools of 'God knows what' potential.

No doubt. This was a crazy bastard in front of him, one to handle with care.

"And so, Danny, just like this great city of ours, the part you play in its rambling, rumbling history is about to change."

They were at the foot of one of the new high-rises, walking behind it to an expanse where an area about the size of a house had been staked out on the ground. Next to it a cement lorry, its body gently turning, a load obviously sloshing around within.

"When it's done this will be a security station, a place for small men in blue uniforms to sit in and watch TV and get fat, all so that the wealthy homeowners who will fill up this space can feel safe at night. Yes, a security hut, but a fucking fancy one mind, all CCTV and alarm systems going full speed. What better place to secure one's own, changing future?"

They were looking down into the trenches that would hold the concrete foundations of the guardhouse. More trepidation built in Danny's always-to-be-trusted gut. Was he about to meet a clichéd, cement bath end? For pulling an security van job? Had he stepped on organized crime toes? Upset some Eastern European gang? His mind raced through the possibilities as fast as a synapse can snap, but none were reasons for being executed.

Harkness grabbed Danny's shoulder, interrupting his mental checklist. They were now face to face, the tall cop looking into him with those eyes. He spoke gently, almost in a whisper, as if worried someone might overhear them.

"Now, Danny, what we found at your flat earlier. Not a bad little haul, one might say, enough for all of us, as the Old Bill saying goes. The word is that you are excellent at what you do. I like excellence. Whether it is in my wine, my football team, or my women, I like excellence. And that little pile of money pretty much proves your reputation of having a cracking set of light fingers.

"So, here is your future. You are now working for me. We will treat the wallpaper as my consultation fee, as I guide you to bigger and better things. Don't worry about paperwork and red tape. Every single cop who tore up your sparse abode this morning also works for me. I say the word, and stuff gets forgotten, or lost... or both.

"Welcome to your new life, son. I know most people hate change; they resist it. But the ones who do, often they are the ones who don't make it. I can help you and you can help me. This change will be good for us both... you'll soon see.

"A wise man once said, 'All great changes are preceded by chaos'... Danny, here we are. I. Am. Your. Chaos."

Harkness accompanied his last words with a big meaty hand on the back of Danny's neck, jostling his head at each syllable.

A black Ford transit van crept across the site towards them, pulling up alongside them. Two men got out and went around the back to open the doors.

"And just so that you know that I am very serious, and indeed, committed to our future together, Danny Felix, I thought I would give you something, a little signing on gift... so you wouldn't doubt my sincerity."

At that, the two men came from behind the transit van, each

carrying a body on their shoulders, heading straight to the foundation trench directly beside the cement truck.

Harkness guided Danny by the neck over towards the same spot, only letting go when the two heavy lifters caught up with them.

And there it was: the reason for the anxiety in Danny's oh-so-ever-reliable gut. He couldn't keep the shock off his face as the two bodies were unceremoniously flopped into the trench, landing face up, blank-eyed and staring.

Danny was looking at the obviously recently deceased bodies of Janusz Piesakowska and Frankie Nelson, the two men who had helped him rob the cash van. Both had been garrotted, blood cascading down their fronts, eyes still bulging from sadistically brutal deaths.

Dragging his gaze from his two ex-partners, Danny looked over to where Harkness was standing by the cement lorry.

"You see? I'm very serious about the pursuit of excellence. I'll be in touch soon, Danny."

And with that, Harkness pulled a lever on the big truck and its contents poured onto the staring corpses.

CHAPTER 4
LITTLE 'UN

JUST BEFORE ENTERING THE WARD, CHRISTINE CHANCE WENT TO THE ladies' loo.

After splashing a little water onto her face, she gripped the sides of the sink and took a long, deep breath as she raised her eyes to meet her face in the mirror.

She looked tired. But that was no surprise. Crow's feet were beginning to make their presence known around her clear, green eyes. Her mousy blonde bob framed her almond-shaped face, a face that was once quick to light up with a smile, but now wore a heaviness that was nothing to do with her job and all to do with the fact that she felt daunted by the task ahead.

She pulled herself up to her full five-feet-nine, and silently counted to ten.

It was this way every time for her. One last attempt to steady herself before facing her worst fears.

It was very late at night, but the nurses, with her daughter's help, had long ago worked out what she did for a living and so never seemed to mind that her visiting hours bore no relation to common sense. She was never challenged, never asked to leave, never given even so much as an odd look. Sometimes, when her child was having a rough day, Christine wished they would stop her at the heavy double doors, but that had never happened.

CC made her way to the furthest corner of the small ward. The rectangular room housed just five beds. Five souls waited for their last step into whatever next life they chose to believe in.

And there, in a bed that had once seemed regular size but now appeared giant by the way it dwarfed its frail occupant, lay Christine's daughter, Shauna Elizabeth Chance. The scale of the child to the scale of the bed was the most telling sign, in Christine's mind at least, of just how ravaged her child was by her cancer. She had been a vibrant, joyous kid. She loved music, dancing and, much to Christine's constant surprise, WWE wrestling.

But what started as an achy back that they both attributed to camping out with friends turned out to be something much more sinister and insidious.

Shauna's breathing was shallow, raspy but regular. The eleven-year-old was asleep in a chemically enhanced haze. Machines gently monitored and beeped, keeping track of the decline that Christine knew was accelerating.

It was in these quiet moments that CC's mind wandered to thoughts of what was right and wrong, what seemed fair and unjust. How did you measure a life? And how could it be endangered when it had only really just begun? To Christine, her daughter's slow and undoubtedly painful trek to this point, where Ewing Sarcoma clenched its fist around her spine, seemed a fate that should only be reserved for the worst human, not an innocent child. When those thoughts and feelings crept up on Christine, she felt the worst pangs of guilt, hurt, and anticipation of loss. But she also realised that what she really felt was anger.

Angry with her daughter, angry with the world, angry with nature, angry with God.

Cancer toyed with this girl, her little girl, and made Shauna dance to a dirge of pain.

At first, she prayed that it would be all okay. God's good, it'll all be fine, the doctors will find a way. And Christine needed to believe they would. Needed to know that by being a good person, daughter, mother, copper, friend and the Almighty might give them a fighting chance at recovery.

But as time and the cancer rushed on, she felt foolish for hoping. And that led her to anger.

What could she do about it? What could anyone do about it?

Nothing.

Deal with that, CC girl, she thought.

And while she tried to reason with herself, Christine sat there and listened. Every beep, each ragged breath, soon realisingshe, herself, was holding hers until her daughter's next vital intake, however weak.

Movement in the bed, a flutter of papery eyelids. Her daughter was awake.

"Mum, is that you?"

"Hiya, sweetheart. Here at some crazy hour as usual."

"I don't mind, Mum."

"Want to sit up the bed? I can get those pillows a little higher?"

As they worked together; Christine understood how skeletal her daughter was.

"What's the latest? Catch any bad men today?"

It never failed to surprise Christine how much Shauna loved to chat about police work. Most girls her age wanted to talk about celebrity gossip, the male nurses, or pop stars. But Shauna never seemed to tire of her mum's latest news.

Christine obliged with a child-friendly version of the day's events. And Christine felt better for it, they both did. Certainly, easier than conversations about chemo or surgical options — which were running out — or new-fangled drugs that no one could afford (there were tons).

When the day's news had been talked out, Shauna motioned to the drawer of her dresser. "Keith, that male nurse, the tall one. He gave me something today, look in the top drawer."

Christine reached over and pulled out a newspaper.

It was folded to a double page spread with a big photo of Shauna's favourite boy band at its centre.

"That was nice of him, love. A whole page dedicated to your crushes. And their shirts seemed to have disappeared! I'm not sure this is suitable for a young mind like yours!"

"Mum! Stop being a weirdo! And look at the other page; I spotted it ages after Keith gave it to me."

Christine flipped the page to another double spread story. There was a huge photo leading the editorial line.

The shot was taken from a long way off, so it was grainy but clear enough to make out the shape of several men prone on the ground with a lot of other people around them. The peaked caps with black and white checkers singled out the police easily enough. The men on the ground were, of course, the baddies, under a headline that declared: Grounded! Heathrow Haul Record As Cops Foil Huge Drug Ring.

Looking closely at the shot, Christine realised, with a little surprise, that she could see herself in the foreground. Not that anyone could have instantly recognized her, but she knew her own time and place, and she had definitely been there.

She looked at Shauna.

"I thought that was you up front, but I couldn't be sure."

"It's me but this stuff is supposed to just happen and fly under the radar."

"I knew I was right... but anyway, back to the nurse. He was asking all about you... I think he thinks you're sexy!"

"Shauna Chance!"

The exclamation full of mock indignation prompting a fit of giggles from both of them.

"Just, you know, saying, he has nice eyes."

"Enough, you, you'll be getting both of us into trouble. Anyway, what would I want with a man, they're just hassle."

"Yeah, but fit hassle, and anyway, they love me in here, I can get away with loads."

Christine immediately felt sad when her daughter said this. She knew Shauna would feel it too, so no need to go there. Being a cancer ward's best customer was never a title to aspire to.

Tiredness finally hit Christine like a heavyweight in the third round and she tried to stifle a yawn.

Before CC could protest, her kid told her goodnight. "Go on, get some sleep, Mum. We can talk more in the morning."

CC nodded. "I'll be in tomorrow, we need to talk doctors and stuff, find out the latest."

Shauna dropped her eyes to her chest, and agreed softly, before adding, "Will you get another gold star, commendation thingy? For the airport job?"

"There's talk."

"And you still won't go along..."

"Who needs gold stars, eh?"

"I like them. I get to keep them in my shoebox, with the others, and my old Teddy bears and stuff."

"G'night, Shauna. Love you." A kiss on the forehead.

"G'night, Mum. Love you too... I'll tell Keith you said hello."

CC waved off her comment and walked away from the bed.

She felt like she was on the end of a string, like a yo-yo, spinning away from her fears as far as possible, only to shoot back on herself again as fast as the pull of the string allowed, engulfing her in every horror scenario she could imagine for her daughter and even more afraid of the ones she couldn't.

Danny looked into Celeste's eyes. Green-flecked with hazel, they radiated so much emotion, more, he thought, than any other he had known. Belonging as they did to one of the few people he trusted, these eyes gave him a sense of calm, as though nothing could rock or blow him off whatever course he might be set upon. The irony of this was not lost on Danny since he knew Celeste rarely approved of any of his escapades, and today was to be no exception.

What would you expect from your big sister?

"Bloody hell, Danny. I hate it when you do that!" slapping him on the chest as she said it.

Danny did like appearing in her kitchen when she least expected him to, standing there enjoying the aroma of fresh coffee and toast, the table bearing the aftermath of a breakfast enjoyed by two kids who had already left for school, and a husband to whatever it was he did in the big city firm.

As Danny had silently let himself in through the back door, his sister was standing with her back to him, staring intently at her mobile, her thumbs a blur over the virtual keyboard.

Growing up, people were always mistaking them for twins, when in fact Celeste had three years on him. She was tall and dark haired like Danny. She moved with the same easy fluidity he did. Now a working mother with a high-powered job and high maintenance kids, Danny thought she was amazing, while she thought he was still a kid like her own two.

Except this big kid had a taste for trouble.

Celeste was the only remnant of his family Danny cared about. When he was with her, he was glad to be there, even if she was judging him, lecturing him or both at the same time.

"Danny, I hate it when you creep up on me... and where have you been? You look like shit." Then a manicured finger in the air. "Don't answer that, I don't want to know..."

"I had some unexpected visitors."

Her eyes instantly widened. "Were you arrested? What are you into now, for Christ's sake?"

Danny only shook his head in reply and pointed his finger in the direction of the coffee pot.

She took the hint, grabbing a mug and pouring. "I haven't got long; I have to be at the office by nine. What's going on?"

"I have made some new friends, and I am not sure I like them. I just came to pick something up."

Celeste arched one of her eyebrows. "What? From your old things you left in the garage a couple of years ago?"

Danny had a habit of moving about once every year, Celeste sometimes helping with interim storage, sometimes not, if she was in one of her 'I don't approve of your life choices' moods.

"Who are these people, Danny? What kind of a fuck-up are you setting up for yourself?"

The pitch of her voice rose in tandem with her sense of alarm.

"I do just fine, Celeste. My life is my own... I am not like you. I was not built for all... of this."

Danny gestured to the room, house... the family home. "I do just fine, don't measure me by your standards, sis."

They both knew they were spiralling towards a very familiar argument, one which neither liked, but felt strongly enough to dig their heels in over. Danny tried to head it off. "I just need to get into your garage."

"It's not locked, but you already know that. Let yourself in, you do most other places..."

"Come on, sis... Don't be like that."

A pause fattened between them, both circling their love for one another as well as their frustrations.

Celeste broke first. "Dad was asking for you..."

"Really? I'll write the date down. I don't know how you can even talk to that old man."

"Danny!"

The tensions threatened to build again so he made for the utility room door that led to the garage.

Once in there, he didn't need the assistance of the overhead lights to locate what he was looking for, lifting up his sister's beloved treadmill from the front end, reaching underneath.

His fingers soon located the black leather pouch he had sequestered there nearly eighteen months previously. He unzipped it and checked its contents. Satisfied, he turned to go, only to bump straight into his sister, who, it seemed could be as quiet on her feet as he was.

She reached up instinctively to cushion the impact of their collision, her hand pressing the black leather pouch flat against Danny's midriff.

Her eyes widened, shock flashed across her face, replaced by fury in the next instant. "Danny, is that what I fucking think it is?"

"I have to go, sis. It's just a tool of the trade and a little money. They cleaned me out... I'm sorry."

He was brushing past her, trying to get out before the storm of her ire really hit, and God did she know how to get angry.

Mind you, who could blame her? How many sisters with small kids would be that happy about a Glock 19 handgun, holding seventeen rounds and a spare clip, being stored in their garage?

CHAPTER 5
DUE DILIGENCE

A FEW, UNSETTLING DAYS PASSED SINCE DANNY WALKED AWAY FROM Harkness. Unsettling was the right word, in fact the only word, simply because everything else around him seemed so unchanged and normal.

Danny had a lot of thinking to do as he made his way through a central London evening.

Harkness and his mates drove away and had left Danny to find his own way back home from the building site.

Once back at his flat, Danny was amazed to find that while all the walls had been stripped and the money gone, the flat had been left tidy.

Life seemed to trundle on. No strange cars in the street, no catching half glimpses of a face, a shadow sent to keep an eye on Harkness's newest acolyte... you know, to make sure that a disappearing act was not imminent.

No, Danny was not being followed. Nor was there any sign in the papers or the broadcast news about his recently, dearly departed collaborators, Frank, and Janusz.

Life was unnervingly quiet in Danny's opinion. Of the three basic, instinctual human reactions to trauma: fight, flight, or freeze... he couldn't find great enthusiasm for any of them. He reckoned if he tried flight, Harkness would somehow know where to look. He seemed a resourceful type. As for freeze, Danny Felix never allowed himself to give in to panic. God knows he had been in enough high stress situations to know his own heart and mind, and they had never, thus far, strayed to flapping or fluster.

As for fight? Now, that was the trickiest of options.

Danny was not a traditionally violent man. He felt that sometimes force could be a useful tool; more precisely he knew that the threat of implied or impending violence could be just as good and way more efficient as the act itself. But then again on some occasions a fist, a flash of blade, or, at the worst, the bang flash wallop of a discharged sawn-off was the only way left to go.

Not that he was against killing someone if they got in the way. Danny didn't much like people. They had an unerring way of letting you down in almost any situation. But equally, he felt that if you resorted to killing, it must be a sign that you were not fully prepared in the first place, or you were trying to steal something so big, that the lives lost were worth the pay off.

Fighting unknown quantities was nothing short of stupid, Danny thought. Know who it is you are about to slap. Know how they like to slap back. Know where they least want and expect to be slapped. Due diligence, see? Preparation was crucial in every job, big or small. What was that irritating phrase that boring people who did boring jobs used? Fail to prepare... prepare to fail. That was it. Now if someone ever used that phrase to your face, you'd go ahead and slap them straight away. What would a man who used handy phrases like that ever have in his locker to hurt you with?

Danny preferred his wisdom a little more elegiac. Street philosophy made a lot of sense to him. If someone wanted a fistfight, bring a knife. If they had a knife...step it up to a gun. Shift the odds in your favour in whatever way you could. He remembered a schoolyard fight of his own. A bigger boy taunting him, older, stronger, more experienced. Danny needed something, anything to give him an edge. And then it came to him. His coat. It had a particularly big zipper, the end of it metal and heavy. So, as the bigger boy charged at him, fists cocked, Danny casually shook off his coat and started swinging it around his head. Before his enemy had a chance to reach him, the zipper had done its work. It connected with the boy's eye, eliciting a sharp squeal of pain. In a second the confrontation was over. Street philosophy. When you haven't a chance...use anything to give yourself one. And the best way to do that was to be prepared. From that day on, Danny was always ready. He preferred planning to improvisation, even though he was lucky with his own on that school day.

Danny Felix became a devotee of due diligence. Ask a few questions, put the right queries to the right people, and you had something to conjure with.

Not that Danny was preparing for all-out war with Inspector Harkness.

Not right out the gate anyway.

If he was honest, Harkness was intriguing. Danny didn't think he'd ever heard of him. That made him an interesting quantity straight away. But he had to admit, Harkness had burst upon the scene in the most colourful of ways. He made sure his agenda was set out with some panache. Danny had liked Frank. Janusz he tolerated because of his skill set, but he wasn't married to them, so when they turned up all glassy eyed and limp at the building site, he hadn't been heartbroken... more surprised. No mean feat for one member of the criminal fraternity to surprise another, even if this member was a game-keeper with aspirations of poaching.

So, the mystery needed to be unravelled a little, the unknown quantity needed to become a known one.

Questions asked and hopefully answered. Which meant a trip to see Dexy.

In London, the saying goes that you are never more than twenty feet from a rat. In some parts of the city though, Danny figured you could probably revise that estimate down to about ten feet. Especially in the centre of the city, where tourists, trannies, showbiz agents, media luvvies, hookers, actors, pickpockets, pimps, publishers, drug dealers and even the odd cop all rub shoulders: Soho. Danny loved it.

Clubs and coffee shops festooned what used to be the most luridly colourful section of the bustling, busy West End. Peep shows and strip bars had been marginalized, but the underbelly still existed... just in a more stylishly acceptable way. Soho had gentrified. But not completely.

Dexy's place was a perfect case in point.

From the outside, Dexy's was just a door. An anonymous looking door, but one that lead to a place where people gathered. They talked, ate, drank, caroused, and completed all manner of transactions, some financial, some sexual and even some political. Whatever your trade, if you could afford the membership or had a special arrangement with the owner, then Dexy's would open its door to your knock - a private members' club where the management was as discreet as the clientele was varied.

Danny Felix approached the door, pushing the button on the security system and heard the buzz and click as the entrance to this furtive wonderland opened for him.

Dexy's had an air of informal opulence. The walls were

plain coloured but finished with velvet. The art was like a greatest hits collection of the bright new young things on the market, with the paintings, etchings, and hangings refreshed regularly due to the never-ending sway of what was on trend. The bar and restaurant were dotted with battered old leather sofas that still managed to take on the weight of even the most indulgent of members.

Despite their proximity, the seating areas all managed to dull the constant, confidential chatter. The fabric walls absorbed the sound of the most delicate conversations.

Even the toilets proved a bohemian surprise. Here walls were covered in a collage of nudes — both male and female— engaged in mundane activities, just without the aid of clothing. Danny only noticed what made the pattern on his umpteenth visit. When he did, he had laughed out loud, drawing an askance look from the city gent peeing next to him.

But the real 'surprise' about Dexy's was that it was created and maintained by filthy, rotten drug money.

Dexy, the owner, was not really called Dexy, of course. It was a nickname from back in the day when money was made by delivering the intoxicant of choice to the rich, famous, or just plain fabulous. After a daylight brush with the law in the early days, Dexy swore to only ever to deliver after midnight... hence the nickname was born, after the eighties pop band: Dexys Midnight Runners.

Dexy's business boomed. Investments were made until enough cash was generated and, in turn, laundered to buy some respectability and fulfil a vision... a vision of a sanctuary where customers could get just about anything they wanted, or achieve whatever they needed to, legal or not, in an air of polite sophistication, away from the prying eyes and ears of the outside world.

"Monsieur Felix, what a pleasure to see you again." Francois, the maître d', had long eyelashes, snake hips, and an appetite for young men of questionable virtue. He liked Danny and impressed him endlessly by knowing every member by name.

"Will you be dining with us? The Sea Bass is exquisite this evening."

"Not tonight, Francois. But I would like a quiet word with you-know-who."

This was greeted with the arch of an exquisitely manicured eyebrow. "Let me see."

Francois flicked through a leather-bound diary he produced from a small drawer in his rostrum.

"Hmmm... company. Let me slip a note through. You might be lucky. Have a drink at the bar and I will let you know."

Danny moved through to his favourite room in the club. He loved that the lounge was a celebration of every type of alcoholic endeavour. Aged whiskies rubbed shoulders with specialty bourbons, the relatively young contenders on the hard liquor block.

Absinthe, gin, designer vodkas, brandies that were as rare as they were expensive, all draped in soft lighting that allowed their myriad, shimmering hues to splash the walls and ceiling in the kind of light that made you want to drink whether you needed to or not. Danny always thought that if you achieved the right lighting and atmosphere in a bar it was as effective as a siren song, beckoning you onto the rocks of boozy ruin — for him, it was a call easy to indulge.

He made his way through a maze of sofas that created cover for a Member of Parliament, corporate giants, several models, and an aging movie star Danny once quite liked. The MP was in conversation with a particularly notorious entrepreneur once linked to a huge counterfeit money scam. While damning evidence never materialized, the whiff of suspicion never quite dissipated either.

"Sir?"

"High West Whisky please, a double..."

"One ice cube as usual?"

Danny nodded, impressed that the Croatian bartender remembered correctly. Mind you, Danny remembered her too, especially the thick dark hair, and the grey eyes.

His reverie was cut short by a polite cough just behind him. A waitress.

"Monsieur Felix, Francois would like to invite you to go upstairs in exactly five minutes."

A few sips and exactly five minutes later, Danny climbed the stairs leading to a dark red door at the very top of the town-house. This, he knew, led to a sumptuous apartment built into the attic. Now, it was a very private space, one for only a few chosen guests. He was one of them.

The door opened and a young, lean-bodied man exited, all dark eyes and designer shirt and jeans, looking a little flushed of face.

"Danny Felix..." came the soft call from beyond the door. Danny stepped through to see Dexy.

"Danny, Danny, Danny... if I had known you were coming, I would have changed my plans... but, as you may have noticed, I have just put one out... as it were."

Danny couldn't help but smile at Dexy. Here she lived in her ultra-smart apartment, totally set apart, at the pinnacle of her mini empire. All of it built on the strength of London's predilection for white powder, whacky-backy, and pill-popping.

Dexy was the kind of woman you noticed. Just turned fifty, six feet tall, red haired and Amazonian, with a temper to match and as much street savvy as you could ever wish to pack into one human being. Danny found her bewitching, but then just about every man who entered Dexy's orbit could not fail but be entranced. You would never describe her as beautiful, but her face had character in every pore. High cheekbones down to a chin that was a little too long. Some light acne scarring on her cheeks, with eyes that were just a little too far apart. But for some reason she fascinated Danny, always had. She reminded him of a Siamese cat whose features had been drawn out a little too long. Not beautiful, no, but undeniably attractive.

"Now, Dexy, behave. We haven't 'seen' each other for a long time, and anyway, I know you like them younger and prettier than me nowadays."

Dexy tilted back her head and closed her eyes, smiling softly at the memory. "Yes, but you know me Danny, I like rarities and you, as I recall, would be a most welcome distraction to repeat. A bit like a grand vintage car... polished, smooth... a beautiful ride."

"Hey hey... less of the vintage, I'm only twenty-eight." Mock outrage on his face, Danny moved to her, kissing her on both cheeks, trying not to let his gaze fall to the gape in her silk dressing gown, loosely tied around her waist.

A laugh from her caused Danny to have his own flashback. He had always found Dexy's cut glass English accent with its huskiness at the edges one of the most alluring things about her.

"And so, Mr. Felix, why have you beaten a path to my door this evening?"

Without his asking, she had poured Bourbon for him, sliding a single ice cube into the crystal tumbler as she waited for him to answer.

"I need to do a little digging, and I know you are always an excellent place to start."

Dexy lifted a television remote control, flicking a wall-mounted screen into life. Images from the club below appeared on the screen.

"Isn't that a Minister from Her Majesty's Treasury talking to Fake Freddie? I knew things were bad on the economic front, but really?"

Danny smiled, knowing that she was waiting for him to tell her why he was here.

"Dexy, I seem to have picked up a new friend, maybe an unwanted friend, and the thing is, I've never come across him before."

"Are we talking a colourful character or a serious man in a blue uniform, darling?"

"Well that's just it, a bit of both. The name is Detective Inspector Harkness."

Dexy's face clouded for a second, before recovering. Danny took note, but said nothing, waiting for this woman who knew just about all that you needed to know about London's trickier side of life to share her own thoughts.

Her eyes met his over the rim of her champagne glass.

"Ahhh, Detective Inspector James Harkness... a relatively new addition to the ranks of ambitious boys in blue. How have you managed to catch his eye, Danny? Let me rack my brain for a second."

She stared off beyond the room's plush curtains onto the babbling throng on the streets of Soho below, a smile playing at the corners of her lips.

"A cash-in-transit van, about two weeks ago. You poured petrol over the guard as he came out of the van and stepped back while you levelled a gun at him in one hand and smoked a cigar in the other until he handed the bag over."

Danny spread his hands wide, sitting down on a chaise longue as he did so. "I couldn't possibly comment, madam."

"Harkness really is fresh meat, but I hear his star is rising at a phenomenal rate. He is... let's say... enthusiastic."

"He knew a lot about me, which I never like."

"Oh, darling, someone been chatting? Not like you. I don't know an awful lot about your new admirer, but that is easily rectified. What I do know is that some of his colleagues think he is a little... unorthodox?"

"What? They suspect he's dirty?"

"No, I don't think it's that, rather they consider him to be an individualist. He likes to accelerate the game plan whether anyone else is strapped in or not."

Danny flashed back to London buildings whizzing passed the car window with Harkness howling his feral cry. "That I can believe. So, can you help me with my due diligence, Dexy? You know me, I never like surprises unless they come packaged with red hair holding a glass of Tattinger."

Dexy liked the compliment, he knew, and she would help him, but first: "Of course I will take a closer look at Harkness for you. But maybe, in return, you can do a small favour for me."

Danny sipped his drink, feeling the dark brown heat in his throat.

"We have a member here, she is about to enter a new phase of her life — music deal, high profile TV presence, probably a candidate for the 'Nation's Next Sweetheart' etc. etc. Problem is, and it is a particularly twenty-first century problem, she was a little cavalier in her private life before her newfound success."

"I dread to think... has someone got a little souvenir of their time with this starlet?"

"Exactly, a moving picture type souvenir, and he seems to be intent on grabbing his opportunity for mischief. You can imagine the kind of upset this might cause our friend. She has a chance at a fabulous life. Do you think you could find a way to acquire this mini movie for us, if I were to point you to its director?"

"It would be impolite to refuse, Dexy, especially as you asked so graciously — and you know I love the movies."

"Excellent. The subject of the film is a young talent called Honey Sister. Her real name is..."

Danny cut her off. "Sarah Grimes. I read the papers, Dexy. I couldn't have *not* seen her picture in the last month or so."

"Yes, and her former flame is one Barry Blount, a reality TV star whose 'fifteen minutes' was more like three and those are very definitely up. The footage is about two years old but can still pack a heavy punch for our Honey."

"A reality TV muppet? It will be a pleasure to make his acquaintance."

"Thank you, Danny. Francois will slip you his whereabouts as you leave. And now, I must get dressed and ready myself to press the flesh in my humble little club here. It has been a pleasure to see you again." With that, Dexy slid her arms around Danny's neck, whispered good night in his ear and kissed him slowly, fully on the lips.

Danny could still taste the sweet, heady mix of lipstick and champagne as he descended the stairs back into the main part of the townhouse.

CHAPTER 6
A DAY'S WORK

"I SHOULDN'T EVEN BE TALKING TO YOU! I MEAN REALLY, WHO WEARS A yellow tie with a pink shirt!?"

The copper in charge of the interview blushed as he looked down at his tie.

It wasn't every day that CC's colleagues interrogated a grown man wearing an electric blue lycra catsuit festooned with rhinestones. The shiny fake diamonds cascaded down the front in supposed random order until they gathered near the waistline to form a shimmering arrow pointing at the owner's groin.

But then, this was no everyday snitch.

His name was Fisty, a surprisingly talkative drug dealer enjoying some enforced Metropolitan Police hospitality. His invitation to the police station generated panic and led to a tip-off that set CC and her colleagues onto a job that had now been running for four days.

Fisty was eager to ease some of his own troubles through a little chat about other people's, especially as his friendly, arresting officer told him that the police had proof one of his pills caused the death of a sixteen-year-old schoolgirl. Her face laughed hauntingly from the front of newspapers for a whole week. She was found dead in the bathroom of her best friend's house after a party to celebrate the end of exams. What should have been the start of her future turned out to be a full stop. The 'proof' of a link to the girl's sad exit was all a huge dollop of make-believe suggested by Christine Chance. Fisty fell for the hook, the line, and the sinker. CC suspected that Fisty enjoyed his own product as much as his customers did and might have just enough of that paranoid edge to panic at the first sound of a jailer's set of keys. And panic he had.

The interview with Fisty was like a Shakespearean soliloquy, a babbling litany of "he said this", "he did that", "she knew him" and "that's stashed there." Enough leads for an entire law enforcement division to work on for a month. But one scrap of info had leapt out at the interviewing officers, simply because it featured the name of what officials liked to call 'a person of particular interest.'

Ignatius "Iggy" Adesina, a Nigerian, a giant of a man.

He was a suspect in fifteen separate reported incidents and, Christ, did these incidents read like scenes from a Tarantino movie.

The worst, a robbery and aggravated assault with a deadly weapon, made CC's stomach turn when she read the witness accounts: suspect enters a Chinese restaurant with a machete and threatens the staff until he is able to access a back room where about twenty Chinese nationals are in the middle of a high-stakes poker match. All highly illegal of course, but a lucrative takeaway if you can manage to exit the building in one piece. The robber 'convinced' the players to let him leave by casually lopping off one of their hands with one fell swoop of his butcher-sharpened blade and then scalping a second when he tried to raise out of his chair.

The suspect was fully ski-masked but forgot about his

hands. Specifically, he'd neglected to cover a tattoo of a snake coiling around his middle finger, the head seemingly poised to bite the fingernail. Ignatius had been arrested, along with a few other local stars with similar habits, about twenty-four hours later and questioned at length.

Once in the slammer, the arresting officer noted that Iggy's right hand was bandaged. It soon revealed a burn that could only have been attributed to bathing a finger in some kind of acid thus obscuring any trace of a tattoo. Because the police had no photos of Iggy's hands prior to this unfortunate "accident', or any idea where he might have procured the caustic material, there was nothing to connect the six-foot-ten berserker to the crime. Plus, his sister gave him a cast iron alibi; he was at home with her and her two sons watching the Eurovision Song Contest. Iggy, a fan of Europop? Yeah, as if. Still, it gave CC a buzz to think they might get behind such a dangerous player so soon after he'd figuratively given them the finger...

Fisty was telling tales like a penitent sinner on speed, saying that Iggy had been to see him to get a reference for a muscle man who had looked after Fisty during a tricky time of his life. Could the muscle be trusted? Could he handle himself? Was he good with guns? Because, for the job Iggy had in mind, he would have to be, and soon, too, because this opportunity was coming up fast.

And so now Christine and the rest of her team were out and about, bouncing around different parts of north London at five a.m. on a June morning, with London traffic thinking about gearing up.

They'd been on the follow for about an hour, behind a white Ford transit van driven by Adesina. CC was growing increasingly frustrated because the suspect seemed to be leading them on a goose-chase and she needed to pee... like really badly.

Apart from stopping early in their journey to pick up some

thugs, the white van proceeded to do nothing but "dry clean" as the cops called it, driving in a series of squares, backtracking on a route several times to make sure there was no following vehicle or faces that popped up too many times in traffic. None of this was new to the team but, still, it was a pain in the arse to avoid being caught and meant everyone had to be on their toes for every second of the follow. It was weary work.

"I don't think this lot are going to go for it today, Freethy. Traffic will be too heavy for them soon."

Christine was on her mobile to her best friend and colleague, Detective Constable Mark Freeth. She knew better than to have informal chat over her walkie-talkie. Radio scanners were easy to come by and so it was deemed best to only use the radio for formal operational chatter. Freethy was in one of her other follow cars.

"Agreed. I feel like a bleeding cabbie here, except fuck all chance of a tip at the end of it. I'll text the others."

"What are you up to, Iggy? What is it this time, my old China?" CC asked the question out loud to the emptiness of her car.

CC was definitely puzzled, a state of mind she didn't like. She retraced the morning's route over again in her mind looking for a pattern, a reason behind the zigzagging across the leafy suburbs. She became distracted, glancing at the GPS on the dash.

Christine looked up just in time. She had to slam on the brakes to avoid rear ending a van that pulled out in front of her. A black Mercedes van sitting low on its suspension and driving bang on the speed limit.

She took a breath; lucky no one had been in the car with her to see the near accident, which would have been an office fine and a serious dose of banter from the others when they finally arrived back to base.

The Mercedes pulled off to the right into another street when Christine's radio squawked.

"Seven seven seven, if you are still on Percy Avenue, heads up, suspect vehicle is turning into your road now."

'Seven seven seven' was Christine's call sign.

As indicated, Iggy was at the wheel of the white Ford pulling into the road ahead of her car but travelling towards her on the opposite side. CC instantly signalled to turn left, feeling lucky there was a street into which to do so. Once she turned, she knew she was in trouble because she had entered a cul-de-sac. No matter, she was in it now and there were the other team cars slowly triangulating, handing the white van from one to the other, keeping it in visual contact.

CC pulled over to the curb, spotting an alleyway between two houses that looked just about the perfect spot for a long-needed pee.

Christine peed... and peed. God, it felt good, comfort at last returning to her insides, and a chance for a quick leg stretch too. It was one of the knacks of the job, knowing when and where to break off when you had to. She prided herself on her capacity to hold it in; she had the knack of knowing just when to dive behind a bush. She had peed in the most incredible places during her time on the job, once even using the rubbish chute in a block of flats when she thought she might burst.

Back in the car, the soft radio chatter continued while the white van travelled in a big square and headed back on itself yet again, repeating the route it had taken as CC pulled onto this road. She executed a swift but controlled J-turn and crept towards the mouth of the street. Just then, the black van she nearly dented minutes earlier passed in front of the junction.

Killing her engine, Christine sat still for a moment. Her instincts were jangling, thoughts playing at the edge of her brain. There was a pattern. No, not a pattern, but maybe a reason?

What the fuck is going on?

Her gut told her it was time to call the gunships closer to her radius.

Alpha, Bravo... tighten to lead car now, please."

Alpha and Bravo were Christine's gunships, armed response officers who were close by but not fully involved in the direct follow. She only called upon them to engage if events went from puzzling to action packed.

"Received."

"Four oh five position?"

"Sutherland Avenue, westbound. About a hundred yards off target."

"Five one five, position?"

"Parallel on Percy Avenue, westbound."

"Five one five, what other vehicles have you got visual on?"

"Seven seven seven, I have one milk float, a red Audi estate and a black Mercedes van."

"Okay received..."

"Seven seven seven, four oh five here, target turning left onto Casper Vale."

"Five one five, what can you see now?"

"The Audi is breaking every traffic law and swearing as he tries to pass the milk float..."

"The Mercedes van?"

"Turning left onto... Casper Vale, what's on your mind here, guv?"

"Four oh five, target vehicle turning into a dead-end street. Think it's a mews — can't see the street name. He's stopping, I think."

Christine snatched up one of her countless maps... mews, mews, off Casper...

"There, Casper Villas Mews."

"Five one five here... turning onto Casper Vale... are you thinking what I'm thinking?"

That's when she called it: "They are going to go guys... heads up, heads up."

Christine just got it. There was no job site, but there was a job target. It was the black Mercedes van. They had been following the van. Whatever the fuck it was doing, they were tracking it.

"Seven seven seven!! Seven seven seven!! Four oh five, robbery! Robbery! Robbery!"

The black Mercedes had pulled into the mews, and as it did, Iggy's white van reversed, sealing off the mouth of the small, closed off street. Instantly the side doors of both vans were thrust open, spilling three men from each, all of them carrying enough firepower to take out the entire street.

There were shouts, expletives, barked orders, counter orders. Iggy crashed out of the driver's seat of the white Ford van, sprinting at full tilt to the cab of the black van.

The first cop cars sealed off Casper Vale blocking the main road, stopping unsuspecting early morning traffic before innocent bystanders found themselves in the middle of the O-fuckin-K Corral.

As CC arrived, so too did the gunships; six armed officers. Five with sighted rifles scrambled to take cover behind their own vehicle, other members of the team doing the same. The sixth armed cop used a Loud Hallier to command the adrenalin-hyped robbers to cease and desist.

Bullets, shotgun pellets and foul language joined the calls for law and order, as the trigger-happy outlaws realised they were in the middle of a calamitous clusterfuck. Christine knew that the bullets would soon start to fly in her direction.

Somewhere a dog was howling, and sirens were screaming

as more crossfire was dispatched between the two vans. What the hell had they stumbled upon? The confusion quota was rocketing with the arrival of several local police cars, spilling greenhorn local yokels out onto the street, all of them eager to take part in what seemed to them a set piece from a *John Wick* film. And in the middle of it, Christine could see the big Nigerian, Iggy, who used the butt of his full-size shotgun to hammer out the front windscreen of the black van, trying to convince the driver, who was not to be seen but presumably was playing dead under the front seat, that he should open up.

And at that moment one of Iggy's boys did a very strange thing – a full pirouette and fell to the ground at the rear of the white van. When CC saw a vibrant red flower blossom burst on the would-be robber's chest, she realised that the firearms boys had finally decided to settle to their dark work. They nailed him just as he sighted his automatic rifle on one of his rivals.

Another two shots rang out, and suddenly the clatter of metal on the ground was heard, as the latter-day gunslingers began to realize they were not only outmanoeuvred but stood no chance against the Met's marksmen. In securing the mews as the perfect booby trap for their prey, Iggy's boys also ensnared themselves. They literally had nowhere to run ... except straight into the London-blue cordon that now 'bottle-corked' the street.

And just as an eerie silence settled on the scene, Iggy came roaring, bellowing like a rutting stag, trying to cajole his cohorts back into action. "Cowards!! You fucking chickens! Come on!! We can take these poleeece bastards."

Iggy had his shotgun pointed skyward, but as soon as he lowered it, the gun cop with the megaphone ordered him to drop it and himself to the floor or else...

Iggy kept on coming. Then he made his mistake. He blindly fired both barrels of his shotgun in rage, aiming at nothing in particular, and just as he popped the barrel in order to re-load, the local plod boys made their move. In what looked like the best bit of rugby action you were ever likely to see, three burly, pissed off cops were on Iggy like flies on dog shit.

He batted them off in the same way as you might flick fluff off your trousers. All Christine could think was how the fuck are we going to bag this monster up?

More cops flung themselves at the huge man like demons possessed.

The other gunmen who had dropped their weapons assumed positions on the ground. The older, more experienced officers, who recognized a potential arse kicking when they saw one, held back from a tilt at Iggy to break out their handcuffs; the wisdom of age made CC smile.

Iggy finally succumbed when a resourceful young female officer clanged him full pelt with her telescopic baton across the backs of his knees. It did the trick, Iggy went down, the might of his bulk blunted.

And then it was over. The cacophony of sirens rose as Black Mariahs arrived to take away the suspects. Finally, scientific investigations officers rolled up and unravelled their crime scene tape.

And finally, Christine was able to satisfy her curiosity. She approached the rear of the black Mercedes van, to see what Iggy was so crazed to appropriate.

The back doors were wide open, and what a sight it was, prompting a slow exhalation of air from Christine Chance as she surveyed the interior. Black plastic bags, at least thirty of them, some punctured and spilling their contents onto the floor of the van.

Money. Lots and lots of money...

"It's a collection van..."

CC turned. It was her four oh five, Detective Constable Mark Freeth... Freethy to his mates.

"Iggy was being a naughty boy! He was thieving another naughty boy's stash... can only be drug or prostitution money."

For the second time in as many weeks, CC, and her team rid London's criminal underbelly of a record amount of what it loved most dearly.

Filthy lucre.

Letting out a low whistle, Christine turned to survey the remarkable scene just in time to see Iggy bundled into a custody van, a thankless task requiring the efforts of six uniformed locals.

CC laughed out loud for the first time in a very long time.

CHAPTER 7

LIGHT-FINGERED, WARM-HEARTED

IT WAS AN EXERCISE DANNY STARTED WHEN HE WAS MUCH YOUNGER. At first, he despised the task. Now he found it therapeutic, a sharpener that aided his thinking and brought him an almost Zen-like presence of mind. What began as necessary self-education was now a cherished form of meditation.

Arranged in front of him on his kitchen table was a selection of newly bought locks. Two for doors, two padlocks, two window locks and one heavy duty D Ring lock for motorcycles. Danny was picking them one at a time, aiming for each one to surrender in under a minute.

All the while, he was mulling over thoughts about his sister. Danny always felt out of sorts after crossing swords with her. Their perceptions differed; Celeste could never see what he could.

Danny felt the first tumbler in the padlock he was working on shift to one side.

He knew instinctively when something didn't ring true. While others had their noses pressed against their own personal glass, Danny could always see the bigger picture. Mapping the consequences and outcomes was like breathing for him. He picked up patterns in everything. Locks, families, society... everything.

And he knew that was why he and his sister clashed. Not simply because he had an unconventional lifestyle—he could admit that— but because from his teenage years he understood that their family system was not all it could or should be. She couldn't distil the reality from her desire that it be normal. But Danny knew it was not. He could see it was a system built on control, not love.

Angling his second slim pick tool under the first, he felt the second tumbler start to give.

The problem was his father.

Growing up, it was all Danny could do to be in the same house as him, never mind the same room. It wasn't only that he was cruel and violent to them in private, but simply that he was supremely boring. And their home life was modelled in the image of the main man of the house.

Danny endured endless hours of just living; a mantelpiece-clock-tick of an existence. Routine ran everything. They ate at the same time every day. His parents watched the same shit TV every night. His father read the same newspaper. They all attended the same church and spent the same Sunday after-noons with the same relatives, talking in the same banal tones about the same shit... all the fucking time.

Tumblers three and four gave in to his pick's probing.

His father was a bank manager. The purity of numbers and an unshakeable belief in Jesus Christ set the tone for how he approached everything in life, even fatherhood. Everything was ruled by order, symmetry, scripture, compliance. Emotion was frowned upon. To say home life was sterile would have been kind.

Danny's fingers slipped, the lock ejecting his two picks instantly. Bollocks.

Within this stifling atmosphere, Danny grew up to be a model son: achieving the right test results, getting into the right schools, and simply being an all-round goody frigging two-shoes. And even now, after all these years, the memory of his early self made him feel angry.

Then his teenage years hit.

Danny felt a glint grow in his eye just about the same time he discovered a spot on his chin and a stray hair growing where none had appeared before.

Tumblers one, two and three gave way again.

The tipping point for his teenage self seemed innocuous. A trip to the cinema... but it was the film he saw that proved revelatory. Growing up in a religious household, he was fed the usual diet of Disney and *Ben-Hur*, never getting the chance to see anything that would challenge his father's values. Until one wet Saturday afternoon, on a secret trip to central London, he and his mates finished the day at The Prince Charles Cinema off Leicester Square. They were cold and as the ticket prices were cheaper than the big cinemas, they went in and saw a film they were too young to watch.

The film changed Danny's life.

Sean Penn and Gary Oldman, in their wilder days, starred in the absorbing and believable crime thriller called *State of Grace*. Penn was a man who leaves behind his not-so-healthy roots in New York's Hell's Kitchen, then returns. Only this time he's an undercover cop, tasked with infiltrating the criminal group he fled in the first place.

The story went off like a bell in Danny's head, a chime so clear he couldn't ignore it. Here was a man caught in a web constructed solely by his background and circumstance. The undercover cop's inexorable journey to his tragic fate enthralled Danny... and informed him. The pattern of how past constructs present and tees up with the future screamed at Danny from the screen.

He would have to break the cycle developing in his own life.

The lock in his fingers sprang open. A glance at his stop-watch showed a minute and twenty-eight seconds. He immediately snapped the lock closed and started again.

Reflecting back, Danny could see that the film had re-wired his brain. He began to look at the world, his world, in a very different way; seeking out the patterns, systems, trails of emotional breadcrumbs that could lead you back the way you came and help you to recognize where you might have turned left instead of right.

And because of his youthful outlook, Danny believed that if the system didn't serve you, then you could and should just change it. Most systems couldn't handle such simple subversion.

Danny's fingers were flowing now. In his head he could see a mental picture of the innards of the mechanism. It gave more easily. Time: one minute five seconds. He snapped it closed and started again.

His thoughts drifted back to his family. Young Danny resolved to jolt his family system, give it cause to sit up and take notice. If he could shock his father, light a little fire under the all-consuming routine, he might help the whole family shift.

He hadn't just rebelled in one fell swoop. It was gradual, he remembered. A failed exam here, a homework left undone there. All the time trying to push for some sort of a reaction.

Nothing.

The most he got back was a shake of the head and a silence in return. Sometimes there would be a physical reaction, usually a beating carried out to the refrain of some hymn or bible passage. Sometimes, Celeste took up the gauntlet of chastising him, just like she did now. But that was not the change he was after.

The stopwatch was reaching forty seconds when the lock gave way. He repeated this process three more times, getting the lock finally to submit in less than thirty seconds.

Danny paused, stretching out his fingers, feeling the sinews flex, the muscles relax.

The next lock.

He knew Celeste couldn't forgive him for how far he had taken things, never mind the fact that he still refused to go along. The point she missed was that their father's unmovable spirit led Danny to the life he was now leading. No comeback made the teenage Danny more determined. If he could buck the system, the family might become a better version of itself... a version that transformed his father into Dad.

The willingness to challenge the status quo blossomed in his brain like weeds in an untended summer lawn. The urge to rebel coincided with his other adolescent urges, presenting an opportunity to really shake shit up. An opportunity in a very attractive form.

Angela Phillips was the hottest girl at Danny's ever-so-boring school.

She was known as 'The Untouchable Babe'.

She was the headmaster's daughter. That could put a dent in any boy's plans, especially if they involved skipping school for a day of romance, fish and chips and a fumble in the front room. Angela travelled to and from school in the passenger seat of her dad's Ford Sierra. It might as well have been a military tank.

Plus, Angela had a boyfriend. An older boyfriend. From another school. An older boyfriend who no doubt carried an older boy's pair of fists. Neither Danny or his mates knew him, but they all believed he existed and somehow this communicated to them that "older boyfriend" equalled "older minded activities". Ipso facto, Angela most definitely put out on a serious scale. Hence... Angela was mysterious and possibly open to more than just kissing... the perfect combination.

And finally, the third and most important reason Angela Phillips was the 'Untouchable Babe' was the fact that she was beautiful. Intimidatingly, drop dead, stop the traffic, beautiful. Long hair, blue eyes and a laugh that lit up her face, the room, and every teenage boy's loins for miles in every direction. All you had to do was look at Angela to know... untouchable.

Except to Danny Felix. The new, fuck-every-convention, Danny Felix.

He laughed to himself. The locks were melting under his touch, all of them in under a minute each. To push himself that extra mile he wanted to pick them one after another in under two minutes.

He pushed back then too, egged on by his friends and his own boundary-breaking momentum. He knew he had to take a run at Angela Phillips.

And like that, his future was sealed.

He just didn't know it.

~

"You are full of shit, Felix."

Not the most promising start to a flirtation. Nevertheless, Danny felt the fact that Angela Phillips was talking to him meant something.

"I'm telling you I can. I know the bouncers on the door."

"Hollywood's is an over-eighteen club, except for those stupid Sunday afternoon gigs for little kids."

"Listen, if you want to go to Hollywood's on a Saturday

night with me, I can get us in this Saturday night. Simple and sweet as. I have a fake ID."

"What's in it for me? Why should I go anywhere with you?"

"Cos... I'm fit... and no one else round here can get you in to Hollywood's on a full-on Saturday night. And as far as I can see, no one else round here is asking you. They all think you're untouchable. Up your own arse."

It was a gamble, saying that she had a reputation for thinking she was above everyone else, but he figured he had nothing to lose.

"Hollywood's? On a Saturday? I don't believe you."

"I can get into anywhere I like, girl."

"Big words come cheap, mate. I tell you what, prove it to me. On Monday bring me something from somewhere impossible, proper proof of something, and if you do, you can take me to Hollywood's next Saturday."

The course was set.

Danny remembered it all like it was yesterday, and at the same time it felt like a lifetime ago. His stopwatch showed he was still over two minutes as he decided to take a final run at all of the locks in a row. Who was he kidding? He would keep going until it was easily under two minutes. He couldn't let a challenge lie, now or even way back then. Which was why he had gone as far as he had to try to impress Angela. If he succeeded, he might just kill the second bird with one stone.

Danny thought about grabbing an ashtray from Hollywood's, but there was a problem. Every Sunday afternoon the nightclub was transformed into a throbbing youth club. An under-eighteen disco without a hint of alcohol or even dark corners. Angela might assume he'd nicked the ashtray during the kiddie fest.

Danny needed a game winner. And he thought he knew where he would find it.

At four in the morning.

Fourteen-year-olds are lithe.

Danny was living proof of it.

The kitchen was the way in. Old-fashioned sash windows topped the longer windows in the kitchen. And one sash was open.

With the assistance of a gas bottle meant for the barbecue, Danny was able to step up to the windowsill, reach down through the opening and grab the handle of the larger window underneath, pulling it free.

Dropping lightly to the kitchen floor, Danny began his careful search for his intended target. No joy.

Fuck.

He registered he was still over two minutes into his current lock challenge, smiling as he recalled how his initial nerves turned to brass balls back then, understanding that burglary was the logical way forward.

He made his way through the downstairs; his confidence growing by the second until he became aware of a low sound. A snore.

Sweeping his eyes across the gloom of the living room.

Second fuck.

A dog. A big one. Of some kind. Hard to make out.

The journey to the hallway seemed to take forever. Every rustle of his clothes freaked him out. He was sure that any second, the dog would erupt in a cacophony of barking and lights would go on all over the house and he would be left with crap in his pants and a tricky story to tell.

What Danny didn't know was that the dog was called

Napoleon and was also fourteen. He was certainly no longer lithe. To complete the set, he was deaf. Danny could have played the bagpipes at full pelt and Napoleon wouldn't have even stirred for a scratch.

In the hallway, Danny used a trick he stole from an old black and white film — a burglar had mastered the art of scaling stairs in absolute silence.

Placing his left foot into the left corner of the first stair, where the carpet met the banister, he tentatively put his weight on that foot, making sure the weight was transferred to the outer edge of his trainer. He then did the same thing with his right foot into the right corner of the same stair. In effect, he was climbing on the edges of his feet. Rolling his weight into the smallest possible surface area of each foot to make his pressure point on each stair as small as possible, and in the corners where the wooden stair boards lent the most support. As demonstrated by the big screen thief, this was the way to eliminate stairs creaking.

Third fuck.

Except a good one this time. It worked. He mounted the stairs silently.

He rested at the top of the landing, peering again through more gloom.

A laundry basket, overfull and spilling over.

Fourth fuck!!!

The laundry basket was made from wicker just like the one in Danny's house. And from experience he knew that if he lifted the hinged lid it would make that dry, raspy squeal.

Kneeling before the basket, Danny prayed to the patron saint of teenage housebreakers for assistance.

He rummaged through the contents which were spilling out of the top. Underpants the size of a small house... urgggh.

A flimsy nightdress and then finally, exactly what he was looking for.

It took another five minutes for Danny to silently exit the house, this time with the help of a dining room window. No point risking the wrath of the family dog a second time.

As he sprinted home at 4:35 in the morning, Danny Felix's felt the thrill of his first real theft.

And with that memory bright in his mind, he was pleased to see the last lock give way to him now, with the stopwatch reading one minute and fifty-five seconds.

The next morning, the teenage Danny laid in bed visualizing how it would go down. His whole being was still racing with the adrenalin of his night's work...

Unfuckingbelievable!

The pure rush!

Then school.

Break time.

Angela Phillips' locker.

"So, you came back?"

"I like a challenge, Miss Untouchable. Not that you set me much of one."

"What have you got me, a little present? Let me guess? You spent your Sunday afternoon trying to nick something from Hollywood's that would convince me you can get us in there?"

Danny smiled. He flipped his school bag open and handed Miss Untouchable Angela an item of clothing.

A grey, sports bra.

Inside out, so that it showed a name marked on the label.

Blue Pen. Big Letters. Spelling out the name 'A. PHILLIPS'.

"What the fuck?" was all she could manage.

"By the way, Angela, what's your dog's name?"

Danny's labours were rewarded with another closeup experience of how systems worked — this time the school system. Classroom gossip of his exploits found its way to a teacher and then, of course, to Angela's father, the principal. Danny was expelled two days later, and only narrowly avoided a police interview after the pleas from his oh-so-respectable parents. It turned out that Angela's dad was an active and respected member of the local Conservative Party, just like Danny's father.

The day after, an older boy called Rufus kicked the living shit out of Danny in front of the local youth club, telling him, as he did so, to leave his girlfriend alone and then writing the word 'PERV' in marker pen across Danny's forehead.

But that was not Danny's biggest disappointment.

That came in the evening when his father came home from work to find Danny battered and bruised but still defiant. Even now, the memory stung Danny; it twisted in his gut to admit it.

His father simply looked him up and down.

"What is the matter with you, boy?"

And, at that, Danny's held-in emotions burst. He screamed, hurled abuse, poured out his every frustration. It ended as the fourteen-year-old marched out and slammed the front door behind him.

He hoped, about fifty yards down his old street, to feel a tug on his shoulder.

That tug never came.

As he cleared away the locks and his picks from the small table, as he tried to put aside his frustration with his sister Celeste, Danny admitted to himself that his history still had a strong pull on him. The one system he was desperate to affect remained unchanged.

And Celeste wondered why he looked at the world and still tried to see how he could upend it, jolt it into a better version of itself? All right, his methods might be unconventional, but the most obvious thing that the Angela Phillips' incident taught him was that he was good at something.

That romantic, crazy derring-do gave Danny the taste. He was bitten by a bug. The undeniable rush.

He was now a thief.

CHAPTER 8
DIRTY DISHES: DIRTY DEEDS

THE WASH UP. THE DEBRIEF. THE POST-MATCH BISH BASH.

Christine loved this. It was one of the best parts of the job, standing around in a favourite pub, pints in hand, retracing, retelling, reliving a piece of work well done.

And there they were, CC, Freethy and the team standing in the Shakespeare's Head walking each other through their personal angle of the events. The blow-by-blow accounts of who saw what, who said what, and who nicked whom.

It felt good to CC; it was, to her, one of the fundamental parts of being part of the force. It was in these moments that they stood together, having fought together. They could all revel in being part of what was known as The Blue Wall. An old dog of a beat constable once described it as such to her when she was a young probationer.

The Blue Wall... the reason order won out over chaos.

And the members of that wall loved to rip the piss out of each other and now was the perfect time to do it.

Banter.

The release valve that allowed all of them to deal with the violence, the tragedy and disappointment they faced in the job.

A good laugh at your teammates expense, all in the name of being able to deal with their ferocity and consign experiences to memory. In moments of extreme pressure, the touch of humour could make their task bearable.

And Christine was in full flow, enjoying the moment, blossoming within the camaraderie. "So, the Black Mariah's pulled up and our lovely Custody Sergeant Donnelly..."

"Digger!"

The group toasted the cell sergeant sarcastically with his nickname.

"...lovely Digger is at the rear doors trying to act respectful, telling all six-foot-something of Iggy Adesina that it is 'up to him'. Impeccable manners, our lovely Digger."

CC adopted a deeper tone.

"We can do this the hard way, or we can do it the easy way, sir." Nothing in reply, even if lovely Digger was being charming! Donnelly, helped by five other cops, of course, goes ahead and opens the door. Jesus, if Adesina doesn't come out of the cage like a lion screaming 'The fucking hard way!' And all hell broke loose!"

The laughter lifted up to the ceiling in the pub, amplifying the moment.

Freethy raised his pint glass. "Here's to a fucking great month! I mean, what a haul, first Heathrow, now this lot in north London. It is a bad time to be a wrong 'un in this city." As he said it, Freethy saw something fleeting pass across Christine's face, enough to know that some detail or loose end had irked her even if it was just for a nanosecond.

The rounds kept piling up and the day went from late afternoon to evening until CC and Freethy found themselves in front of one of their favourite places in the city. The Pasty Shop on the concourse of Marylebone Train Station, with an Eastern

European girl struggling to understand their slurred requests for two pasties... each.

"Every time I go on the beer with you, Freethy, I wake up the next morning with a mouth full of burns from these fucking pasties you love so much. Do they have to come out thermonuclear? We're so shitfaced and hungry we don't notice we're roasting the roof of our mouths off."

Freethy, giggling now, his eyes taking just a moment too long to shift from her face to the money in his hand, counting it out for the piping hot pies.

"You love them just as much as me! Now, shut up, eat up, and then you can tell me what's troubling you, Detective Chance."

CC was looking at him now, trying to chew and cool the food in her mouth at the same time.

After a third-degree burn of a swallow, "I dunno... it's nothing."

Freethy answered her with a slightly tipsy, arched eyebrow.

"I'm just... it's just... it all feels a bit too... easy."

"What you fucking talking about?" Freethy, incredulous now, as well as drunk.

"The Heathrow thing that made the papers, then this morning. They kind of just fell into our laps."

"You never look a gift horse in the mouth, and you think way too much. They were good police work. The intel, the job, the footwork: all good solid stuff."

"Yeah, yeah, I get that. But still, not saying we were lucky, or we weren't good today, but it just feels like it was on a plate. I mean, how long from the snout stuff to the actual job?"

Freethy tried not to scar his tongue with the heat of the food while also not telling his best mate that she was full of shit. "I know, I know. I'm full of it."

"That's not the half of it, CC. Next, you'll be telling me your

Spidey sense is tingling, and you've consulted a medium who's told you where we can find all the diamonds from that Hatton Garden job."

Freethy cupped his hand on the back of his mate's neck, playfully pushing her aside.

"Let me guess. You gonna go see her now?"

Christine nodded back, pointing at a plastic bag resting on the ground at her feet while she ate the pasty.

"Give her a hug from me. Tell her that she has a crazy mum, but she's still lovely."

"Shauna knows that already. See you tomorrow, Mr. Freeth."

~

Danny wasn't surprised that the lock took him less than a minute to spring open. The real difficulty was keeping his body out of the infrared sensor, which if triggered, bathed the entire walled back garden in white light. Danny gave a rueful smile, thinking that the teenage version of him would have found it way easier to avoid the security lamp's range.

This made his approach to the lock awkward. He couldn't be sure that the house was empty and the lack of security light activity back there would preserve his element of surprise should he find some company in the west London garden flat.

He spotted the sensor while he watched the back of the property before making his move. He was in the shadows in an alley that ran along the back of the Notting Hill houses as he realised the languid slink of a Siamese cat would help his cause. Strutting through the back garden, the cat's swagger triggered the tell-tale red dot that heralded the sudden wash of light meant to deter people like him, and equally make the occupants aware that someone or something was making their way across the manicured lawn.

Danny thanked the cat and got on with breaking and entering.

After feeling the last tumbler on the lock slip under his pressure and persuasion, the door handle began to relent. Then he heard a rustle to his left. There, making its way through the bedding plants was the Siamese, retracing its steps.

Danny discovered the full truth of the breed at exactly the wrong time. As he crouched, holding onto the now fully co-operative door handle, and preparing to make his entrance to the flat, the cat made a beeline for him, meowing like it was greeting a best friend on the way to a mouse hunt. If the cat made it to him, it would break the infrared beam en route and set that light wash off again. Never mind all the racket the mewing made.

Danny hissed at the cat, low and long through his teeth, trying to sound menacing. This only seemed to embolden the cat further. It sauntered closer, weaving its tail in the air in a way that made Danny think of Dexy – her silk dressing gown, the glass of champagne in her hand, the knowing glint in her eye.

Danny looked around for something to toss at the creature but realised that might set the light off anyway.

Just then a huge white moth flittered across the garden, attracted by a streetlight just beyond the wall, and the cat was distracted long enough to change course and followed the erratic path of the big insect.

Seeing his chance, Danny whirled through the doorway, still in a crouch and closed the door behind him as gently as he could.

A dimly lit kitchen.

Alarm? There were no indoor sensors blinking at him, so that was a good start.

The object of the evening's sport was to locate and acquire a laptop. It belonged to Barry Blount, formerly of 22 Unknown Road, Obscurity Town, but now a minor-league celebrity after appearing as a contestant in one of those wretched, overblown pieces of shit TV that was dressed up like a social experiment. Danny didn't mind breaking into a Z-grade celeb's home, they deserved it as far as he was concerned, given that usually they would climb over a pile of their dead relatives to achieve fifteen minutes of fame.

Mind you, fifteen minutes was more like fifteen seconds these days, as the fickle finger of fame, fast-forwarded by the internet, tabloids, and general lack of attention span, continued to degrade the media and the minds of the target audience.

Still, Danny thought, Blount obviously made the most of his flash in the pan. This flat was in a great part of London and would hold its value handsomely as Barry's notoriety flushed itself down the publicity toilet... a process already begun.

Blount gained a 'cheeky Londoner' reputation on his reality show, calling a spade a spade and talking like he was a working-class hero with 'salt of the earth' tattooed on his backside at birth. In fact, he did have 'salt of the earth' tattooed on his backside, but only since the day he found out he had made the show.

Turned out Barry was not really a working-class hero. He was not even working class. He was an out of work, and increasingly desperate, wannabe actor who came from a very moneyed family and actually spoke naturally with a cut-glass accent. Barry flung himself into the 'role' of 'cockney sparrow' because he heard that the producers of 'Trial By TV' were short of that kind of personality for their project.

Having been cast, he knew he would be seen buck-naked in

the showers of the communal house that was the setting for the show. The tattoo, therefore, was a tool, by which Barry could convince the audience that he was a bit of a rough diamond, not a failed actor desperate for a fix of the crack that came along with the fame.

The tabloids loved Barry, especially after a spirited debate about personal hygiene one night with some of the girls on set and in particular the merits of intimate waxing. Barry couldn't see the contradiction in expecting women to be fully waxed and buffed to within an inch of their lives while men could sport hair for hair's sake in every orifice.

What happened next gave Barry his fifteen seconds; four of the girls held him down, waxing him live on national television in a place where the sun don't shine. For the remainder of his time on the show, as his hair steadily grew back, all Barry could be heard to intone regularly was, "Me nuts, me nuts", and a catchphrase bereft of wit or guile was born.

Back in the real world, after the show finished, Barry became the face of a brand of salted peanuts sold all over Europe in pubs and bars. That alone paid for the flat where Danny Felix now stood.

Danny was here to nick Barry Blount's laptop in return for Dexy's due diligence on his new friend Inspector Harkness. Obviously, Honey Sister was one of Dexy's newest, and prized, members.

It was obvious that Blount understood how the gutter press worked their worthless magic, given that it was their indulgence which created his fame in the first place. And when they tired of him, they also set about revealing his actual roots. His upper-class background now relegated him to the small stories used to fill up celebrity pages each time he turned up in a West End nightclub with a horsey set girl on his arm.

Danny figured the footage catching Honey Sister doing

something compromising was Barry's latest attempt to climb back up the ladder of tabloid newsworthiness.

Dexy and Danny were going to stop that.

Moving through the silent apartment, Danny was all eyes, looking for the flat outline of a laptop, or its tell-tale pulsing light if it was still plugged in. No joy, until he found himself in a hallway in front of what was undoubtedly the lounge door.

Danny kept light on the balls of his feet, moving silently. He cracked open the door.

He didn't go all the way in because there was a low light on in the room, and he could smell something familiar.

Whisky. Drunkenness.

Through the crack, he could see two big L-shaped sofas dividing the room, the closest one with its back to the door.

Miaowww, miaooowww.

The fucking cat.

Fucking useless-cupboard-loving-aloof-until-you-feed-it–cannot-even-take–them-for-a-fucking-walk-cat.

From the other side of the sofa: a grunt.

"Do shut up, Teasie!"

The cat pushed past Danny, through the partially open door.

A live one after all — a person unknown, at home, but probably Mr. Nuts himself, Barry Blount.

Danny slowly and quietly pushed the door of the lounge open and pulled a ski mask over his head as he did.

That's the thing about Rubicons, Danny thought, *if they weren't for crossing, what the hell were they for?*

In he went. Danny could now see over the back of the sofa. On the long bit of the L, lay the underpants-and-nothing-else-clad body of Mr. Barry Blount holding a bottle of Johnny W., the top off. On the short part of the sofa was a laptop computer, the browser open at a page of Google searches.

Barry Blount was home alone, chugging down whisky and googling himself.

Danny was weighing the next move, when...

"You might as well come in. Teasie has already alerted me of your presence, haven't you darling?"

The cat made a figure-of-eight in front of the sofa and used the overhanging cushions as a scent marking post. Barry didn't get up.

"Come on, show yourself. I'm too sloshed to put up a fight and I have no money in the flat, but I do have some primo marijuana; as a compromise, we can light up. I'm depressed anyway, nothing new about me on Google for a week. A facking fortnight!" It was a truly a modern-day moan (that only the twenty-first century could have produced.)

Danny rounded the sofa and looked down at Barry Blount, waxy skinned and wan in the glow of the Google search that was evidence of the fickle finger of fame.

Barry was, to use a common phrase, hammered. If the Johnny Walker was new when he cracked it, it was now down to the last quarter.

Seeing Danny's masked head, Barry decided there was more jeopardy to the scenario than he first considered. Still, it took a good twenty seconds and a lot of effort and heavy breathing for him to lift himself to sitting position. He almost lost the bottle on the way but managed to rescue it before the good whisky went to waste.

Danny had one thought. *Get this over quick.* "Give me the laptop, your mobile phone and your wallet and I am out of here. No one has to get hurt." Danny wasn't ready for the reply he got.

"You must be jolly well kidding... my laptop is my blood life... I mean lifeblood. I can't do without. I have a lovely Tag watch. Maybe that instead, hmm?"

Danny couldn't believe his ears. Barry was negotiating. With a burglar.

"My stash is in the armoire against the wall over there. Come on, let's have a toke and a chat..."

Barry moved towards the cupboard against the opposite wall, only for Danny to do the unthinkable. He grabbed the waistband of Barry's underpants, producing a painful wedgie.

"Owww, owww, owww, come on! That's a bit much, isn't it? Owww."

Barry Blount began to sob. Big, heaving, can't catch your breath sobs. His naked shoulders quivering in time to the sad noise.

"I... I... sob. I have nothing here of value to... sob... give you... I have nothing to give... sob... anyone. Can't we just have a quick... sob... puff and then you can hit me or do whatever you like, but don't... sob... take my Mac Air. I'm a celebrity!!"

The last bit was accompanied by the biggest sob.

But Danny just bent down and grabbed the laptop. He'd seen enough... a grown man, crying, over an Apple Mac and a miserable Google result.

Barry went to stand up but then thought better of it when he saw Danny draw back his arm, ready to lash out.

"iPhone. Now. Where?"

"On the top of the armoire, you... sob... bastard."

Danny could see it. He grabbed it, and as a second thought, he opened the drawers of the dresser until he found the plastic bag of hash. There were three joints rolled already along with a sizeable cube of resin.

"Ooo now... Come on! Not my doobies too!"

Barry, you need to look to your priorities, Danny thought, but returned to stand in front of the hapless has-been.

"Here... light up and take a big old hit."

Barry was clearly confused as Danny handed him one of the

pre-rolleds and the lighter from the stash bag. He did as he was told, lighting then pulling in on the joint like a man coming up for air.

Danny watched Barry's eyes go glassy.

"Again... deep drag."

Barry did as he was told.

"Now, more smoke. And take your pants down."

"What? Are you some kind of bumbandit?"

Danny almost laughed, but held back, feigning another punch in Barry's direction.

"Now toke again and play with yourself."

The naked and unsteady Barry listlessly touched himself. "You are a strange one..."

What Barry hadn't noticed was that from the first moment he lit up the joint Danny was filming him with his iPhone.

When he reckoned that he'd had enough, Danny planted a foot in Barry's chest, knocking him back onto the sofa.

The hash and booze combo fully kicked in; Barry was incapable of stringing many words together.

Danny reckoned it was time to do one out the door.

"Barry, listen to a voice of reason. Don't call the police mate. I have kept your stash bag and if they come looking it has your fingerprints all over it, okay? Just put this down to bad luck, mate."

"You... you... know me?" Barry slurring, off his tits, circling the airport.

"You..." Big pause. Barry trying to grasp the words out of his addled brain...

"You... recognize me!!"

And Barry Blount laughed and clapped, suddenly happy in the drug-addled knowledge that he still had it... he was still a celeb.

Danny just rolled his eyes, scooped up the laptop, placed it in his black rucksack with the newly acquired mobile phone, and said goodbye to Teasie the traitorous cat, pulling his mask off as he went.

~

Walking back towards Notting Hill Gate Tube, Danny couldn't shake off the pitiful sight of Barry, there in his underpants, confronting an intruder and being more concerned about the death of his public profile rather than death itself.

Just as he was about to enter the Tube station, Danny caught sight of someone in his peripheral vision. Big guy. A really big guy, steaming towards him, right up to him, grabbing Danny by the elbow, something sharp and hard pressed into his ribs.

In order to avoid that sharpness going between those ribs, Danny relented, moving towards a car pulled up to the curb. An Audi, back door swinging open. A face Danny didn't recognize framed within. But Danny knew he had to do what that face was telling him, especially as it uttered only one word: Harkness!

Danny ducked into the back of the Audi, sandwiched between the stranger and the guy with the knife.

"Harkness," was all Danny said in return to his new travel companions, nodding gently as he did so, and the car took off into the night.

CHAPTER 9

VISITING TIME

It was all in the timing. It was a ritual that over the last few weeks quickly became a routine.

Shauna opened the bag of Haribo gummy sweets to match her mum's faked coughing fit. That way the nurses wouldn't hear the rustle as the plastic bag gave way and she would be able to taste her favourite sweets for the first time in a week. Shauna didn't care what the doctors told her mum. How could a mini cola bottle gummy kill you?

They could if you ate a mountain of them. Christine invented the ban in order to give Shauna a secret treat, an indulgence to compensate for some of the others denied to her. It felt like an overly simplistic conspiracy, but the way in which Shauna dedicated herself to the subterfuge once CC planted its seed in her head proved that it was fun and sufficiently naughty to make it feel like defiance in the face of her illness. A defiant sense of fight that Christine found hard to summon up sometimes.

"Awww, Mum, you're a legend! Sooo much tastier when they're not allowed."

She looked tired, though Christine didn't mention it. Tired

in a weary to the bone way, as if she just had enough of everything.

CC produced a copy of the Evening Standard, London's main daily newspaper, turning it around so Shauna could see the cover. It was a full-page story on the arrest of Iggy Adesina and the gun battle. Once again, Christine was struck at how good fortune lumped a stack of illicitly gained cash into the laps of the Met Police.

"Uh oh, Mum. Were you in this? Heavy shit!"

"Shauna Chance! Language."

"Seriously, Mum. If you keep going like this, you'll put your-self out of a job, no baddies left to catch." This last sentence was slightly garbled through a mouth full of jelly sweets.

Shauna pushed herself up onto a Matterhorn's worth of hospital pillows.

"That's just it, sweetie... there's something not right about it." Christine sank into the chair beside the bed, alcohol and work fatigue claiming her all at once.

"Wah? Since when did taking baddies off the street make for bad news?"

"Listen to you trying to talk like Old Bill. It just feels a little weird, like it was meant to happen. We were in the right place at the right time *twice* in a few weeks, and I'm beginning to ask why?"

Shauna's eyes were now closed, the click of her drying throat as she swallowed a jelly ring and a little bear.

"D'you remember last year, in the summer holidays, that girl Bethany told us all she could get us backstage to meet BTS?"

CC was a little thrown by the conversational change of direction.

"Umm, I think so. The concert in Shepherd's Bush or somewhere...?"

"Yes, and you didn't let me go because you thought it might

be too much for me. Plus, you said not to believe everything Bethany said?"

"Uh huh..."

"It was just like you said, Mum. If it looks too good to be true, then it usually is. The girls ended up waiting outside the Empire until midnight without even so much as a signed photo to show for it."

CC didn't know whether to smile or feel sad. Had she passed on her cynical police sense of fate that made her daughter question everything, or was it the hand that fate had dealt Shauna? Christine couldn't be sure, but Shauna certainly showed a wisdom beyond her years.

"You might just be right there, 'Detective Inspector Know It All'."

Christine stood to kiss Shauna on the top of her head, careful to manoeuvre past the drip that was providing her with morphine.

"I could go on, Mum. You also told me you make your own luck and you always say, if something is wrong, go back and look at the details. You even told the doctors that before they got my diagnosis right."

"...Details." Christine repeated her own mantra. It was a line she had heard a million times from her own dad.

Except sometimes she wished it wasn't such good advice. She remembered when she had to force her doctor to look at Shauna's symptoms again, and now when she should be cheering job success, her gut was saying something else.

CC sighed, longer than she meant to.

As if reading her thoughts, Shauna changed the subject. "Mum, did you bring any ice cream?"

A smile, reaching into the plastic bag. "Why'd you think the gummies feel cold?"

"Ahhh, the clues are in the details, Mum."

"Yeah... except it's probably melted by now..."

The car journey took Danny all the way from the west side of London to the West End, the colourful bright lights of the theatres and restaurants splashing before his eyes as he watched out the window. Then out the other side of the kaleidoscope of tourist traps and into the real powerhouse of London... The City.

They finally came to a stop outside a venue that looked like a rundown church, sitting uncomfortably cheek by jowl with shiny skyscraper offices and a smattering of high-end restaurants.

It wasn't a part of London Danny felt comfortable in. During the day, office workers scurried around like insects, barely able to look each other in the eye. Then at night it became a kind of ghost town—a place abandoned as though people were frightened to be caught here after dark or be shackled to their desks forever.

Danny was bundled out of the Audi. His backpack was searched but returned to him. After all, what harm could a laptop and a mobile phone do? Little did they know, thought Danny, as he was pointed towards a pathway that led down the right-hand side of the old church.

His escorts were taking no chances. The big guy behind him, the driver and his other passenger led the way. As they rounded the front end of the building, the noise of a crowd rose. A lot of voices. Excitement. He could see an entrance ahead, right in the middle of the building, a wide set of steps leading under the main wall. A banner proclaimed some kind of charity function and the letters M.M.A. As they drew level with the steps, the noise increased. And then Danny realised. They were entering the crypt of the church, a space that ran the entire length of the building. Tables arranged in circles out from the centre, scattered with men in city gent suits, cigar smoke hanging low in the air though indoor smoking was banned years earlier. And in the very centre of this large underground space was a huge cage. Danny got it...

M.M.A. Mixed Martial Arts. He had been brought to a cage fight.

He was shown to a table at 'cage-side' just as a slight Japanese lad took a roundhouse kick to the head from a heavily tattooed opponent. Danny could hear the thud of the impact despite the bays of the crowd around him. The boy collapsed like a slinky toy on a flight of stairs, going down onto the canvas in stages: a little stagger, the knees first, then a full-face plant, out for a count that even the referee must have known was unnecessary.

The crowd went wild.

Torn betting slips peppered the air. Men who were pillars of society in any other context leapt out of their seats, sending drinks and plates flying, howling like rabid dogs at the scent of blood. The victorious fighter strutted, inked arms aloft in the cage, as though he had delivered some great moral justice rather than a flying foot.

A number of greying men were around his table, two standing now, applauding the end of the bout, another chugging on a cigar that was roughly the length and girth of a baby's arm. None of the men acknowledged Danny, but he did note that there was still one free chair left in the round. The strong arms who had led him there backed off, content to watch him from a distance.

In the centre of the table was a sweating ice bucket, filled with decent looking champagne. Three bottles were already turned upside down to show they were decommissioned, but another three proudly pointed at the ceiling. Danny thought, *if you can't beat them...*

As he poured himself a glass, the hubbub settled. The stricken fighter was being helped out of the ring and replaced by a dinner-jacketed 'master of ceremonies.' His voice was like every local radio DJ Danny had ever heard, all oil and rounded vowels.

"Gentlemen... I hope you are all enjoying our entertainment. I think you'll agree we have witnessed some great sport this evening. We have just one bout left to rock your world. The young ladies will pass among you to collect the betting papers for our final fight, and don't forget this is all for a fabulous cause, The Freemasons Grand Trust. Doing good for the people in the community who most need our help. Bet generously gentlemen, and remember this worthy cause gets to keep all the forfeited bets plus ten percent of any winnings."

At this, a gaggle of girls passed between the tables. Danny realised they were the only women in the subterranean venue. Using champagne buckets, they were collecting betting slips and wads of cash from the tables.

So far, so posh boys big night out. But where was his host? When would Danny's new boss show his face?

"Gentlemen, tonight as always we have reserved the very best to last. A heavyweight contest in every sense of the word. Three five-minute rounds. I think you'll all agree it is a fitting finale. So, without further ado, it's mayhem time! Let me introduce our final pair of gladiators. First, the challenger to last year's champion, a veteran of both Afghanistan and Iraq, at a height of six feet five and weighing in at two hundred pounds even, Grant Corky Corkhill."

The crowd erupted again, as a skin-headed ex-corporal

entered the basement hall. All swagger and arms aloft, tattoos covering his upper chest and arms in the manner of an ex-con, the blue and red ink depicting a lion standing over a fresh kill, blood dripping from defiant jaws. A side door in the cage was opened to allow the fighter to enter, skipping around the canvas inside, jabbing at the air and rolling his shoulders, ducking, and weaving.

"And now to the defending champion, all six feet eight of him, 230 pounds of machine-like muscle. The man with the flying fists, the legend that is the Darkness we call Harkness!"

Danny's surprise level rocketed. Making his way through the tables towards the cage, bare-chested, long shorts, and wearing those little half-leather gloves that cage fighters love – was Harkness. His skin glistening in the lights. Men were patting him on the ass and arms as he passed them, and bellowed support as he progressed to the centre of the room. And as he made it to the entrance to the cage, Harkness looked straight at Danny and winked. Fucking winked.

Either you really are bat-shit crazy or you have balls of solid steel, Danny thought.

The referee brought both fighters into the middle of the cage, giving them cursory instructions and making them bump fists.

An air horn sounded, and the two combatants made straight for each other. No sparring or dancing around to size each other up. Oh no. This had the feel of grudge match. Memories of Hagler/Hearns, Tyson/Holyfield, now Corky/Darkness Harkness. Both men were swinging big roundhouse punches at each other. Corky ducking, dropping fists trying to work into Harkness's ribs, stepping back to then re-join with another flurry of punches, this time aiming for the solar plexus. But Harkness was ready for him, meeting the bruiser square in the midriff with a lightning quick knee, rocking the man back on his heels. Then Harkness was on him, a rapid combination of jabs to his head and face, then a step back to deliver a high kick, his foot connecting soundly to the side of Corkhill's skull.

The crowd was up and screaming as Corky tried to get his head back in the game, trying his own forward-lunging knee jerk, only for Harkness to catch the knee and flip his opponent onto his back like you might flick a beermat in the air.

But the war hero wasn't so easily dealt with, athletically springing back to his feet from a horizontal start before Harkness could finish him, using his jumping momentum to meet his rival with a pile driver punch, evading Harkness's guard-up fists, delivering a head-snapping, bone-crunching blow to the nose. Boom! Harkness's face was now covered in claret, his nose pushed over to one side. Danny was certain he was done for. But he should have known better.

Harkness laughed. While the rest of the room was going ballistic at the sight and smell of the blood all over his face, Harkness howled, the same feral noise he used that first time he drove Danny on the joyride to see his ex-partners form foundations for a security hut.

And there it was. A twitch, just a twitch in Corky's eyes. He knew, Danny knew, the crowd knew, and Harkness knew... Corky was shit-in-his-pants frightened.

The Tall Man made his move then, ducking under a flash of punches from the soldier, wrapping his big arms round his rival's waist and hoisting him up, high into the air, only then to double over and spring with his legs. Both men then took off, toppling in slow motion until they hit the canvas. The cage shuddered with the force and weight of the impact, an audible whoosh was heard as all the air was slammed out of Corky's lungs, as his head smacked into the canvas. Harkness mounted

Corky and sat astride him, his blood dripping down onto his opponent's hair and face. The referee was hovering, waiting for the coup de grace, but when it came, even he was taken aback by its ferocity.

Harkness began what could only be described as a barrage of full-on punches and blows to Corky's head and face, fists literally a blur until splashes of crimson joined his gloved hands in the air.

The referee tried to intervene, grabbing Harkness by the shoulders to drag him off. He was thrust away for his trouble and Harkness returned to his stricken opponent, swinging down with more vicious blows. The ref made a second attempt, this time with help of the ringside trainers, and finally they managed to haul Harkness off.

The room was a tumult of screams, cheers, howls, and bedlam.

The whole fight took less than three minutes.

All Danny Felix could do was to watch, open-mouthed, as Harkness once again turned to look in his direction, a snarl of a grin on his face spitting out his mouth guard, a crazed look in his eyes, as he pointed at Danny and bellowed, "I'm alive!!!"

Danny was escorted upstairs through a series of corridors until he and his captors came to what must have been the original sacristy, the room where the priest would have prepared for service.

As Danny entered, a doctor was just sticking two tubular bandages up Harkness's nostrils. Then, taking a tight grip on the bridge of his out-of-place appendage, the doctor yanked. A crack and a roar from Harkness signified his nose was back to its rightful place in the middle of his face.

The first bloom of bruising was already forming under his eyes, which were tearing from held-in pain. He finally sat on the edge of a chair.

"Danny Boy, a delight to see you again. How did you find this evening's... ah, how shall we describe it... entertainment? Yes, that fits... 'entertainment'?"

Danny just held his stare.

"Ah, the silent treatment again. All steely eyed and quiet of mouth... I invited you here this evening for two reasons."

As he spoke, a trickle of blood ran from his nose, the two tubular bandages were evidently to no avail.

"First, to show you that I will not tolerate any brinkmanship. If I enter an arena it is with single-minded determination. Secondly, I want to put you on notice. I have a job for you; it will be imminent. Show your fucking mettle. No drugs, no excessive intake of alcohol, and no pointless games of hide and fucking seek."

Harkness paused to breathe through his mouth for a second, his tongue snaking out to mop up the single line of blood that now breached the top of his lip. He stood up and paced the room, slowly rolling his head on his shoulders, flexing his neck muscles, trying to release some of the ache.

"At seven a.m. and nine p.m. sharp every day you will check in using the phone number that Skelly here will give you before you leave. Don't neglect this. It is not a request. If I need you in between times I will send either Skelly or Denzel to fetch you. You will drop everything and come, no matter what. Is that understood?"

Danny watched for a second and then gently cleared his throat. "I am not your pet dog. You don't own me," he said evenly, without emotion, just stating the fact.

A smile raked across Harkness's face. "Let me ask you a question? What do you want from this life, Danny? What do you want to remember when your last breath is ready to rattle from your chest?"

Harkness was now moving towards Danny, looking down to meet his eyes solidly, without blinking.

"When opportunity comes calling, do you want to be able to say that you were all ears, ready to reach out and grasp tightly onto the thrill of a lifetime? Do you want to write your own bit of history and see it mean something? To you? To this city? To those like me and you?

"Men like you and me, Danny, we need to be seen, we need to leave a mark, we need to be like Churchill, mate. He said, 'History will be kind to me, for I intend to write it.' That's our kind of life. If you step out on this journey with me, I promise you we will make history. And you will be handsomely rewarded for it. If you don't...? Then I will just have to swat you like a pointless fly."

"Jesus, Harkness, you do love a speech," countered Danny calmly. "Listen, I don't know you, so I don't trust you. I only work when I want and with whom I want to. Why should I help someone who is supposed to be a cop? And while you're at it... how about this, didn't Henry Ford say that all history is more or less bunk?"

Harkness laughed, reached out, and placed two hands on Danny's shoulders. "You sound like a man with a choice in the room. Ford did say that, but all Ford ever did was make very dull family cars. You, Danny, want to have a life. I know the likes of you: you don't just steal to put money in your pocket. You like thieving. That's what makes you so good at it. And that is why you're here, to help me steal something. Something fucking spectacular. Do me the honour... stay in touch, Danny, just like I've told you to. Don't make me come looking – it won't go well for you. But I will make it worth your while, sunshine. I promise you that. Take him home, boys."

The three muscle men shifted in their positions. Skelly, the driver, and Denzel stepped out of the doorway, which left the enforcer who held a knife in Danny's ribs earlier that evening to shepherd him out of the room.

Sidestepping them, making as if to take a run at Harkness, Danny caused the big bodyguard to move between them, his right arm coming up in anticipation of a blow, which was exactly what the thief wanted.

At lightning speed, Danny grabbed the enforcer's arm, throwing his weight in the opposite direction and up, twisting. The bodyguard doubled over to stop his arm getting wrenched out of its socket.

But Danny then shifted his weight immediately again, a satisfying crunch as he drove his victim face first into the door-jamb, his own size and heft doing most of the work against him. Wood and bone both splintered in the impact.

The other two were unable to come to their colleague's aid because in their joint surprise and haste they blocked each other from actually getting back through the doorway.

Danny now had the big guy on the floor at his feet. Meeting Harkness's gaze full on, Danny calmly raised his foot knee high. Then brought it down. Hard.

He stomped on the man's collarbone. The sickening snap was loud and soon followed by the victim's scream of pain.

"I'm not going anywhere, Harkness. You're not the only one in the room who can fight. And let me be clear, I'll meet with you one more time, later this week. And when I see you, do *me* the honour— reveal your hand or fuck off out of my life. I can't bear grandstanding. Come and get me when you're ready to talk business instead of just filling the room with bullshit. I'll make my own way home, gentlemen. You'll be busy taking your friend to casualty."

As he walked out of the re-purposed church, all Danny

could hear in his ears was the echo of Harkness laughing.

CHAPTER 10
NEW CREW, OLD HABITS

As Christine parked her car, she marvelled that so few of the local residents realised that their neighbours were one of London's most effective anti-crime squads. The west London base for the Barnes Flying Squad was an anonymous looking building, a scruffy 1970s red brick affair, boxy, unremarkable.

For such a well-to-do area, the team handled gritty cases across the whole of Southeast England and sometimes beyond. Criminals didn't tend to think about jurisdiction when they were identifying their targets. But, if they came from London, chances were that no matter where their job was pulled, the Barnes team would be the ones on the hunt for them.

As she walked from her parking bay into the office, she raised her face to the sun. She sighed out loud. This was something she knew she was doing frequently these days. Christine came straight from Shauna's bedside. It was another night of fitful, shallow sleep, punctuated by random beeping, imagined and real, as the equipment told the story of her daughter's slow decline.

On such sunny mornings it felt cruel to her that a world was

85

still going about its natural business while Shauna clung to what little of her life was left. Christine wanted everything to stop and have an almighty pause of breath while she and her little girl dealt with whatever fate God meted out. But then wasn't she equally scared of stopping to face the eventuality that lay ahead?

When she reached her desk, a yellow post-it note summoned her to a meeting with her Detective Chief Inspector, "as soon as you get your arse in".

Entering the 'guvnor's' cramped office, Christine pretended she couldn't smell the smoke from the crafty cigarette her boss lit up before anyone else came in for the day's work.

DCI Collinson was round and becoming rounder. He was a copper from the old school. An ex-beat bobby who rose through the ranks when experience mattered more than politics and was now close to retiring. He had a month left in the job. The expanding waistline, a severe smoking habit, commendations coming out of his ears, and a regular pension on its way. He was plain speaking, politically incorrect in private, and a cracking good policeman. CC respected her DCI almost as much as she had loved her own father. She would miss this man whom many underestimated when they met him... and all went on to regret it.

"All right, Chance, come in, have a seat. Who's on coffee run this morning? I'm parched." Collinson's voice was craggy and gruff with a cockney accent carved out by a lifetime of Embassy Regals.

"Freethy, sir... late as usual."

"For his own funeral, mate, his own funeral. I better open the windows, bit stuffy in here."

CC looked down to hide the smile she couldn't stifle.

"We've had an excellent few weeks haven't we? Good numbers, good results, lot of wrong'uns taken off the streets. And, I have another job that looks like it might pop sooner rather than later. Another chance to tick some boxes without too much overtime."

"Another? We've had a lot of luck of late, guv."

"Yes, but good intel is our oxygen, young lady. Don't knock it."

He threw a buff-coloured folder across the desk at her. "Looks like we have a bead on a team of Russkies. They've been running a load of high-class tarts in the West End for the last eighteen months or so. Now before you say it, yes, I do know that we aren't vice, but get this – it's a cash industry, as you know..."

Christine frowned mock indignation at this suggestion.

"You know CC, get it where you can... ha ha. Anyway, these Russkies and their dirty money have caught someone's attention. In the folder you'll find details, some useful, some not, for a gentleman called Abasin Yusufzai. He's of Pakistani origin but was brought up in Bradford. He moved to the bright lights of our fair city three years ago. He is either the founder or, at least, a major player in a group of Radical Muslims called Mohammed's Way. Usual thing, death to the west... virgins waiting in heaven... all that good stuff. Anyway, he's had a team of lads on the sniff around this Russian outfit for six weeks. Seems they want a slice of the cash business, without having to sully themselves with the sordid business of trafficking girls and all that untidiness. We have confidential informant intel that says the job is imminent. Especially since we're playing host to that big football conference... UEFA, FIFA all in town. Our Allah-loving-friends figure that it could be a cash-rich few days for the likes of the vodka drinkers. The girls will be working their arses off."

CC winced inwardly at the bias and the unintentional pun, but there was logic in the rest of it, for all its insensitivity. She leafed through the contents of the folder as her boss talked, noticing that many of the evidence sheets were severely redacted.

"Sir, there are a lot of blacked out passages here. Is this from anti-terrorist by any chance?"

"On the money, sunshine. Names, paragraphs, details removed all over the place, but I have been told the rest is reliable. The full bill of the race."

"Sir, excuse me for saying, I don't like doing dirty work for SO15. They usually drip-feed us and sit back and watch as we chase our tails."

Collinson sat back, taking Christine in for a second. She thought she was about to get a lecture.

"Listen, young Chance, I dislike those MI5 wannabe wankers as much as you do, but this looks credible. We can take a few players off the board and everyone gets to sleep soundly in their beds. You'll find that this file is not as drip-drip as they usually are. Frankly, it surprised me. Quite a bit of detail once you read through it. They've even given last known addresses for the entire crew. We're on a roll at the minute, so why don't we just get our heads round this and see if we can't keep that going. Any old nonsense with the detail or any interference from the spooks, just let me know. I'll kill it dead. Okay?"

At that moment, Freethy knocked on the door, carrying several takeaway coffee cups.

"Freeth! You're late! A man could have died of fucking thirst before you got the water to him! Ten quid fine!"

"Aww, guv. It was packed in there. Yummy mummies and all that..."

"Fine stands!"

CC chuckled. Office fines were handed out regularly. The money was split between an office beer fund and a donation to charity once every few months. Fines could be for anything deemed annoying by the guv or on a majority of opinion of the team—anything from referring to an Irish national as a "Paddy" to crashing a service vehicle while in pursuit of a suspect.

Once Freethy delivered the drinks, mumbling about the "bleeding coffee run", Christine looked to her DCI for the rest of the briefing.

"You'll have to have armed support once you've established contact. Not only are the ragheads well-armed but we're sure the Commies are too."

The guvnor had just racked up about fifty quid in fines in that one sentence.

He continued with a bellow.

"Bleedin' hell, Freeth, where'd you get these? One inch of coffee and seven of fucking foam!"

When she finished laughing, Christine asked what she knew to be a crucial question.

"So SO15 has a man inside? Any chance they'll let us know who? Is he one of the crew? Is there someone we will be picking up but then letting go... anyone to avoid?"

"Not that they have directly shared, but that may come later. No such thing as a free lunch. They will want us to manipulate someone most likely. The key to this is to get behind them, make sure that we know the location of the counting house that holds the money and get the stopper on it before you have another wild-fucking-west style shoot-out in a leafy suburb."

"The counting house isn't in the file?"

"Not yet. Might be another drip to come. Now why are you pulling a face?"

"Nothing guv. It just seems this run of luck is all very convenient."

"Read the fucking file and clean up their radical jihad bullshit before anyone gets their balls blown off. I hope that's not beyond you. Now out of my sight. My one inch of coffee is getting fucking cold."

CHAPTER 11
SHOULD'VE WOULD'VE COULD'VE

THE FIRST THING DANNY NOTICED AS HE DUCKED HIS HEAD INTO THE back seat of the silver, chauffeur-driven Lexus was the black designer business suit she was wearing. It was cut like a man's, but you couldn't get any more feminine than the way Dexy wore it. Danny had to focus in order to brush aside the hot, intense flashback it gave him, his memories ignited by the rich spice of her perfume in the car.

It was early and the pickup was in Regent's Park, just as arranged. Danny had Barry Blount's laptop with him.

"Good morning, young man. How are we?"

"Always pleased to see you, Dexy. I think you wanted this?" He passed the computer across.

"I saw your girl on breakfast TV this morning. Looks like she really is flavour of the month. Mind you, the interview was so sickly sweet it gave me diabetes."

Dexy was already busy powering up the machine, the chime of the operating system greeted her efforts.

"The nation's sweetheart should be exactly that, Danny! She has a chance to make it. Recovering this should certainly prolong her window of opportunity, so thank you. She doesn't know you, but she does owe you."

Danny waved a hand gently in the air, knowing it was Dexy who would honour the debt.

A "log on" screen presented itself. Dexy looked quizzically to Danny once the machine prompted them for a password for access. "Barry's not the sharpest spoon in the drawer... is he?"

Danny smiled and nodded agreement. Dexy typed 'password' into the password box, and sure enough the desktop came to life in front of them. Danny gave a short laugh. His next guess would have been 'misternuts,' all lower case.

It didn't take them long to locate the video file that was so precious to Honey Sister. Barry Blount, once again, proved not to be a candidate for MI5. He had saved it to the desktop itself, unencrypted and filed as 'Honey Movie'.

"Before I double-click, darling," purred Dexy, "please remember I am an innocent soul, so you may have to explain what is going on..."

"Ever the convent girl, Dexy..."

This earned Danny an elbow in the ribs, which hurt more than it should because of his tussle with Harkness's henchmen and his bladed enforcer from the previous night.

Dexy double-clicked and a video box filled a quarter of the computer screen. After taking a few moments to load, the frame jumped to life. It was a beach on a sunny day.

"Oh, a little al fresco romance," purred Dexy, leaning into Danny a little as the video played.

It wasn't what either of them was expecting.

Waves lapping gently, Barry Blount's voice was clear from behind the camera or camera phone. He was directing, asking Sarah Grimes, or Honey Sister as she would become more widely known, to stop being shy and perform. After a few minutes of back and forth, the budding starlet relented.

She finally walked into view, looking younger, a little more fresh-faced, a little less manufactured. It was unmistakably the same girl who giggled on Danny's TV earlier that morning. But, on the computer screen she was carrying a little girl. A little girl with sunny blonde hair and grey-specked eyes. She had a cute button nose dappled with freckles. A smaller, identical copy of the woman carrying her. For clarity's sake, about fifteen seconds into her appearance on screen, the little girl tightens the grip of her arms around Honey's neck and says, clearly "Mummy... ice cream... ice cream."

Dexy hit pause.

"That's an unexpected development. She really does want her fame."

Danny sighed. "I'm out of my comfort zone here, Dexy. I am capable of doing a lot of things, but denying a child..."

"Danny, darling, you can wipe that look off your face. You and I are capable of everything if put in the right position. Holier than thou is not becoming of you."

"I don't like manipulation, Dexy."

"Then don't play the game, my love."

Before their version of the moral maze could escalate, the driver of the car cleared his throat. "Ma'am, apologies, but I think we have someone following us."

Their route took them north out of London's centre, and they were now circling the stadium dedicated to the national game – Wembley.

"Go through the sports complex. Plenty of blind turns in there," Danny barked, as he shifted in his seat to see who or what was behind them.

A Ford transit van. A black one, Danny recognized instantly as the one that had ferried his ex-accomplices to their cement grave.

Harkness and his team.

Instinctively, Danny felt under his arm. The gap his hand found made his heart sink. He'd almost brought the gun retrieved from his sister's garage, but decided it wasn't necessary.

"Pick up the pace," said Danny, the Lexus now speeding through various warehouse zones, swerving to avoid a cement mixer in attempt to put distance between them and the black van.

"What the fuck is going on, darling?" Dexy looked a little less composed than usual.

"It's Harkness, the guy I asked you about."

"I heard he's quite the action man," said Dexy. "Three tours in the Gulf for the first war, another three in the sequel, and just three years ago he was in Afghanistan. Trouble is no one seems to be able to pinpoint his regiment."

"Flying under a black flag?"

"Maybe, but not so covert. I was able to find out he was there and the number of times. No, the real mystery about your Harkness is how he has risen so quickly at the Metropolitan Police Service. Did you know he's Anti-Terrorist Squad?"

"I assumed Flying Squad..."

"I thought you might, but no, he is definitely SO15. It fits, given his recent military experience. Anyway, his colleagues all seem to like him. No whiff of anything corrupt or dirty. No wife or kids, an elderly father who's also ex-service, originally from Aldershot. Aside from that, I really can't find anything of great value."

They were interrupted as their driver took a corner too tightly and the car lurched sharply to the left. The rear wheel bounced off the curb, the clang of the alloy audible even inside the vehicle.

The urgency was clear. The black van was joined by a

motorcycle carrying two riders, the driver brandishing a hammer while the passenger gripped a sawed-off shotgun.

"Brace yourselves" was all the driver could say, as Dexy turned to look at Danny, urgency now in her voice.

"How have you ticked these chaps off, Danny? Don't answer that. One last thing: Harkness was given a dishonourable discharge from the Military. He slit his Afghan translator's throat. The motive was never explained. He's all business, your new friend!"

There was an explosion of glass as the driver's window gave way to the hammer and the double-barrels replaced it.

"Ma'am?"

The driver did the sensible thing. He pulled to a halt before he lost the left side of his face to shotgun pellets.

Instantly, the van pulled tight behind them.

Figures jumped out, yanking the rear doors of the car open.

"Get the fuck out. Now!"

"You do keep very charming company, Danny."

"Careful, Dexy... that list includes you."

And with that, Dexy was dragged by her red hair out of the car.

Danny should have brought the gun. But if he had, would he have used it?

Almost certainly.

The hands now reaching for him received a fine reception. Danny wrapped his arm around the wrist and pulled with all his body strength, enjoying the ping as his assailant's head was smacked against the car's door frame. Danny shuffled over to Dexy's side, the door still hanging open. He pushed himself out with both hands. His body straightened as the rider on the bike reached him.

Knocking the shotgun to the side with lightning speed, he used his upward momentum and right arm to smash into the soft flesh of the biker's throat, crushing his windpipe all the way back, mashing it against his spine.

Leaving him to collapse on the curb, Danny whirled around, trying to get a fix on where the first set of hands dragged Dexy. Setting off towards the black van, he saw the last flash of her red hair as she was bundled in through the side door.

In his haste, Danny got too close to the front end of the van. As he drew level with it, the passenger door was flung open with full force, cracking into his knees, his momentum causing his nose and head to follow suit.

Down he went.

Eyes swimming, head clanging and woozy, gravel forcing up under fingernails as he scrambled to stand up. Only for a heavy foot in the chest to smash him back down.

Danny didn't need his vision to clear to know who was standing over him.

"Danny, my son. A good man knows when his race is run."

Harkness surveyed the scene around him briefly. He then turned to his remaining men. "Get rid of the driver and get Spikey back in the van and get the fuck out of here. Leave me the keys of the Lexus."

Spikey was choking. He was doubled in two at the side of the road, coughing up blood, fighting for air.

Danny slowly sat up. Harkness was now hunkered down beside him.

"I couldn't let you think your insubordination last night was even the smallest of triumphs, Danny. So here we are, letting you know the lie of the land... again. And just to hammer home the fact, I have your friend too. Maybe now, you will start to listen to me."

Danny just stared at him, taking on board the magnitude of what Harkness told him.

The Tall Man grabbed him. He pulled him to his feet taking

him towards the rear of the Lexus. Harkness pressed the button on the key he'd just been handed. The boot popped open.

"In you go."

Danny resisted, pulling back on Harkness with as much energy as he had left. "If you think I'm getting in there..."

His words broke off as Harkness swept Danny's legs from under him using his own left leg. He hefted his upper body weight into Danny's waist simultaneously, folding him into the boot of the big executive car.

"Get in and shut the fuck up. I don't want you to see where we're going. Once there, all will be revealed."

As the boot door closed, the daylight shrank. Danny had the second flashback of the day, this one a lot less pleasurable than the one Dexy inspired.

In his mind, he saw a man standing over him, closing a door tight, blocking out the light on an equally small space. Danny shivered, both at his enclosed space and the sight of who was shutting him into this black hole. In that instant he was back, a small boy... and the man standing over him was his father.

CHAPTER 12

CULTURE CLASH

WHEN KATERINA KNOCKED ON THE DOOR OF ROOM 520 OF THE Grosvenor House Hotel, she looked particularly stunning, if she said so herself. A chic, tailored, wool suit worn over Agent Provocateur lingerie. She felt confident and ready. The persona she created in her own imagination allowed her to screen the real her from these moments of exploitation. She waited for the door to be answered.

It was opened by a Middle Eastern man. He had a smile on his bearded face, his eyes not able to help but look her up and down as she stepped over the threshold. She recognized the naked desire in his eyes; she had seen it many times as she stepped into rooms like this one. To Katerina, the refinement of luxury hotels belied the animal purpose that the room was about to accommodate.

"Good afternoon, handsome, sir."

Though she flashed her best smile at him, Katerina's thoughts were full of contempt for the latest pathetic imbecile to rent her body. What was it today? Three hours? A cool £5,000 for the privilege, she believed, even though she wasn't supposed to know her own price point.

Her next thought was disappointment. He was Arab, so she wouldn't even have a glass of champagne or wine to break the ice, to help take the edge off the first exchanges.

"Excuse me, darling. I need to prepare," Katerina said, her high heels clicking on the tiled bathroom floor as she closed the door behind her.

She took her time. Not because she wanted to be just right, but because she wanted to delay the inevitable. Her instincts told her to be alarmed. There was something about this one she didn't like. She hoped he wasn't going to be one of the rough ones who felt that once they'd paid, they could do whatever they fucking liked.

When she finally emerged into the bedroom, he sat on the edge of the bed, his hands spread out on either side of him. He took an involuntary gasp at the sight of her in her high heels and expensive lingerie.

She walked towards him. She stood over him letting him smell her perfume. Her smile was stiff, plastered across her face by the force of her own will.

He stood up. Meeting her eyes, he kissed her full on the lips. Something swished in her peripheral vision, a reflection in the mirror that hung on the wall facing the end of the king size bed.

And then she could see what he held— a black silk scarf which he gently draped across her wrists once he pulled them in front of her. Her instincts were right.

A kink.

Was he someone who could only get it up by having the woman completely under his control?

He tied the scarf in a tight knot, and then produced a second, identical scarf. Katerina waited to see if this one was for her eyes or to tie her to the bed. But he had a surprise again for her. The scarf came up over her head, down round her neck and then, suddenly, viciously, he pulled across her mouth, swiftly tying a large, tight double knot, which pushed its way into her mouth as well as held it in place.

And then he reached behind him, under the pillow nearest to them on the bed. She waited to see another scarf, except this time it was a brute-ugly handgun.

And now Katerina was scared. Scared enough to weep.

~

The 'intel' had been spot-on. CC's team followed the Mohammed's Way acolytes for forty-eight hours, and today it was clear they were gearing up for action.

Her guys trailed the suspects in West End traffic, their edge of expectation building. But there was a problem.

They had lost the main man, Yusufzai. He separated off in the afternoon. Despite her team having split in order to stick with him, he slipped the tail via the London Underground. The follow lost him in the labyrinth that was the new King's Cross network, too many interchanges and people in the way.

At least they were still behind the rest of Yusufzai's men in their battered Renault van.

CC was driving a short distance back from the van, following as it snaked its way round Marble Arch and down onto Park Lane. The radio chatter offered constant commentary on their movements. The van signalled a left-hand turn. Christine looked at Freethy in the passenger seat next to her.

"Let me jump out here, CC. If they turn up and head back towards Oxford Street, I can intercept them on foot. You won't see where they go if you make the turn behind them now, we're just a touch too far back."

CC pulled the car to a stop at the curb, Freethy leapt out straight away, checking he had his radio covered up as he sprinted down the blocked off street.

CC gunned her BMW back into the traffic, a few blared horns greeting her for the apparent aggression.

She made the turn around the front of The Grosvenor House Hotel about twenty-five seconds behind the Renault, and just at that her radio crackled into life. Freethy.

"I'm by the taxi entrance of The Grosvenor. Two have switched into the back of the van. Good news is we have our main man again. Abasin Yusufzai just got into the front seat. But he's not alone. Can't say for definite if it is a woman, but it's someone dressed in a burka."

The Arab man forced Katerina into the burka. Cleverly, the black silk scarf blended in with the deep black of the covering. She was still gagged, but of course behind the hood, no one could see that she was tied at the mouth.

Katerina fought her rising fear and pushed the bile back down into her throat, as panic forced her to gag. As she walked next to the man, particularly through the hotel reception, she fought with herself. Should she try to pull away from him? Scream?

The hard pressure of the gun just to the left of her spine was enough to keep her compliant, hidden in the folds of his sleeve and the cloth of her new outfit.

As she put it on, he babbled at her in heavily accented English. It was a few minutes before she could comprehend that he was taking her somewhere, somewhere to meet some men she might know. Still, as she was none the wiser, Katerina's panic and fear fluttered like a captured bird in her chest. This all felt to her like the last straw, the latest indignity that might just break her resolve. The incident left her bereft, stole her self-respect, robbed her of her carefully constructed façade.

She felt like a piece of meat, cheated of the one thing she could cling to: hope.

Was this man taking her somewhere to be forced into something completely debased and debauched at a gang bang? Would she live? Could she bear to live if that was to be her fate? Katerina thought she had developed a tough outer shell over these last months of abuse, but now she knew how fragile she was, how little her life was worth in this world, just how disposable she was.

CC saw the burka-clad figure get into the van milliseconds after she turned the corner into Park Street. What the fuck was this? A woman? On a job? An Islamic woman? Unless it was no woman under the get up?

The Renault van started off again, heading north towards Oxford Street, as Freethy predicted. CC slowed to a partial stop at the Grosvenor to allow him back in the car.

She had a choice to make. Keep the follow going, or if anything, tighten it up. But then what? Knowing the chaos her next decision might cause, she had to be sure. Her instincts had to be totally on point. Would they slip up and give away something that might allow her to call it? Exactly when should she radio in the gunships?

"Any signs of coercion? Do you think it's actually a woman under that outfit?"

Freethy was already shaking his head, a rueful expression across his face.

"To be honest, I'm not sure. I wasn't paying them much mind, not expecting to see a man and woman even approach our target vehicle. When they reached it, I realised it was our main man. As for whether that's a woman? Could be, slight enough build, but can't swear to it."

"Fuck." That was all she could manage as she picked her way behind the Renault, which turned left, back towards Marble Arch once again.

~

Katerina was in the middle seat in the front cab of some kind of van, sandwiched between her 'client' and another man. He wore a scarf and a baseball cap, but it couldn't hide his beard, dark eyes, and Middle Eastern complexion. Both men were babbling to each other in a language she neither knew nor could identify.

Her captor spoke to her again in poor English, prodding her ribs with his gun. "Look up, keep head still, no look down, until I say, whore."

She did as she was told, only to feel him bring her tethered hands up and in front of her. Something round, cold, and metallic was forced between her fingers, then the sticky pressure of heavy-duty tape was wound around her hands, the object was now wedged between them. Finally, there was some fiddling with the end of the metallic object, where it protruded from both her fingers and the tightly wound tape.

"Fuck," was all Katerina could think. "What the fuck?"

~

The Renault van meandered through west London down into Knightsbridge then deeper into Kensington, until eventually it pulled into a dead-end street.

CC had to cruise past it, instructing one of the other cars to deposit a man on foot to see if he could get a closer look and see why they'd stopped.

But before they could get someone in position, the van was on its way again. It pulled back onto the road it turned off and once again started to retrace its route, back into the streets of Knightsbridge, towards the rear of Harrods department store. It wasn't a long journey.

Christine concentrated on her gut for twenty seconds, and then reached for the radio. She called the gunships in closer.

The short stop was a simple one. It allowed the suspects to pull on masks and distribute weapons from the rear of the van. Katerina was still up front, still being forced to look up, her neck now beginning to ache from the prolonged pose.

She could sense that the atmosphere in the van changed. There was an added tension in the voices of the men. The van pulled off, and after what seemed like hours, she was given instructions, once more in broken English.

"When we stop, we get out, you no fight, whore. No fight, you will live. Understood?"

She nodded affirmation.

"When we get to door, you move when I say."

The van came to a halt. Her handlers pulled her roughly out of the door, onto a plush west London street. They pushed her up the steps of one of the large terrace houses. From the looks of it the building had seen better days. She was placed front and centre before the door of the house, and her 'client' rapidly banged his fist on the door. As he did, he whipped the hood of the burka off her head.

As she waited for a response, she had the presence of mind to look down at her bound hands. There, sticking out from the tape was some sort of metal egg, with a ring on the top of it. A clear wire was attached to the ring and led all the way to her left, where her captor held his gun pointed at her with one hand and the end of this wire in the other. And then it struck her, like a horse kick to her chest.

A hand grenade was trussed between her palms.

~

It was a fucking nightmare. The street where they stopped was wide and fairly clear of traffic but there was nowhere to hide. CC didn't dare pull into it, she hurriedly dispatched Freethy on foot to get a fix on what was happening.

Then her mobile phone rang. Freethy on the other end.

"We're fucked."

~

Panic was blooming in her chest. Katerina wildly whipped her head from side to side, looking from her captor on one side of the entryway to the rest of his gang on the other side. Then the sound of a peephole being opened on the door itself, a puzzled shout from behind it.

In Russian.

The bouncer's mistake was to follow his instinct and open the door when he recognized one of the boss's girls on the doorstep. But why was she wearing a gag?

Suddenly there were masked men in his face, guns pointing, one of them babbling in crazy English something about "boss" and "grenade". When the talker thrust the girl's hands under his nose, he understood the bit about the hand grenade. The proximity of the explosive and a gun under his chin forced him to lead them down a long hallway. They finally turned into a big room on the ground floor. It was a kitchen. At a table in the middle of the room sat five men, all eating a meal as a sixth man served them. Dinner was about to be ruined.

∼

"They've gone in, armed, with the girl. It's definitely a woman. They seemed to force their way in. But unless we hear shots, we can't follow. If we roll up too early this has fucking 'siege' written all over it."

Freethy was right. All they could do was to block the van's escape route and hope they didn't force the issue. But that might be too loose. There could be back alleys between the houses that would give them passage out.

Christine doled out instructions on the radio, getting the gunships to shut off both ends of the street, but not too close. The next thing she did was hit the panic button on her mobile, calling in the big boys. If this was going 'siege', she wasn't going to be able to hold on to the scene on her own for very long, nor did she want to.

∼

The bouncer was pistol-whipped from behind as soon as he crossed the kitchen threshold, and Katerina was shoved through the door straight after him.

Despite her terror, because that is what it was now— out and out terror—she couldn't help but recognise one or two faces.

At the head the table was Losif. The man who laid the ground rules for her new life when she was first brought to London. He became her 'boss'.

The other face, however, was far more shocking. Like a knife twisting in her chest, this final indignity delivered a 'coup de grace' and added to this nightmare of hers.

It was the man who courted her back home in her native Russia. She was a waitress in a Moscow nightclub. He waited for her after work and whispered sweet nothings to her throughout the night. Wooed her. Romanced her over many months. He took her heart as easily as you might pick up an apple and take a bite. When he suggested a trip to London for a romantic weekend, she was convinced he was going to propose. On arrival, they didn't check into a beautiful hotel or book a lavish restaurant for dinner. He simply handed her over to Losif. Her descent into exploitation had begun. Kirill was her lover's name, or so he had told her. Now, here he was, directly in front of her.

Sitting there. Eating. Here in this London house. The first time she had seen him since he walked away from the speeding car that abducted her.

Her new captor spoke directly to Losif.

"Everyone still, please. Look to her hands. See? Grenade."

He jangled the ring on the grenade by gently tugging on the catgut he tied to it earlier.

"Anyone moves, I pull. Anyone not answer my questions, I pull. Anyone try trick me, I pull. Yes?"

Losif nodded, coolly wiping his mouth with a paper napkin as he did so. His movements were cautious, deliberate, trying to show that he was no threat to the intruders.

Her captor spoke again. "More men?"

Losif shook his head slowly. "No."

"Money. Where is money? Show my men."

Losif nodded to the pistol-whipped but still conscious bouncer and said, in Russian, "Show them."

Katerina, taking it all in, was too terrified to move. She

didn't turn to watch as the men left the room for the money. She could not take her eyes off Kirill.

She loved this man. She dreamed of a life with him. She put her faith in him. And now look. She was here, a grenade in her tethered hands. Her body defiled and disrespected. Over and over again by so many strangers. Her dignity stripped from her. All because of this man, Kirill, who had once held her face in his hands and told her she was an angel, a gift to him from God. She was just a product to be traded. A business transaction.

Katerina felt sick.

The Arab men were now ferrying money in large canvas bags out to their van.

CC ordered the street blocked at both ends, a gunship just around a slight bend, about a hundred yards from the target house, but far enough away so it was not visible to the men who were now piling bags into the back of their battered Renault van. The other armed response team was close enough that once the suspects tried to make their exit, the hit could be put into place easily.

One of her team was now trying to edge along the opposite pavement, using parked cars for cover, trying to get photographic evidence of the theft as it happened. When the mystery woman was added to the mix, CC radioed that she hoped the photographer on the team managed to 'smudge' her, to photograph her, not just for evidential purposes but for identification should they need to let her slip while in pursuit of the main suspects.

Freethy was also trying to get a better angle on the proceedings from a vantage point behind some bushes at a property diagonally opposite the target house. All the while he was on both the radio and the mobile phone to Christine, one conversation clipped and professional for the radio records, the mobile phone chatter much more informal and useful.

Mobile: "Looks like they're loading up, no sign of the bird. Maybe she is a hostage but can't tell at this point."

Radio: "Standby all assets, suspects loading cargo."

Mobile: "They are pointing to the west end of the street, so make sure the pistol packers at your end are ready to move their arses this way."

"They are itching, don't worry about that, Freethy. They love this kind of shit."

CC hoped she wouldn't be sniffing gunpowder in the air that evening.

Katerina started to shake. She knew how her boss thought. She would be blamed for this, even though she neither knew the Arabs nor understood their intent. The pimps would assume she helped set this up; they would want to dispose of her. Robberies attracted unwanted attention. Loose ends needed to be tidied up.

Yet all she could do now was stare at Kirill. The man she loved. The man who would probably be given the job of killing her.

Five very long minutes passed until the bag carriers returned to the kitchen, telling their boss, Abasin, that they had all the money.

Abasin nodded gently, his eyes never leaving Losif's face. His stare was fixed on him from the moment he walked in. "We leave. No one follows to door; the grenade stays safe."

"I will find you. This is a very bad day for you." There was no threat in Losif's voice. He was simply stating a fact.

"Allah is great," was the reply. Abasin slowly backed towards the door, his cohorts aiming their guns, doing the same. Katerina was being drawn backwards by Abasin's gun hand.

And then something changed. She changed.

She was flooded with rage. Every hand, every mouth, every touch, every degradation, every fear, every tearful sleepless night, every self-recrimination, every humiliation, every faked smile, and orgasm.

Every. Single. Misery.

They all boiled up in Katerina, her heart fit to explode. She'd had enough. Enough of their control, enough of their lies, enough of their objectification. It was over. In that instant she knew what she would do. The element of surprise was to her advantage.

Whipping her bound hands from left to right in front of her, Katerina pulled the catgut taut from where it was attached to the grenade all the way back to Abasin's hands, and then with a swift flick of her forearms, she felt and heard the ping of the metal pin and round handle across the top of the explosive spin free into mid-air.

She leapt forward for all she was worth, her head burying into Kirill's chest. He rose out of his chair to try to escape this woman who had launched herself at him. But he was too slow, her momentum knocked him against the stove behind them.

Abasin was the first to react. Turning to run, screaming in his native language to his men. "Get out, get out, get out!"

But they weren't quick enough.

The grenade fulfilled its deadly purpose, exploding next to the gas burner that just cooked the Russians' last meal.

There was a heavy crack, followed by a deeper boom. Freethy heard it first, CC a second later. Confusion struck each of them at the same time, but the roar that followed surprised and shocked them.

The gas explosion triggered by the grenade took out the whole front of the house. Bricks, plaster, and debris were flung high in the air. The Renault was rocked from side-to-side by the force of the blast. The driver was at first wide-eyed and unsure of what to do, and then the burden of choice was removed from him. A large slab of portico slammed into the bonnet of the van, pushing the engine free of its mooring and onto the road beneath it.

And now CC was screaming into her radio: "Go! Go! Go!" The gunships hurtled in, along with the rest of the team, crowding round the van, hauling the driver out of the door. Christine stood looking at the front of the ruined house, whispering out loud: "Fuck, Fuck, Fuck."

CHAPTER 13
THE WRONG FOOT

DARK, ENCLOSED SPACES HELD A TERRIBLE FEAR FOR DANNY. IT HAD been a long time since he had found himself in such an unwelcome position. Now that he was here, he was struggling.

Entombed in the car boot, he tried to focus his mind in order to wipe away images from his past. But as he concentrated on his battered body and the throbbing cramp in his knees, the memory of his father was a stubborn spectre. Flashes intruded on his attempts at slow-breathing — his father forcing a five-year-old Danny into the cupboard under the stairs, reading from a bible as he did so. Dark and cramped, the hours passed until light flooded all around him, only for his father's form to block it out as his raised arm brought a belt down with a vicious swish. These beatings were always accompanied by a shrill rendition of the Lord's Prayer.

His sister, Celeste, would sometimes try to sneak food or drink to him, but Danny always refused to take them, his young mind knowing instinctively that if caught, his sister might pay a price.

As the car slowed, he finally pushed away the memories. Instinct kicked in as he listened to the sound of tyres on the road. Then he heard a change, the wheels hit a ramp of some kind as the angle of the car shifted and forced him to slip back against the end of the car. And then a stop. A door opened. The balance of the vehicle shifted as he felt Harkness get out.

The boot was opened. Danny blinked and held his hands out in front of his face, squinting in an attempt to adjust his vision.

"Ah, Danny. I think we got off on the wrong foot."

This bloke is fucking nuts, was all Danny could think in return.

They were in a multi-story car park, the only vehicle on that particular level. Danny bent over, trying to stretch off the ache of being curled up in enclosed space.

He straightened up and looked at Harkness, wiping dried blood from his face.

"Danny, we will not harm her. She's just a little insurance policy is all. A keepsake to keep you on the straight and narrow."

"What are we doing here, wherever here is, and why?"

"I like your attitude, young man. All business. Cutting to the chase. You don't need to know exactly where we are, but I have a little mission for you. Think of this as a sort of job interview. I've heard from all sorts that you are good, Danny. I want to see it myself. A little Doubting Thomas, I am. Need to put my fingers in the wounds."

Danny just stared at him, his level gaze never wavering.

"What do you notice about this car park, Danny?"

Danny took his time before breaking his gaze away from Harkness's face.

"It's new. No tire marks or debris. The dust is still settling."

Harkness clapped his hands together.

"Correct! And as it is brand new, it is empty... except for the lower levels, the basement. Where just about now, an illegal event is happening. All very naughty! And we're about to make it even naughtier, you and me. A little thievery to brighten our day."

"Why the fuck would I want to rob somewhere without even the chance of a reconnaissance or planning of any kind? Getting fucking killed is no measure of how good I am at anything other than dying."

"Where has all that positivity gone? It was here a second ago. Danny, I have thought of everything. No need for you to reconnoitre. One of my boys is doing it for you right now. Take a look."

Harkness produced a small device from his inside pocket, activated it and tapped an icon to open an app. As he handed the device to Danny, it came to life with a black and white image of the basement several levels below.

The screen showed a crowd of men, all huddled round each other. Try as he might, he couldn't fathom what they were doing. Plus, he was still busy trying to work out just how he might get the hell out of Harkness's crazy scenario intact.

"My boy is down there now, wearing a pair of glasses that also happen to have a camera in them right here," explained Harkness, touching the bridge of his nose by way of illustration. "Genius, isn't it... have you worked out what they are doing yet? It's a dogfight. Easy money, a load of gypsies, all flashing cash. Now there is probably only about twenty grand changing hands, give or take. I don't really need the money, but I want to see you in action, Danny, see the fabled Felix magic."

Danny was about to protest. He took a step towards Harkness, only to see him reach inside his coat pocket, the hand emerging with a gun in it.

"Play the fucking game, Danny. It's what we do. I'll even show you a little trust."

Harkness flipped the gun around in his hand proffering it butt-first to Danny.

"This is insane. We could get torn apart down there. They must have security of their own. They must be tooled up already."

"Yes, they do, but the beauty is that I provided them with the heavies. They are all my boys, undercover. Once you make your move the bouncers won't interfere. Of course, I can't vouch for the gypsies and their customers, but I'm sure you will think of something."

Instinctively, Danny checked the gun, slipped the cartridge out of the butt, and was surprised by the sight of live bullets in it.

He looked again at the screen. Harkness's man swept his eyes around the site in a slow pan so that Danny could form a layout of the place in his own mind.

"Exit strategy? How do we get out once we have the money?"

"There will be a car waiting at the top of the basement ramp, driver aboard, ready to whisk us away. How we get there is your challenge, my son."

"We'll need to distract them somehow."

"Again, I'm sure you'll think of something..."

Danny blew out his cheeks, knowing in that moment he was going to do this. He knew he was going to do the one thing he never thought he would — *wing it* on a job. But apart from trepidation, there was another emotion at play in Danny's heart.

Excitement.

He wanted to have a go. It was too delicious to resist. He

would never want Harkness to see that in him, but he couldn't deny it.

"C'mon Danny, think of it as a game. It'll be fun!"

"Alright, let's be reckless then, Harkness, but here's the deal. The money, it's all mine. No split. You've already said you don't need it."

"Cheeky bugger," he said as he applauded and laughed, mirth dancing in his eyes. A light playing in them that scared the living shit out of Danny but thrilled him just a little, too.

There were about a hundred men, of all shapes, shades, sizes, and ages. The air was thick with feral excitement, expectation of the brutal entertainment in front of them. As Danny and Harkness approached the rear of the throng, one man spread sawdust onto the concrete floor, soaking up blood from a fight just finished. Another man loaded a limp-looking Staffordshire bull terrier into the back of a blacked-out van, actual tears in his eyes and tenderness in his movements.

Nearby, another two vans were parked, one of them rocking from the force of the dogs inside. They were eager to get going, to fight. Bloodlust.

Danny began doing what he did best.

His eyes were 'all about', processing information rapidly. As he stood at the back of the throng, he linked the images from the screen with what he could now see for real. In moments like these, Danny seemed to go inward on himself. It was as if he could float above the room. The set-up was clear in his mind, a snapshot of his immediate surroundings. He now had a clear understanding of the size and shape of the venue and crowd. Next, he scanned the faces, taking each individual in, making instant judgements about whether they presented a threat, a hindrance, or were just other bystanders. A combination of experience and gut instinct provided him with all of this data in an instant.

His next move was to take in the physical evidence around him. He was keenly aware of the smell of the body odour of the man next to him at the back of the crowd. He was sweating profusely, and Danny knew he had either a lot to lose or had lost already.

Danny scanned the gathering again, this time isolating the big men. He scouted for bulges in their waistbands or under-arms revealing who was carrying and who wasn't. He assumed that those who were belonged to Harkness. At the same time, he absorbed snatches of conversation, picking out little titbits of information. There was a Seamus here, a fuck-off there, a David calling odds for the next fight. All a jumble that Danny was filtering for anything useful as he moved through the crowd.

Then back to their faces. Danny's gaze swept the assembled throng, deliberately making direct eye contact, using the split-second engagements to measure the reactions his stare provoked. The shift in a face might sometimes barely be percep-tible, but Danny never missed even a flicker or unconscious twitch. He read an article about it once. They were known as 'microfacial movements.' A whole plethora of 'telling info' in literally the blink of an eye or less. He could spot a minute flinch from fifty paces and know whether the person who just gave himself away was a 'lover' or a 'fighter.'

Last but not least, Danny looked at the floor, because in his experience, feet never lie.

He read people's subconscious intentions and feelings with a quick glance at the way they positioned their feet. When the action kicked off, he could tell who might lose his cool or who would bolt for it.

Danny assessed the situation in just over one minute.

Once done, he let his eyes settle on the man running the show. He identified him as soon as he laid eyes on him.

Older, about fifty-five, with reddish-brown hair turning silver at the edges, his small, dark piggy eyes sat beneath a forehead that was slightly too big for the rest of his face. This was completed with a thin-lipped mouth that gave him an overall look of someone who could be cruel or kind in the same heartbeat.

This gig was obviously his because of the number of men standing unnaturally close to him. And the fact they were paying no mind to the action about to unfold on the concrete before them. They, like Danny, were too busy scanning. Their no-nonsense glares kept everyone just far enough away from the main man. One particularly tall bouncer leant in to whisper in his boss' ear every now and again, a small nod or shake of the head each time a question was asked.

No doubt Piggy-eyes was the guv'nor.

"What you thinking, Felix? Talk me through it," said Harkness, doing some whispering of his own.

Danny laid it out for him. "We'll have to be quick, incisive. To our left, eight o'clock. Heavy set man, black, short, bald. He's tooled up, but not one of yours, not ex-military so keep an eye. Dead ahead. Small guy. Leather jacket. He's a fighter, meets a look full-on. I'll have to take him out of the game straight away. The one we need to talk to is over at three o'clock. Piggy-eyes. He's got plenty round him but it's his game. He's the one we have to convince we aren't joking."

Harkness was nodding gently, clearly impressed that Danny took the scene in so quickly. "Leave the convincing to me, Danny. Just nod when you are ready to kick-start the fun."

Danny stepped away, not liking the sound of the last comment. Convincing? Apart from winging a job, the only other thing Danny never liked in a plan was a teammate as unpredictable as Harkness.

Two men were now in the centre, each holding a dog. Danny was surprised to see two Jack Russells, both snarling, snapping, pulling at their leads, the smell of the blood from the previous fight firing them up. The flaring of their nostrils and curling of their lips adding to the anticipation of the spectators. The men were goading them, edging the dogs towards each other close enough to provoke a bite then hauling them back at the last possible second before contact was made.

Money was furiously changing hands, with wagers being placed and side bets multiplied before the start of the bout. Finally, Mr. Piggy-eyes raised his voice. He had a thick, rough cockney accent.

"Let's get on with it. Get ready to release."

Danny stood just behind the short man in the leather jacket, the one he had told Harkness was up for a fight.

It was show time.

Danny tapped him on the shoulder, and as he turned to react, Danny calmly reached up and bounced the butt of his gun on the bridge of the guy's nose. Blood shot everywhere as he fell to his knees, and the blow caused the crowd around them to divide like someone had just declared the plague. Danny then levelled his gun across the circle at Mr. Piggy-eyes, and at the top of his lungs shouted, "Don't fucking move an inch!"

At the same instant, two of the bigger men Danny had observed earlier, one wearing glasses, put a hand on the shoulders of two of Mr. Piggy-eyes' closest associates, their expressions enough to discourage any reaction.

At Danny's feet, the short guy was struggling to stand up, ready to strike back, even through a blood-soaked face, when Danny calmly sideswiped him again with the gun, barrel first this time, opening a huge welt on his cheek. More haemor-rhaging.

As the hubbub subsided, Mr. Piggy-eyes spoke up. "Who the fuck do you think you are? Are you fucking mad?"

One of Harkness's men tossed a black sack into the middle of the fight ring, just in front of the dogs.

Danny answered. "All the Money. In the bag. Now. We have enough guns and men to make a right mess of this place. Don't be fucking stupid. Just get on with it. Nobody wants to try to be Mad Max here. Okay? No fucking heroics."

A movement to Danny's right caught his eye. The dog handler shifted his feet, pointing them his way.

A dog as a weapon, thought Danny.

The handler released the lead. At almost the same instant a gunshot rang out. The fierce little dog's head exploded across the feet of the crowd.

Harkness was holding his gun level on the other side of the circle, just behind Mr. Piggy-eyes, who was clasping his hands over his obviously ringing ears.

"See? The man means business. The money, gentlemen. Fucking now!" Harkness looked very pleased with himself at that point. He turned his gun towards Piggy-eyes, whose face showed both rage and resignation.

Danny picked up the sack and used his gun to encourage everyone in the room to hand over wads of money they might be holding. It didn't take long for the bag to bulge.

In a matter of minutes, Danny gathered what he thought was enough and nodded to Harkness that he was ready to make an exit.

Then turning to the throng, his gun cocked and visible to all, he declared, "Gentlemen, a pleasure doing business with you. We will now take our leave. Don't try to come after us. It's easier for me to pick out a target from above you on this ramp than it is for you to dodge a bullet down below."

Danny backed towards the incline. Harkness and his men joined him, dragging Piggy-eyes with them as they did so, a gun at the back of the boss man's head.

As they reached the bottom of the ramp, Danny saw it. The 'tell' he had been expecting. The one that proved to him that Piggy was too stupid or too proud to just roll with the punch. It was slight, but it was clear to Danny.

Piggy tensed his core muscles in anticipation of launching himself at Harkness. The element of surprise was meant to deflect the gun away from the back of his head while he swiped at The Tall Man. But Danny was ready. As Piggy shifted his weight and started to spin, Danny calmly shot him in the thigh, the smell of gunpowder, burnt cloth and blood suddenly all around them.

Harkness was incredulous. Danny laughed. He knew he may have just saved Harkness's life and he could see from the expression on the big cop's face that he didn't know how to feel about that.

Danny raised his voice, instructing the crowd again.

"Now, Gentlemen, see what I mean. No foolishness,"

And then he put in his insurance policy, a distraction that would guarantee them a little time to get the fuck out of there.

Looking at the guy who called the odds, he shouted, "Hey, David, thanks for the tip-off…"

The bloke was gob smacked and then horrified as the rest of the men all turned to look at him.

Danny didn't want to look back as he and Harkness's crew sprinted up the concrete slope.

CHAPTER 14
KISS AND TELL

FISTY WAS ENJOYING THE SPOTLIGHT.

To describe him as flamboyant would be like saying Lady Gaga wore sensible clothes.

He was renowned as being London's campest man alive. Given to wearing outrageous outfits to big club nights in the heart of London's Soho, Fisty could always be relied upon to turn the eccentric level up to max. Paparazzi loved catching sight of him at some of London's hottest venues. His flamboyance inspired a weekly column in one influential fashion blog dedicated to nothing else.

And that evening was no different. In the Parrot Feathers Club, a basement venue on Old Compton Street, the music was loud, the dance floor heaving and in the middle of it was Fisty, holding court like a twenty-first century Liberace.

He was shouting at the top of his voice.

"I just knew that a summer's evening of naughtiness called for my green mankini with matching tutu ensemble. It enhances my eyes."

Fisty dipped and turned. His matching fluorescent green sunglasses looked like they were designed for a child and then

122

made three sizes too big. The young, muscled man wearing the tightest 'Keep Calm and Carry On Cruising' T-shirt could only laugh.

"But Fisty, babe, aren't those platform high heels more suited to strippers?"

"I can dance in anything, darling. And as for stripping, what would make you think I was that type of cheap queen?"

In this room, Christine Chance stuck out like a nun at an orgy.

As she made her way down the stairs into the throbbing nightclub, she was half amazed and half uncomfortable. Some of the young men looked like Michelangelo statues, their physiques cut like stone, their tight clothes leaving nothing to the imagination. She felt a little jealous of the fun of being gay in these days of tolerance, cheap gym membership, and social networking. But some of the clientele greeted her with openly aggressive glances and the odd, "Dyke night is on Tuesdays, love," as she scanned the room in front of her, looking for the snitch who informed on big Iggy Adesina.

When she spotted him dancing, she couldn't stop herself from laughing out loud. Another cop told her where to look for Fisty, saying she won't be able to miss him once she was there. Jesus, he wasn't wrong.

CC had never liked Kylie Minogue, and she liked her even less now. The music was loud enough to make CC feel almost dizzy. As she pushed her way through the crowd she was reminded of a school of sharks circling a shoal of fish, just waiting for the moment to swoop and feed.

When she finally reached him, Fisty was whirling like a dust devil, his arms flailing in time to the incessant beat. When he finally spun to face her, CC grabbed him, stopping him dead.

"Fisty, I need you to come with me for a little chat. Now."

He said something, but as Kylie was being 'shocked by the

power of love', CC couldn't hear it. The bloke next to him tried to pull Fisty away. CC simply grabbed the guy's wrist, twisting and using his straightened arm to push Fisty's mate to the floor, face first.

She had Fisty's full attention now.

Horrified at his protector's new angle on life, Fisty did what any chemically enhanced diva would... he threw a tantrum. A bitchy, vicious one that went from zero to one hundred in a flash. Coming at CC with a blur of fake nails, fake tan, sweaty mankini and a high-pitched scream. She reckoned that if she was going to avoid having her eyes scratched out, there was only one thing to do. She sidestepped calmly and grabbed Fisty by the balls and twisted.

He squealed; his face drained to white. His body gave way on him, his legs folding under him like a broken deckchair. This was completed by an unfortunate realignment of the mankini.

"Ugh," was all CC could manage.

Suddenly a pair of powerful arms wrapped around her waist picking her up, turning her away from the stricken informant. However, she was quick enough to pull her Met Police brief up before the eyes of a second bouncer who was just arriving on the scene. A little late, it had to be said.

The flash of the badge was enough for her to be set back down and the big lads to back off.

She turned, grabbing hold of a whimpering Fisty. His right-hand man was now less inclined to interfere, not wanting another chance to kiss the dance floor with his face. Plus, he saw the badge.

CC pushed through the crowd, with the informant in front of her, up out of the venue, into the bustle of Soho and finally into the back of the waiting car. A car being driven by Freethy.

Once they were underway, Christine gave Fisty a wedge of tissues pulled from a box stuck in the car's door compartment.

Fisty wiped away the tears streaming down his face, leaving his once immaculate make-up in ruins. His fully dilated eyes told Freethy and CC that their passenger had been sampling a little of his own product that summer evening.

Between sobs, he managed: "You frigging bitch, why'd you have to grab me like that?"

CC just looked at him.

"I mean, I just asked Craig to take you outside so he could find out what you wanted, you didn't have to go all frigging mental. I should be calling the police and my solicitor, you fucking breeder."

He didn't see my badge. That might be useful, CC thought.

"Okay, enough now, Fisty. I'll tell you why you are here once you stop whining. Understand?"

Fisty shifted in the seat, adjusting his ridiculous mankini. CC didn't dare to look to see if he had been successful.

"Talk to me about Iggy Adesina," she instructed.

This prompted a look from Fisty. One of camp irritation. She had to admit she liked this guy's chutzpah.

"I don't know who or what you are talking about, darling. Do I look like I know anyone called Iggy?"

"You were arrested in Soho and detained at Finchley Road Police Station on the eleventh of this month. What did you tell them?"

Fisty squirmed ever so slightly at the mention of Finchley Road.

"Listen, Tinker Bell, you can kiss my arse! You should know when you do what we do for a living, getting arrested is simply all part of the musical. I wasn't asked about anyone called Piggy, or Iggy or 'getting Jiggy with it'. I was being quizzed about matters I know nothing about. Hence, I am a free walking bitch."

"Fisty. Look at me."

He did. Now staring directly into CC's Met Police badge.

"Awww, fuck. You buggers don't play fair. And I've chipped a nail!"

"Fisty, cut the crap and just tell me everything you told them about Iggy Adesina."

"I didn't know too much. My interest in him was purely personal, you know. Everyone likes a challenge, a nice big black man like that. I figured I could turn him. I dreamt I could, anyway."

"I'm not asking you if you fancied him, Fisty. Freethy, if he dodges another question, I'm gonna roll him out the back door. Okay? Just give me a little room, I don't want to ding the paintwork on the car."

Fisty looked wide-eyed now. "You wouldn't! You can't! You bitch!"

"Iggy Adesina."

"I don't know that much!" The whine was one hundred percent back into his voice.

"He was sent to me. He wanted some muscle. And if there is one thing I know, it's muscle. He wanted some boys to help with some heavy lifting. I just passed on the fact that he was asking to one of your friends in blue. They put two-and-two together. I'm just a free-spirited entrepreneur."

"You are a drug-peddling degenerate, Fisty. Don't try and dress it up. If it deals in shit, takes shit, and looks like shit, it's generally shitty. So, you put Iggy next to some heavy lifters then? And what did you get out of it?"

"I want my phone call!"

"You fucking idiot. I'm not arresting you. I just want information. This is not official, just a little fishing. That's why I can throw you out the car if I want."

Fisty was panicking now. The look on CC's face was just

about believable, especially if your last line of cocaine was still fully motoring in your veins.

"I... I put him in touch with some boys. I'm like Gumtree, just trying to be helpful. I didn't get anything from it, nor would I have. I just liked the look of him... you know, that skin... it's almost blue it's so black. And he's so big. You have to believe me. He was just a crush!"

Christine reached across Fisty, hooking her fingers into the pull on the rear passenger door, ready to lever it open, perfectly positioned to shift her weight and dump the snitch onto Tottenham Court Road.

Fisty let out a girlish scream. "I'm telling you the truth, the truth! Stop frigging scaring me! You lot are all the same, fucking crazy bastards!"

Christine thought she might actually have got some honesty after all but decided to push for one last question. "Who sent Iggy to you? Who was the connection? Don't tell me you met on Grinder!"

Her fingers were still curled around the door release.

Fisty just looked, a new, deeper terror creeping across his face now, something CC didn't expect.

"Nobody! No, nobody important. Just some fuckwit. I've told you everything."

Freethy pulled the car to the side of the road. Christine met his eyes in the rear-view mirror. The message between the two of them was clear.

That was to be their lot. If they held Fisty any longer and under more duress, there was nothing but trouble in it for them. There were plenty of people about who saw CC flash her badge. There would be CCTV and if Fisty wanted to make a real complaint it would be pretty straightforward to do so.

She opened the door on the other side of Fisty. She looked at the man in the ridiculously garish outfit, ruined makeup drying on his chin and chest. "Get out."

Fisty didn't need a second invitation. He was gone, the sound of whimpering tears trailing behind him like the scent of his overpowering cologne.

CC closed the door and Freethy pulled out into the traffic.

"I think we need to sit down with Iggy."

Christine nodded her agreement, a troubled look on her face. "Did Fisty seem genuinely scared to you?"

"You had your psycho face on, Mrs. I don't blame him."

"No, over and above that. When I asked him about the connection? That was when he looked really spooked."

"Maybe. But you're right. Iggy might tell us a bit more than Fisty. He looks like the type who doesn't panic too easily."

"Hmmm. Let's have a chat with our Nigerian friend, then."

"Tomorrow?"

"Yeah, not now. It's getting late."

"You'd have to change your clothes if we were going now anyway."

"What do you mean?"

"Take a look at yourself," grinned Freethy, beginning a chuckle that would soon develop into a full belly laugh.

CC looked down at herself, only then realising she was covered in glitter. Obviously, the snitch had been wearing some kind of body paint or make up... and now she was too... pretty as a picture, all covered in sparkles...

And before she could do anything about it, Freethy was snapping a picture of her with his iPhone. The flash, she was sure, was bringing all that glitter to life in a photo that was certain to end up on the office notice board.

"You cheeky bastard!"

CHAPTER 15

IMMEDIATE FUTURES

IT WAS THE DRIVER WHO RELEASED DANNY, BLINKING, FROM THE BOOT of the car.

Stretching slowly while eyeing the six-foot lump who freed him, Danny had two questions.

Where was Harkness? Where was the bag of money they had just liberated?

Danny didn't bother asking. He wouldn't reply, and anyway the lump was already climbing back into the car, driving off without so much as a "cheerio", leaving Danny outside his flat.

As he went through his front door, the smell hit him instantly.

Aftershave. A scent he recognized but was not surprised by.

He walked into the small kitchen. The little two-seater table was pushed up against one wall. On it a bottle of Gentleman Jack Single Barrel, two shot glasses and two cold bottles of beer.

On the other side of the table sat Harkness, relaxed, smiling. He gave a little wave of hello.

"You could have knocked..."

"Where would the surprise be in that, Danny, eh?"

Danny shucked off his jacket, pulled the remaining chair

towards him and sat down, an unexpected weariness settling upon him. When'd he become so tired?

"Danny, first of all. Let me apologize. I have not shown you proper professional courtesy or respect."

Here we go, Danny thought.

"Here is the deal, young man."

Harkness paused, long enough to pour the Jack Daniels into the two shot glasses in front of him, gesturing to them as he sat back. Danny waited silently.

"Oh... I get it." Harkness leant forward again and took the glass nearest Danny, sank the shot in one, and chased it with a mouthful of the beer next to it, condensation sliding down the side of the cold bottle as he tipped it to his lips. He then took a second, smaller swig from the other beer bottle and set it down, pushing it towards Danny.

"Okay? Now that you can see that you won't keel over. Have a drink, Danny. Chill out a little and hear me out."

Danny reached across and shot the bourbon, then chased it with the beer. It tasted great.

"When we first met, I told you we would make history in London Town. I was not lying. You caught my attention because you are, not to put too fine a point on it... fucking good. I saw that for myself tonight. Oh, and I almost forgot."

Harkness shifted in his seat, uncrossed his legs, and slid a canvas bag full of money across the floor, leaving it at Danny's feet.

"You have pulled at least thirty-five jobs. Never been arrested. Been looked at a couple of times, but nothing to stick you with. By my estimation you have probably socked away a cool three or four million in the last five years or so.

What I want to offer you is a chance to do twice, maybe three times that in one hit... your share."

Danny was anxious to know what was on Harkness's mind.

And now here they were, shooting Jackie D and Coors and finally getting down to it. *Good numbers, too*, Danny had to admit. He was interested but did he want to play with Harkness?

"You can plan an armoured car job better than anyone. The job in Willesden Green, the petrol, the cigar... classy. You gave yourself maximum impact in minimum time and used the chaos that is Cricklewood to make good your escape. How did you get away so quickly, by the way? The car was dumped, where? The bottom of Walm Lane? What's that, a mile from the job site?"

"Bike," Danny stated simply.

"Motorcycle? Hmm, that'll work."

"No, bike... bicycles. Three of them. I divided the money into backpacks, and we went our separate ways. The cops weren't looking for cyclists panting their way down into Kilburn. They went up into Cricklewood looking for speeding cars and some 'Fast and Furious' action."

Chuckling, Harkness reached for the JD again, pouring and shooting straight away.

"See... fucking great. What about the Rickmansworth gig? Used a stolen bus to pin the replenishment van to the wall of the bank while you got the delivery boy to cough up."

"Now, that was motorcycles. Straight out and up onto the M25. It was like a car park, roadworks everywhere, and we sailed through. They closed the exits in both directions, but we'd ditched before then. Had a car waiting in Denham to spirit us away."

"That's why you've turned my head, sunshine. That's what I need, right there. And I have the fucking mother of all jobs for you. But it will need your imagination, mate, I won't lie to you."

"Stop knocking off my best men and I might be interested."

Harkness pulled a face, as though offended. "Forgive me,

Danny. You would not have even had a conversation with me if I had not applied a little... persuasive pressure. Anyway, I wanted the organ grinder. The monkeys mean nothing to me... or you. They knew the game they were playing. The game just caught up with them."

Nothing from Danny. He let the casual dismissal of two lives hang in the air.

Harkness took another pull of his beer, and finally added, "Over the last few days, a substantial pile of cash has become a little bit more enticing. You may or may not have been reading the papers, but the force has been enjoying a tiny bit of a purple patch."

"Heathrow. The drugs shipments and money involved. North London, with a money pick-up van."

"That's right, Danny. Yesterday, another little job came off. A bit messy from what I hear but a substantial wad of cash has been liberated from undesirable hands in Knightsbridge."

Danny thought about this for a second. "Russian money?"

"They do love a bit of Knightsbridge, don't they? Our Eastern European friends. Thing is, those three hits all came out of the one office. And now, the evidence room is overflowing, not to mention being a bit of a security nightmare."

Danny suddenly knew where this might be going. Fucking crazy. "You're having a laugh, mate. I know what you are suggesting, but I am not going to rob a frigging cop shop."

"But, my dear, Danny, that is the beauty of it. You won't have to. I will know when they are going to move the money, and where to as well. And let me tell you, because of the most perfect mix of arrogance and beautiful budget cuts, the police don't use a cash in transit van, or a G4S guard. They move their cash in an unmarked Luton, sunshine. With only one or two escorting vehicles, because they assume that no one knows what's in the van, and even if they did, nobody would have the balls..."

Harkness paused for effect, tilting his bottle, looking Danny in the eyes.

"But you and me, Danny? You and me, son, we've got balls of steel!"

Danny was staring at the shot glass in front of him. He tipped some more Gentleman Jack into it, and before raising it to his lips he asked the main question.

"How much Harkness? In total?"

"Twenty million, Danny. Twenty million or maybe even a little more. The final total is still to be weighed in."

"Unmarked van? One or two escorts? Even for that amount? That's fucking nuts."

"The Metropolitan Police, never knowingly overestimated. But I need the Felix magic, because the thieving will be easy... but the getting away will be fucking murder. Over to you, young man."

"What share will I scoop if there is twenty at least up for grabs?"

"Whatever I decide to give you. Remember how your old buddies ended up helping to support a building in White City? When it comes to the share, I'll make the decisions."

Harkness stood to leave, picking up the bottle of Gentleman Jack.

"Harkness... I'll think about it. But there will have to be a rebalance in our relationship. Starting now."

The Tall Man stopped. Turning to look at Danny, he cocked his head to one side.

"You've left the money. Leave the Jack Daniels too..."

"I'm going to enjoy working with you, Danny. You've a brass neck to go with those steel balls..."

Harkness smiled, looking like a cat that had just caught a

canary, savouring the fluttering of the delicate wings inside its mouth just before the first tightening of its jaws.

Christine was watching Shauna sleep. It was a moment of calm after a vomiting bout caused by radiation therapy had greeted CC on her arrival at the bedside.

Shauna's face was serene. Her breath was regular. The skin of her hairless head pale, almost translucent. CC traced the blue of the veins with her eyes, wondering about the mix of chemicals flowing through them.

What were the odds? Christine grappled with this almost daily. A bone cancer that typically attacks the limbs turning up in her child's spine.

CC felt raw. She was someone who spent her life assessing the odds, deciding when and where to engage. Yet here were odds that came from nowhere, that didn't play fair. Like stepping on a needle in the deepest, softest carpet. A sharp, hot pain from the least likely source.

CC felt immobilised. Caught in paralysis, just as her daughter would eventually be. She could not move past her fears. Her heartbreak, her agony, all were tumbling on top of her to the point that she couldn't even speak any of it out loud. She couldn't give form to the emotions.

At work, she could tidy it all away, but she knew this was only avoidance. The reality lurked for her as soon as a shift ended, or a suspect was apprehended. When she put down her tools, out came her own, very private ghosts.

Shauna's approach? She was head-on, matter of fact, no messing. Who was the child and who was the parent? In this situation, CC wasn't sure.

"Hi, Mum."

"Hey, sweetheart... how you feeling over there?"

"Rough. Can you pass me my drink?"

CC brought the orange squash to her. Sitting on the edge of the bed, she guided the straw in the glass towards Shauna's lips.

"Let's see how long this stays down..."

Silence settled between them. CC shifted onto the bed, lying parallel with Shauna, who nestled into the crook of Christine's neck.

"What's it like, Mum? What is it like to fall in love?"

The question took Christine by surprise, so left field she didn't know how to even begin to answer. "Open with an easy one why don't you... What's this about?"

"Just... I was reading earlier."

CC knew it was a mistake to buy her the *Twilight* books.

"It's not something you can sum up in a sentence, sweetie. It's more a... state of mind kind of thing. It's like you don't own yourself anymore. You belong to something... I don't know... greater?"

"That doesn't sound much like tummy flips and butterflies. They sound much more straightforward."

"You can get those without being in love. They can come just because that male nurse comes 'round!"

They both giggled.

"I knew you fancied him..."

"He is fit... and I'm a sucker for anyone who is nice to my girl..."

"What do you mean, something greater though?"

"You feel like you've been seen, I suppose. You've been recognized, picked out, and you have a sort of secret. It's one that makes you different from everybody, because the person you love has chosen to love you back, really."

"That's a bit like how I feel about being ill."

Christine's breath caught as Shauna angled herself to look up at her mum.

"Not the being loved bit, but I do feel like I've been chosen. Picked out. And to begin with it was a secret. We didn't know that I was sick, did we? We just thought I'd hurt my back. But now I am part of something greater... it is something very big, isn't it?"

Christine's eyes were welling up as she tried to regulate her breathing. She attempted not to dissolve into tears of helplessness. It took more than a moment.

"You're not special because you got sick, my little 'un. You were special from the minute I first felt you kick in my tummy. More so when I heard your first cry in the delivery room. You've been special every day of your life. And you don't need a boy or the bad luck of an illness to prove that. And never let anyone or anything make you believe otherwise."

A pause. More quiet.

"It's a shame, though."

"What?"

"Just... I suppose I will never get to know. You know... feel it."

"Yes, perhaps. But we get to love each other right now. You have me, if that's okay?"

"You rock, Mum... how was your day or night or whatever?"

Smiling. "Oh... you know, the usual. I grabbed one bloke by the nuts and threatened to throw him out of a moving car."

"Nice... How was he with that?"

"Frightened."

"We can show him frightened..."

"No... he was. Really. But actually, not by me... by someone else, I think."

"Can you scratch my back? My sunburn is really going for it."

136

The 'sunburn' was where Shauna's skin was burnt by her radiation therapy, but they much preferred to dress it up as something from a day at the beach. Shauna shifted so CC could hit the right spot, the skin looking flushed and irritated.

"Looks angry. No wonder it's itching."

"That's good there... oh. Maybe that means it's doing some good. We can't really tell with the symptoms though, can we? It's the cause we need to kick in the butt. More to the left..."

She was right, the symptoms might be irritating, but the sarcoma was the real bad guy, pulling the strings in the background.

The background... who was in Fisty's background? Someone who scared him obviously...

"How'd you know he was frightened? Did he start crying?"

"No, he told me he was scared." CC adopted Fisty's camp whine for the next bit, "Stop scaring me... You lot are all the same..."

And as Shauna laughed at her mum's voice, Christine's mind was off in a different direction. *"You lot are all the same..."* *What did the snitch mean by that?*

"Mum... you stopped scratching..."

CHAPTER 16
AT THE PICTURES

Danny needed to think.

So, he went to the one place he knew he could keep a clear head with no distractions.

He went to the cinema.

The Prince Charles cinema just off London's Leicester Square had a late night showing of his favourite film, *Blade Runner*.

Slouched down in his favourite seat, in his favourite row, watching his favourite movie, Danny let the spectacular images wash over him. At the same time, he mulled over what Harkness had set out for him.

It felt too good to be true with too much of a golden payday promise. Maybe it was all too good to be true? One he should body swerve without ever looking back. For Danny the answers were always there, you just had to know where and, crucially, how to look. So, he did just that.

Questions tumbled through his mind. Did he want the job? What about Dexy and her enforced detainment? Would Harkness really cut him in on the takings?

Danny traced the patterns, predicting how it could pan out,

thinking through the logical next steps. How would the corrupt cop behave? What choices would he make? What counter moves could Danny then make?

Consequences and outcomes, all clicking together in his mind, Ridley Scott's vision of a world filled to overflowing helping carry Danny's rumination.

On the big screen, teeming civilization made its way through 2019 Los Angeles, drenched in acid rain. Cities overrun with people, neighbourhoods overrun with decay or lavish luxury. The film never failed to leave an impression.

Helter Skelter. This vision of all our tomorrows was key to the film's message. 2019? Danny felt the Helter had been and gone and he was now well into the Skelter.

Harkness spoke of how cities were beacons of progress. How they never ceased changing, morphing, rebranding, and re-launching. But for Danny, this also signified that in order for rebirth to occur there had to be a little death first. Sometimes not so little.

And there was the rub for Danny.

The possibility of 'death'.

For Harkness to achieve his own future in this never-ending city, did Danny have to serve a purpose and then die to help Harkness reach that goal?

Was such a job, the robbing of a police transport laden with untraceable cash, simply an unachievable one? Even if they did intercept the cargo, how could they make their escape? With London and its own teeming civilization blocking the arteries of the city, how could you spirit all that filthy lucre away, off into the ether, never to be seen again? Wouldn't every copper be hunting you down in the same way that Harrison Ford hunted down the 'replicants' on the screen? Chase you down until you felt a hot bullet in your back?

If only he could empty the city... just for one day, the very day that the Met Police moved the cash. Now that would be a fine plan wouldn't it? Empty London out like you would pour away the water from the washing-up.

Or stop it from filling in the first place?

And now, up on the big screen, Rutger Hauer's murderous synthetic human was grasping redemption and glory from the jaws of defeat and damnation. Hauling his tormentor, Harrison Ford, up over the precipice of a building, saving the life of the one man charged with ending his. Pulling off the impossible, confounding all expectation.

"I've... seen things you people wouldn't believe," Hauer tells Ford.

"Attack ships on fire off the shore of Orion. I watched C-beams glitter in the dark near the Tannhauser Gate. All these moments will be lost... in time. Like tears in rain."

It was, for Danny, an electric moment of cinema. A brilliant set piece in which the supposed hero's life is saved by the most amazing U-turn, one version of fate being replaced by an improbable alternative. And now Danny was beginning to see it. A way for him to maybe, just maybe, do exactly the same thing.

CHAPTER 17

FORWARD MOTION

Iggy Adesina was still in custody, awaiting his first appearance at the magistrates' court after the event the tabloid press dubbed 'Wild West London.'

And he was in a foul mood.

Not that CC could give a damn, except it would have been better to be the one who put him in a bad mood rather than being the one negotiating a way through it.

There was light at the end of the tunnel. Seemingly, Iggy didn't much care for the food that Her Majesty's catering offered a gentleman criminal like him. After almost an hour of talking to the big Nigerian without any sign of progress, Freethy whispered a suggestion into Christine's ear that was met, at first, with a snort of derision but on reflection was actually a pretty decent idea.

Iggy wanted better food and while they didn't know of any Nigerian restaurants nearby, there was a Jamaican Jerk House just around the corner from the notorious Paddington Green custody centre where he was currently housed. Caribbean meat pasties were almost identical to Nigerian meat pies. A peace offering might work wonders in a very dull, ill-tempered situation.

It took twenty minutes, but soon the interview room, and most of the corridor outside smelled of the savouries. In fact, they smelled and looked so good, Freethy returned with enough for himself, CC, and Iggy's attorney. The solicitor sat quietly through the morning's proceedings, waiting to see if there were an angle he might work on behalf of his gun-toting client.

Not that Christine or Freethy offered much encouragement on that score. They simply said that, given the nature of Adesina's recent exploits, any information he might pass on *might* encourage the court to look favourably on him. Everyone understood this was not to be counted on; it was not a promise.

They talked for hours, back and forth, about how the Nigerian knew where to recruit his team and where the tip-off came from. "I cannot remember," was all Adesina would say, punctuated by the sucking of teeth and shaking of the head.

But now, with a full belly, Adesina seemed to mellow a little, enough to let slip a smile when Freethy played out a little gamble.

"We know who tipped you off, Iggy. We know who pointed you in the direction of the armoured vehicle."

Freethy levelled his gaze at his suspect, who was busy picking crumbs off his chest.

Another suck of the teeth. A barely noticeable shrug.

"We all know that we have you by the balls for the gun disaster. We have the gun. We have witnesses. Your clothes are covered in gunshot residue. Fuck me, we even have the mobile phone footage from three idiots who happened to think YouTube rather than personal safety once you decided to go gun crazy."

CC's turn... "Anything you give us now, Iggy, will help the judge see you are a right-thinking person of sound judgement.

You help us... we will try to help you. Christ, you'd be helping yourself, Iggy."

The lawyer moved closer to the brink of his seat. He looked from Iggy to the cops and back, seeing a glimmer of a way out and a deal to be made.

But Iggy stayed quiet.

CC weighed in again.

"Iggy, we like a big fish, you know we do. Means we all come out looking like heroes. We can even make it sound like you were coerced to act, but we need you to point the finger first. Knowing is one thing, having a statement to back it up is way more valuable..."

The Nigerian shifted a little.

CC thought he wasn't going to go for the bluff.

"I know, Mrs. poleecewoman."

CC held her breath.

"He tell you about me. The ho-mo-sex-u-al." Iggy dragged the word out, contempt in his voice. CC couldn't judge whether this was a comment on Fisty's sexuality or the fact that he ratted on the job.

She spread her hands in a gesture of 'I don't know what you are talking about.'

"Fisty, he tell you what I am up to. He has no brain." Iggy tapping his head, as he says it. "Man must know when to be strong. But also when to be a-frayed. If I were Fisty, I would be in fear now."

"Is that a threat, Iggy, against a third party?"

The lawyer cleared his throat. About to jump in between. He did not like how this formerly promising opportunity was starting to develop.

"What can I do from here? You shut me in and feed me sheeet. I cannot threat-en. But I can know."

"Iggy, whatever you know, if it prevents more harm, you can

help us, others and ultimately yourself if you just speak up. Now."

Adesina let out a bellow of a laugh. His head arched back, the noise filling the holding cell.

"I help you and help me too? You think I am foolish."

Iggy was the one leaning forward in his seat. His lawyer moved to intervene, but Adesina pressed his arm sharply to shut him up.

"I tell you, I meet the devil. I know heem when I see heem. You say you know his name? You want me to say his name? In my country you say the devil's name three times and he will appear. This man, you do not want heem to appear."

Iggy's eyes were ablaze as he said all of this, looking directly at Christine, burning into her, telling her what he knew to be true. And CC believed him.

"Mrs. Poleecewoman, the devil you say you know would have killed you by now if you really did have his name. He knows about your kind. He knows about me. He. Knows. Go find your help somewhere else, and do not spill my blood in the doing of it."

"I... uhm, I think this interview is over, officers." The lawyer finding his voice at last, not really quite knowing what had just transpired, but pushed his chair back, trying to bring it all to a halt with his own physicality.

But Christine had one last throw of the dice... "Not all police are bad, Iggy. One bad policeman cannot stop the rest of us doing our work."

She played out her hunch, hoping rather than expecting anything back. An act of desperation at the chance of a lead on her growing gut instinct, a firm chance to prove herself right... or at least that she was nosing in the right direction.

Iggy and the lawyer both stood. CC thought it all slipped by, but as the guard was unlocking the door, the Nigerian let out a breath and turned to her.

"It is not that he is Poleece. It is that he is the only man ever to make Iggy Adesina feel a-frayed..."

Once the lawyer and the Nigerian left the suite Christine and Freethy were alone, looking at each other. She finally broke the silence. "Fuck me."

∾

The Tube train pulled in. The signature, low level whine-cum-hum of the Jubilee line train was a sound that Danny always associated with home. His home, his city, his manor.

Danny directed himself towards the last carriage as it pulled into the Westminster Station. This late at night, there weren't too many passengers to jostle with for a seat. Heading north, the train took off on its predetermined path, sliding out of the uber-modern architecture of the station that always made Danny think of the iconic silent film *Metropolis*.

Once at Green Park, the next stop, the doors opened and in came the tall figure of Harkness, looking city smart. He wore a linen suit - better for dealing with the dense, inescapable humidity of the tunnels of London's subway system in the summer months.

He took the spot next to Danny but waited for the train to exit the station before shifting sideways in his seat. They were alone in their half of the carriage. There was only a drunken man and an older lady at the opposite end, both too absorbed in their individual existences to take any notice of two seemingly ordinary men who were about to discuss an extraordinary crime.

"So, Danny, are we about to make a little London history?"

Danny took a second before looking at Harkness. He knew

that whatever he said next, he was crossing some kind of line, some blurred boundary that divided him from a fate that, no matter what his answer, was steeped in danger, treachery, and risk.

But fuck it.

If you didn't take a risk in this life, thought Danny, you would never leave the house.

"I'm going to need money. Call it seed capital, grease for the wheel, whatever, but I'm going to need it. One hundred thousand in cash, untraceable of course, this week. I pick the team; you have no veto, say or influence. Also, you will never know who they are. After our previous meetings, I can't trust you around good talent. And last but not least, this is a one-off deal. We are not partners. We are not mates. We are not collaborators. I execute this job and this job only, then I am like a summer breeze... gone."

"And here was I thinking this was the start of a beautiful relationship. Proust once said that the bonds that unite another person to ourselves exist only in our mind. I think all of this skittishness is in your mind, Danny. The money is no problem. The job is yours to plan, but I will have no secrets here. You know how dirty little secrets can lead to doubt, and doubt can lead to mistrust and misunderstanding. I don't want to end up misunderstanding you, Danny. You know where that kind of mindset leads me."

Danny stared straight at him, no discernible emotion on his face.

"Let's make a little mischief together, Danny. The evidence money gets shifted in nine days' time. That is about as long a delay as I can manage. Be ready. Work your magic but keep me informed all the way. I will give you your seed capital myself tomorrow morning, six a.m. sharp. Be at the car park beneath the Olympic Way at Wembley Stadium. You'll see me coming."

Finally, Danny nodded. His eyes never broke away from Harkness's face, even as he stood to exit the train as it pulled into Baker Street.

As the door opened, Harkness turned to look over his shoulder, blowing a kiss at Danny as he did so.

For his part, Danny didn't know if the decision he just made was reckless, suicidal or, at best, foolhardy.

He was going to find out.

But first, Danny had a team to build.

CHAPTER 18
BIG MAN BOOM

THE M25, LIKE MOST OF PARTS OF LONDON IN GENERAL, IS A contradiction. A fiendish gate to hell on one hand and a stroke of genius on the other. A huge road circling the perimeter of the capital, designed to help manage the city and its clogged arteries of traffic. It funnels people and their vehicles to the right points of entry into the city on routes that are set up like exit points on the face of a huge, lumbering, heaving clock. A bypass meant to put all others in the shade.

Except it grinds to a halt.

All the time.

A gentle fender bender in a jam or a full-scale pile up, doesn't matter what it is, anything can, and often will, transform it into a huge parking lot.

At best, the M25 was designed to make London accessible. At worst, it made London infuriatingly out of reach because a seventy-seven-year-old old grandmother didn't mirror, signal, manoeuvre from the inside lane to the middle one.

And that day, to make matters worse, it was festooned with roadworks. An attempt to widen the road even farther, so that more people could get stuck.

"Enda, why the fuck is the assessment not done yet for this stretch? Get your arse in gear, sunshine, will ya?"

Enda Crilley was a huge tree trunk of an Irishman currently employed on the roadworks.

"I can't be fucking bothered, ya hooer," was the response he wanted to give to his section foreman but, for now, Enda didn't say it out loud.

He took a step over one of the impromptu rivers caused by yet another summer shower. The gush almost obscured where the new, wider highway was supposed to be taking shape.

The avoidance of the water brought him unnaturally close to his superior, causing the engineer to swallow involuntarily as Enda towered over him.

"Now... now listen. You know the delay penalties we're working to, and I know the rain isn't helping but..."

Enda could make a sloth appear like a workaholic and, for him, being screwed by this weaselly Englishman was a good excuse to stand still and work even less. As he tuned out the supervisor's high-pitched whine, Enda idly wondered if they gave him a set of new balls along with the engineering diploma.

Enda was just about to vocalise his "fuck off" to the boss man, already anticipating the pint he could be having instead, when the sound of metal on metal interrupted his thoughts. The crash and a handful of workmen shouting heralded a car leaving the main carriageway at speed.

"Holy Jesus on a bicycle," was what Enda ended up saying as the Ford Mondeo careened into one of the freshly dug road channels.

He whipped round, taking the opportunity to put his big meaty hand onto his boss' face, pushing with all his might, sending his least favourite engineer sprawling about fifteen feet away.

"Crilley... Crilley... you fucking wanker..."

Enda stifled a chuckle. "Ah, sorry sir, I was sure he might hit us. I was trying to save you, sir..."

The car would never have gotten to them, but why waste an opportunity was Enda's way of thinking.

He turned back to where the Ford Mondeo had ground to a halt. Enda watched with a faint twinge of recognition as the driver's door creaked open and a short ginger-haired lad got out. Big Man Boom, as some knew Enda, started towards the car.

"Enda don't be getting a hold of him. It looks like an accident," said one of his colleagues, suspecting that the shove on the boss was not the end of the action.

Enda waved him off, mumbling under his breath to himself. "I think I know you, lad."

A knot of other road workers formed around the driver. They bombarded him with a salty mix of questions about his health, both mental and physical, with other entreaties as to whether he was a "fucking fuckwit?" But the redheaded driver ignored all of this.

He was now pushing his way out of the throng, striding to cut the distance between himself and Enda in sharp, purposeful steps. In no time at all, they were stood facing each other. The ginger kid opened his mouth and spoke in a very thick Cork accent. "You're Big Enda, ay?"

"What now?"

"Big Enda... Belfast Enda. I need to talk to you," the kid sing-songed through his freckled, gingery nose.

"Jesus Mary and Joseph, son, you might have used a mobile phone or something." Enda looked at where the Mondeo was bleeding oil onto the freshly dug road.

"Sure, I have no credit on it," came the reply.

"Ay well, right enough," mumbled Enda to himself.

CHAPTER 19
MR. RIGHT NOW

"Hello Fisty, darling... loving your leather hot pants!"

Fisty executed a beautifully poised 360 for the topless body builder who served drinks at The Bearhug Arms in Soho.

"Jason, you either have it or you don't... but if you like I could give it to you!" came the response, accompanied by a lascivious wink.

"What an offer... but I think I'd rather take it from the Mr. Straight who just walked in."

The waiter nodded over Fisty's shoulder with his chin, prompting another pirouette so that the fresh meat might be appraised.

"Oh, Jason... sadly you'll be too busy serving drinks, love. I'll have to take a run at him for you. I have a weakness for the part timers! You know how they are." Then adopting a deeper voice, Fisty added: "I have two-point-four-kids, drive a Volvo, like rugby, but I'm not averse to a little fumble in the dark room now and again."

He was tall, very straight-looking, with a shaven head but dressed like he'd come from a very stuffy office job.

This was one of Fisty's particular peccadilloes. The rush of seducing an outwardly straight man was truly thrilling sport for him. And when he knew they definitely had a wife at home, Fisty liked it even better.

And so, the evening's entertainment began. Fisty flirting, making occasional eye contact, watching but not watching as the man drank from his beer bottle (subtle, my arse) and his eyes scanned the room taking in every tight little backside that passed him by.

Fisty was feeling supremely confident that evening, dressed as he was in a shimmering silk blouse and those leather hot pants. He had a feeling that the night would be a wild one now that Mr. Respectable seemed to return his stolen glances.

After about an hour of sipping Budweiser and tracking backsides, the straight-looking man made his way to the gents. This took him directly past Fisty, who deliberately took a step back into his path as he drew alongside.

"Are you sure you should be in here, darling?" pouted Fisty, sipping on the straw of his mojito and cocking an eyebrow as he waited for an answer.

"I was just curious. You know. See how it works in a place like this."

"Oh, darling. Rule one is you don't come here to meet Mr. Right, just Mr. Right Now! A place like this is far too exotic for the likes of you... You may need a little training before taking a swim with the big boys."

"And who would you suggest shows me the ropes?"

Fisty cackled throatily at that.

"Oh, love, I have more than ropes to show you."

And that was how it started. Double entendre, innuendo, and at least two more mojitos and a few bottles of beer.

Some time around midnight, Fisty suggested that they switch from alcohol to something a little more medicinal and a little less likely to inhibit performance. A line each in the toilets, and a furious session of heavy petting and suddenly Mr. Straight was telling Fisty to take him home with him.

Taxi!

And so, they left for Fisty's little, one bedroom flat in Covent Garden.

The evening was progressing exactly as Fisty hoped, and soon they were both naked and swallowing a dose of ketamine, letting the mellow high flow over them. Fisty allowed Mr. Straight to experiment with some of the more unusual bedroom accessories that adorned his king size bed.

"What should I call you, Mr. Straight?"

"My name is Clive..."

Fisty greeted this with another throaty laugh. "Clive! How much more straight can you be?"

He pushed Clive down onto the mattress.

"Last Christmas I had these leather straps fitted to my bedstead. Santa knew I'd been a bad boy! I first tried them on a young Polish bike courier. Love him, he had more energy than sense!"

Clive giggled... a little nervous sound.

"Sometimes the straps are for me to use on others and sometimes I have a go myself. Tonight, I want to feel powerless and exploited, a shackled slut. Will you be a darling?"

It would be interesting, Fisty thought, to see how rough anyone called Clive could be.

Soon Fisty was hyper extended in all directions, aroused and ready to be toyed with by his supposedly hetero hunk.

But as he tightened the last strap, Clive surprised Fisty.

"Where's the stash of ket? I want another little hit; this one wasn't enough."

And so, they both took another shot of ketamine, Fisty

making sure that it was a half this time, no need to overdose tonight, not with all the fun he was having.

Not long after, the room danced before his eyes, colours sliding around, Fisty noting how red and lush Clive's lips looked in the glow from the nightlights round his bed. Fisty felt warm, floaty, and horny all at the same time.

But then Clive's face seemed to change. Or had it? Was Fisty tripping a little too hard?

Then it was Clive again, standing over him. Yes, something had changed. Fisty at first couldn't quite make it out, but then he noticed that Clive had... clothes on. And then he wasn't Clive again. He was someone else, someone Fisty knew and didn't like. Didn't feel safe around. Now Fisty didn't feel so dreamy, he felt cold. Very cold... and very aware that he was naked and tethered.

And then the glint.

Just a flash in the flickering of the night lights, a blink of a reflection off a transparent object.

And someone was singing, softly. Something Fisty recognized from his childhood. A song his mother used to sing to him, sing him to sleep with.

Hush, little baby, don't say a word, Mama's gonna buy you a mockingbird. And if that mockingbird don't sing, Mama's gonna buy you a diamond ring.

It was soothing, bringing Fisty back to the warmth again. Bringing Fisty back to feeling calm.

And if that diamond ring turns brass, Mama's gonna buy you a looking glass.

And if that looking glass gets broke, Mama's gonna buy you a Billy goat.

So there was no need. No need to struggle when the man

stood over Fisty and tapped the inside of his forearm just below the crook of his elbow. No need to resist the cold sensation of sharpness penetrating the skin. No need to protest the rush of chemical into his bloodstream.

And as he spiralled off into a darkness, Fisty thought he knew. He recognized who Clive had become. Knew that the man shouldn't be there but there he was. There he was. There he...

And once he loosened the leather straps and rolled Fisty onto his side and into a foetal position, tucking his legs up under his elbows, the man checked for a pulse, waiting a good minute and a half. And when he was convinced there was no pulse, he stood up and set the syringe and the bag of heroin alongside the burnt spoon next to the night light he had used as a burner. Then it was time to go.

Harkness looked down at Fisty one last time and whispered to him gently: "Sleep well, little Mockingbird. You have nothing to worry about anymore."

CHAPTER 20
PETTY CASH

THE ROBBERY WAS OCCUPYING ALL OF DANNY'S WAKING THOUGHTS. HE felt like he was entering a maze. He grappled with each blind alley, picked his way through every false turn until he found the best route to his goal.

Except this was no regular gig. The stakes were high, the rewards were higher, and the unknowns were more complex than any he faced before. Least predictable was Harkness himself.

Danny took a deep breath at that thought, as he stood in the shadow of Wembley Stadium — the monument to national sports and spirit. He looked up.

Swallows were dancing in the cool June air. Danny watched as they zipped and swooped in an aerial display of dazzling joie de vivre, beautifying the morning with their patterns and sheer energy.

Despite all this concrete and steel, there was still room for nature to have some fun.

Fun?

That might be in short supply in the coming days, Danny thought.

He was unable to shake the flash of his father's face when Harkness shut him in the boot of the car a few days earlier. The moment kept replaying itself in his head at night as he was drifting off to sleep. He knew what it was, of course — the vice of control. Harkness wanted to control him, just as his father had.

That Harkness was in complete control provoked greater anxiety. Harkness *was* in control. It was his job. He knew when and where the money would move. Once he revealed the size of the payday, he had Danny's full focus. Let's face it, he showed his serious intentions by knocking off Danny's now very ex-partners and burying them under a west London tower block.

And last, but not at all least, Harkness had Dexy.

Danny looked to the sky again, at the swooping birds, one just behind the other, in perfect formation, the follower being led. Suddenly, the second bird flicked a wing, touching the surface of a huge puddle, at once taking off again to eat whatever insect it just caught.

Was Harkness such a problem? Was he entirely unpredictable? Or was he so busy playing the Billy-big-balls that he might miss Danny's own manoeuvres?

All of Danny's instincts were on high alert. He knew that as soon as the job was over, whether successful or not, he would be in a fight for his life. He would be the one lying glass-eyed in a trench somewhere, waiting for the liquid concrete to fill his eyes, his mouth, his every orifice.

And one other troubling conundrum. Why him? Who talked? Dexy was sure the other night. Whose grubby little finger had picked out Danny?

Jesus, there was a lot to consider here.

Danny's reverie was cut short by a silver van bouncing its way across the car park towards him, bang on six a.m.

Punctual, if nothing else.

157

The van pulled right up to Danny. It came close enough to make him want to involuntarily step back. But Danny stood his ground, not wanting to reveal any nervousness.

Harkness was in the passenger seat. A fat, skin-headed white guy was driving. How many were there in Harkness's private gang? He never saw the same muscle twice. It was quite something given the fact that, in the underworld at least, the more people that knew you were up to no good, the more vulnerable you became.

Harkness stepped out of the silver van, a leather satchel in his hand and a smile on his face. Aviator sunglasses were shading his eyes from the early morning light on a near perfect London day.

"My man, Danny Felix..."

Danny just nodded at the cop. No smile, no words, or barely visible acknowledgement of his presence.

"Here's your petty cash, Danny. I'll want a full spreadsheet of expenditure including VAT receipts for tax-efficient accounting purposes."

Harkness chuckled at his own joke. He placed the satchel in Danny's hands and took hold of him by the shoulders. "There's £50,000 in there. I couldn't let you have it all your own way. I will stake you some more when you need it. Also, I want updates, including a full briefing of the plan. Along with the money, you will find a mobile phone. When it rings you answer... it will only ever be me."

Danny was already shaking his head. "No mobiles, no phones. Ever. You should know better. A mobile is basically a tracking device for the Old Bill. I don't use them. I don't have one. Never have, never will."

Danny fished into the satchel and retrieved an iPhone. It was the latest model, probably capable of all sorts of technological wonders. It smashed very easily under the weight of his boot.

Harkness took a step back, taking Danny in. His face darkened. In a blink, Harkness stepped right up into his face. "Listen boy, when my dog gets out of order, I jerk his fucking leed. Don't make me jerk yours too many times. You hear me?"

Danny could feel spittle hitting his face as Harkness leant in to deliver his threat. The sudden ferocity and aggression would have caused most people to fold. But before he could say another word, Harkness was suddenly aware of something sharp finding purchase in the crotch of his trousers. He looked down to see the wicked glint of the stiletto flick knife that Danny was ever so accurately pressing against his balls.

"Now you listen to me, Harkness, you cunt. I told you before. I will pull the job, but only on my terms. I will keep you updated, but only when I see fit."

Danny now the one sounding fierce. He was telling Harkness what was going to be what.

"Keep your eyes on the Craigslist London website. If I want to see you, there will be a listing in the For Sale section. When you see an ad for a pair of "ruby slippers perfect for the ball", I am ready to meet. We will rendezvous on the Tube at the same time and place as our last meet. Get it? You might have made this job too tempting for me to turn down, and no doubt I am one of the few in this city who could plan and pull it off, but that doesn't mean I am entirely... fucking... stupid."

With each of the last words, Danny leant a little more pressure on the knife, making sure that Harkness could feel that he was in no mood.

"And I *will* need the rest of the fucking money."

With that Danny took a step back. Harkness looked over his shoulder, wondering how in the fuck's name did fat skinhead boy miss what just happened?

Then he applauded – a slow handclap rising in speed and volume until it was joined with that trademark throaty laugh.

"Bravo, Danny. Bra-fucking-vo. I like a little theatricality, a little dash of showbiz... that was cool. Like I said on the Tube, you are a skittish one, aren't you? And I also told you I don't want there to be any secrets or misunderstandings between us. You obviously aren't listening to me, so this might help you to pay some fucking attention."

Harkness reached behind him, tugging on the handle of a sliding side-door on the van. It opened up, revealing to Danny what was inside.

Sitting, tied to a bench welded to the floor of the van was a figure, with a burlap sack over their head. The noise of the door opening caused the figure to start, thrashing against the ties that bound them to the spot.

And Danny felt an increasing sense of dread. Nausea crept into his gut like an ice-cold serpent. Twisting, turning, tightening.

Forget a switchblade to the balls, Danny was being shown that Harkness really was the boss here. He really was the man in charge.

With his own theatrical flourish, Harkness whipped the burlap sack off the head of the captive in the van. Long red hair tumbled down, impeded only by a blindfold wrapped around her head and a gag in her mouth. It was Dexy.

"You are playing with the big boys, Danny Felix. This is to let you know she is still alive."

He slid the door shut again.

"Now, fucking do one. Get planning. We have money to steal. A fuck of a lot of it. Don't let me down. Don't let her down." Harkness flicked his head in the direction of the van. He turned to walk away, and then stopped.

"Oh, and by the way, Danny. How's your sister doing?" he said, without a smile. There was no mirth in his deadpan face. And then he was off, into the van.

Danny was silent.

Harkness had just pulled a rabbit out of the hat.

CHAPTER 21

DIGGING DEEP

By the time Christine arrived at the scene in Covent Garden, the Scientific Investigation Division were just about done. Preparations were underway to move Fisty's body out of the small flat.

CC quickly found the investigating officer, a new young detective called Ayoade. She had never met him before.

CC strode up to the investigator. "Who found him?"

Ayoade was looking at CC and at her Metropolitan Police badge at the same time.

"Good morning, officer. I am Detective Inspector Ayoade of the Metropolitan Police. Why are you at my crime scene?"

CC blew out her cheeks, realising how presumptuous she had just been. "Sorry, Inspector. I'm Detective Inspector Chance. I have had a few recent dealings with your victim, most in relation to the gunfight in north London last week. He provided certain helpful information to us. I was just hoping to get an idea of what happened to him?"

Ayoade relaxed a bit.

"I should just tell you to piss off until I've had a chance to do my work here."

CC gave him a steady look in return.

"I heard about the north London hooha. A lot of fireworks by the sound of it. A bit rock 'n' roll. All I usually get are the dead bodies. Most of them already cold, often homeless."

CC nodded recognition and Ayoade seemed to soften towards her.

"Your boy was a little over enthusiastic with his leisure activities. Track marks on his arm. Fixings left nearby. Alcohol in evidence as well as a recent and familiar visitor given the traces of sexual congress. SOCO reckon he overdosed. A full post-mortem will establish and most likely confirm it."

Sexual congress? Christ, this bloke was fresh into the job, CC thought.

"What about the visitor? Any leads? Any DNA?"

"The body was found by the cleaner. Not much of a cleaner, though, given the number of fingerprints and other physical evidence in the vicinity. It looks like Mr. Scott had many visitors, if you catch my drift."

It took her a second to put Mr. Scott and Fisty together as the same person.

"Listen, none of this should come as a shock. The victim was a local drug dealer, wasn't he? Something of a Soho legend from what I can gather. A patron of Old Compton Street's finer establishments. It looks like he endured the end that most would have predicted for him."

"That's why I am curious, Inspector. Don't you think that a seasoned dealer like Fisty would know how to measure out his hits?"

"There are three empty bottles of mojito mix in the kitchenette and an empty bottle of rum to go with it. Forgive me for making a leap here, but if I had that much cocktail in me, I'm not sure I could unwrap a cough drop correctly."

CC let out her breath, realising she had been shallow

breathing from the moment she arrived.

The fear of culpability gave her cause for concern. When they grilled Fisty, had they alerted whoever was behind the expanding spider web of criminal intent that they were sniffing around? She hadn't exactly been subtle when she pulled Fisty from the nightclub. Had she signed her informant's death warrant? Or, had Fisty been so off his tits that he had recklessly mis-measured?

"Any CCTV of the street outside? Is there a possible ID on who Fisty's visitor might have been?"

"Detective Inspector Chance, are you trying to tell me how to conduct my investigation here?"

CC felt a buzz in her pocket. She pulled out her phone and glanced at it. Freethy's number was flashing up. But this was more important; she had one last chance with her fellow cop. She was pushing her luck, but she knew she would have to dig deeper. So, with a shrug, she tried a different tack.

"Listen, Ayoade. I am sorry but Fisty is a loose end for me... for us. I don't like loose ends. Maybe if you could share the results of the post-mortem. Then I can either give you all the information we have on him, or we can both just put his demise down to over-exuberance. Either way, we can help each other, and I can stop being the arsehole who's annoying you."

Ayoade weighed it up. It was true that if the post-mortem showed any kind of struggle or signs of coercion, then a fuller picture of Mr. Scott's dealings with her office would be invaluable. Maybe this wasn't going to be just another sad sack story. Maybe there would be a little rock n' roll too.

"Give me your number and I'll give you a call when I get Frankenstein's report.

Christine smiled at the slang for the coroner, scribbling down her mobile number on Ayoade's proffered notebook. "Thanks. I appreciate it."

Leaving the scene, she felt her pocket throb again. Thinking Freethy, she pulled out the mobile phone, making a mental note to take the handset off silent.

As she brought the phone up towards her face, she spotted that it was a withheld number.

"Christine Chance."

"Ms. Chance, it's Sister Cavendish here from St Michael's Hospice."

CC's breathing suddenly became shallow. Hyperventilating, she felt like her chest might burst. These were the kind of calls that made her heart leap. "Is Shauna all right?"

"Yes, Ms. Chance, but we felt you should know that she had a very poor night last night. She is stable at the moment, but the Consultant would like to see you and we would suggest that should be today."

"What are you saying? What do you mean?"

"Professor Shobnay would like to speak with you about your daughter's condition and the next steps. It would best be done sooner rather than later."

CC detested the nurse without having met her. She wanted to destroy the person on the other end of the phone, a person simply doing her job. But it was so much more. It was a phone call from reality. An acknowledgement of the truth. A truth she was trying with all her heart and soul to deny.

"Thank you, Sister. I will do my best to come in this afternoon."

"Thank you, Ms. Chance... and my sympathy to you. These are never easy times for anyone in your position. We realise that at St Michael's. Goodbye."

"Bye..."

Christine stood still. As Covent Garden crowds swarmed passed, the reality of what was about to beset her, and her daughter finally pinned her down. She couldn't move.

She felt numbed, stricken, powerless. She was suddenly aware that she wasn't even able to cry. In shock, shocked at herself, she realised that with the exception of a few moments, she hadn't allowed herself to feel the tremendous sadness in her heart.

Her daughter was going to die. And she couldn't do a damn thing about it. Not even weep.

And then, from nowhere, a shrill sound punched its way through and grabbed her attention. A siren sliced into her petrified mind as a police car going who knows where, all lights flashing, whipped passed her in the street.

"I shouldn't even be dignifying you with my presence."

"Aw, sis, please. Can we just play nice together, even for just a half an hour?"

"Play nice... play fucking nice..."

"Celeste, you're hissing... you sound like you might have a puncture."

"Listen, Danny, what you did was no fucking joke. Keeping a gun... at my house. I have kids. And what have I told you about turning up at my work?"

"Sorry, I forgot to bring my bell... unclean... unclean..."

Celeste stopped. and swung her handbag at him. That was the point at which he knew that his sister wasn't really still angry. If Celeste wanted to hit him, she would have just punched him in the face, simple as that.

"Can't a brother just turn up to surprise his sis? Treat her to a little lunch?"

"Not when the lunch is funded by your ill-gotten gains... I'll buy my own."

Now it was Danny's turn to stop. Reaching out, he pulled Celeste round to fully face him.

"Okay, sis. Truce, truce. I know I screwed up. That was not cool stashing something in your garage. I promise I won't do it again. And... wait for it... I apologise."

Celeste let her arms drop by her sides. She tilted her head to the sky, staring at some unseen point in mid-air.

"Danny... I love you. I really do, but you make it soooo hard. I could kill you sometimes. You might have your standards, you've always done everything on your own terms, but you can't just waltz in and out of my life – my family's life – doing as you please. Risk and children do not go together. Especially my kids... my family life. It might be boring to you, but it's my life, my treasure."

Celeste reached out and put a hand on his chest, pushing him gently back on his heels.

"Which is why I'm apologising. I just wanted to let you cool down a bit before coming to see you. Everything is okay at home, isn't it?"

"Yes, yes of course it is. Apart from Dad ..."

"I'm not interested in him, just you. You and the kids and what's his name?"

This earned him a sharp look. "Kidding, kidding... but you're all okay... right?"

"Yes! Jesus, what's got into you? Saying sorry, now acting like some kind of weird family counsellor. Hold on a minute, what's going on?"

It was Danny's turn to look exasperated. It helped cover up his actual sense of relief. "Holy shit, Celeste. I'm not working an angle here, just asking. I can't win with you."

"Okay, okay. It's just, you don't act like this much. Come on, I'll buy you lunch. I need to go to a cash machine."

"I'll buy you—"

"We've covered that already, bro."

Danny gave in. They walked along the high street by Celeste's office to the nearest bank.

"Watch and learn, Danny. This is how you get money from a bank the legit way."

"Ha, bloody ha..."

Celeste tapped in her pin number. She had a moment's hesitation as she thought about shielding it from Danny.

"Celeste!"

She giggled. Her face lit up the way it used to on the rare occasions, as kids, they were able to play together, when their father's presence did not weigh heavily over them.

The money emerged from the cash machine. Celeste snatched it, the receipt and her card into her handbag quickly, laughter still passing between them. "Come on. There's a great Thai café just over here. It does good noodles."

They started to walk again, but as she was getting herself organised, Celeste stopped again.

"Jesus, that can't be right."

She was staring at her receipt from the cash machine.

"What?"

"Naww, the bank must have made a mistake."

"Celeste, what is it?"

"My balance... according to this, I have over £82,000 in my current account."

Danny's heart sank.

"I'll have to go in and see them, after lunch. What do you think?"

Danny was thinking only one thing, but he couldn't say it out loud.

Harkness.

CHAPTER 22
PUZZLE PIECES

In London there are pubs and there are pubs.

Most London pubs are just normal, drinking holes, where tourists and locals gather to have a pint, maybe some food, watch some live sport and socialise.

But then there are the other pubs. These are anything but normal. They are legendary venues steeped in local colour, history, and folklore. These are the mixed watering holes where villains rub shoulders with detectives, where dodgy deals are done, compromises struck, and negotiations conducted, all under the watchful eyes of discreet landlords. New York has Italian restaurants where mafia bosses eat pasta. London has pubs.

The Spotted Dog public house in Willesden Green is one such den. An old-fashioned Irish boozer tucked away in north-west London, it's long been the home to fistfights and riotous drinking. At one point, both the local police force and the Irish mafia, the 'Murphia' as it is known, used the pub for private functions as well as a regular hangout.

Danny loved The Spotted Dog. It was just a great, sawdust, spit-on-the-floor pub that belonged to a different era, a time of fewer complications. Where a spit in the palm handshake was as contractually binding as any legal document. If you had a dispute, it could be sorted out on the small forecourt in front of the pub and then back inside for the next round.

Nobody skipped a beat when Danny walked into the bar. The room was filled with chatter and The Undertones were playing on speakers dotted around the room. Danny soon pinpointed the man he came to meet. He and his companion were the next players in his rapidly forming plan. The smaller of the two men gently raised a hand at him and Danny could not help but feel the smile grow on his face. He liked this crazy Irish bastard and, more importantly, trusted him.

The ginger haired man stood and gripped Danny's hand with all the strength of a man twice his height and breadth. He shook it vigorously, returning Danny's smile with a grin of his own.

"Danny Fucking Felix... has the devil not caught up with ya yet?"

"Not yet, Ciaran. He's too busy hunting you down."

"Nahh, sure he plays poker with me every fuckin' Friday night. That bastard knows just where to find me! Come on, let me introduce you to Big Man Boom. But don't call him that, least not to his fat Fenian face. He prefers Belfast Enda these days."

Danny nodded and followed Ciaran through the body of the pub. His bright orange mop of hair was easy to spot even in the fog. So much for not smoking indoors. The clientele of The Spotted Dog didn't much care for the law.

Sitting behind a round table in one corner of the bar was one of the biggest blokes Danny had ever clapped eyes on. He was huge.

Boulders for shoulders, he was well over six feet, at least twenty stone with meaty fists for hands, one of which was now encircling Danny's own hand making it look like he was a kid taking his dad's hand on a walk.

"I believe you are Danny. Good to meet you. Ciaran says you're a grand lad."

"Nice to meet you, Enda. Ciaran says the same about you."

"We thought you might be thirsty." Enda gestured towards a pint of Guinness on the table, obviously meant for him because there were two others half-drunk beside it.

"Sure. Danny always has a terrible druth on him."

Danny didn't know what a druth was but correctly guessed it meant thirsty. He didn't really have time to make this a social meeting, but he knew it would be rude if he didn't have at least one round and return the favour.

Mind you, despite his urgency, the black as night beer tasted great as it went down, and once he wiped away the foam moustache it left behind, he went straight for it.

"Apologies for cutting straight to the chase here, Enda, but circumstances at my end have become a touch more complicated. Has Ciaran filled you in?"

"Ay, some. He says you want a variety of surprise packages left at different spots all round London. My only question would be how big do you want these surprises to be? And, even more interesting, how deep are your pockets?"

While this discussion took shape, Danny noticed that Ciaran's eyes never stopped sweeping the room, not in an obvious way, but enough to discourage anyone from getting too close to their table.

"It depends. Some of the places will need a bigger surprise than others. Not all need to be the real deal. They just need to look like they might be. It's more about whether you can lay your hands on the stuff and get it prepped... time is tight. As for my pockets...let's just say twenty upfront, another eighty if I get away with it."

Enda was reaching for his beer. Danny was fascinated by the way his huge fist nearly obliterated all sight of the pint glass. He was then further amazed at how the almost half a pint was downed in a single, swift gulp.

"I'll go if you stand 'em, Danny Boy," said Ciaran, offering to recharge the glasses. Danny peeled off a twenty-quid note.

"I was thinking more like forty upfront and a hundred if you make it?"

"I tell you what. Let's say thirty upfront and ninety if I make the grade. And Enda... I fully intend to make the grade."

"I've heard the likes of you before. You say more than your prayers. But Ciaran says you're some boy at this game. You fuckin' better be."

"And what about people? Can you make sure that the surprises end up where they have to be when they have to be? No slip ups?"

"My lads are like the frigging Pony Express. 'Deadline or dead' is what I tell them. On that matter, you know there will be a few..."

"Casualties? Perhaps we can plan to minimise those. Only one surprise needs to be in or around a large crowd. The rest should be like a domino effect."

"I'm with you. Show them the real thing and let them jump to their own conclusions. A scare can be as effective as a big bang. Ciaran was right, you're some boy..."

Danny smiled at the big Ulsterman, nodding, and knowing what came next.

Both men spat in their hands. Danny again marvelled at the huge fist that was now pumping his, neither breaking eye contact across the table.

"Enda, so we understand each other, I have more than just the money riding here so no hitches, please. And I'll pay you out, don't worry on that score."

"Sure, if you don't, I can always beat the living shite outta Ciaran... By the way, you do know if there is any oul nonsense, there'll be more than the coppers to deal with."

It wasn't a question. It was a statement. Danny nodded, thinking if only the police were the only thing he had to worry about.

"Enda, I don't own a car, but if I did, rest assured, I wouldn't want to be looking under it before I drove it."

Ciaran returned with the pints. "Ah sure, Jesus, we don't do that sort of nastiness anymore. Do we, Enda?"

He winked at both men as he said it, leaving Danny to round off the business end of the talk.

"You better do, or else I might have to try buying the Jihadists a drink..."

Ciaran nearly lost half a pint through his nose at the thought of that.

~

Freethy had left Christine a message on her mobile asking her to call.

"Mark Freeth."

"Freethy it's me, what are we doing?"

"Hiya, I managed to get us some face time with DCI Collinson."

"Great. I thought the pub. I want him in a chatty mood. I want to backtrack all of this. All these jobs have been too good to be true."

"What if he won't share? These tips have all been pretty high level."

"They came from somewhere. If they all came from the one place then something stinks, mate."

"We'll have to play it carefully, CC. We might have a can of worms here."

"What time are we meeting?"

"Lunchtime. I thought you'd want to get away to see Shauna as soon as..."

"Okay, see you at the usual."

By the time they were into their third round at The Coach and Horses, Collinson was holding forth with a story that contained at least seven violations of current procedural regulations. Christine wasn't in the mood. She hadn't told her friend about the message from the doctors yet, there would be time enough for that later, and if there was a way to get Collinson to open up quickly, then Freethy would know it.

So, for every pint their guvnor had, unbeknownst to him, they were taking in half in the form of lager shandies, a less alcoholic mix of half beer, half lemonade.

She hated the taste of it, but she had no choice if she wanted to retain information and still make it to the doctor's meeting with a brain clear enough to function. Collinson was finishing up his latest anecdote.

"And all we did was give him a right good battering and sent him home to his old man with a note pinned to his shirt saying: 'Sentence served'. It was a lot easier in those days, I can tell you that for nothing. None of this oversight and procedure shit."

Freethy saw his chance. "Well, guv. You know Christine thinks it's all coming a bit too easy to us right now."

"Yeah, she mentioned something like that to me last time we spoke... Course she then went on to oversee the demolition of an historically significant townhouse in Knightsbridge the same day. Fucking careless if you ask me."

Some phlegmy laughter and a short bout of coughing was followed by a mouthful of Fuller's London Pride ale to clear his throat.

CC went next. "Come on, guv. You have to admit the scoops we've had the last while have all been premier league. All of them. How often has that happened in your time?"

"Swings and fucking roundabouts. You get purple patches, and the commendations that come with them. I don't see why you're fucking whining. I mean, you get the overtime, dontchya?"

Freethy's turn. "Yeah, but there's happenstance, coincidence and then there's too much of a good thing. Anyone would think the SO15 boys were leaving us to do their heavy lifting. Heathrow, north London gunfight... CC's Knightsbridge renovation scheme..."

Collinson laughed at the idea of Christine as a TV makeover host, then swallowed more beer.

CC's turn. "It's not funny, guv. Are we being had over here? I'm thinking there is a connection beyond intel here."

Collinson snapped upright suddenly, like he'd been slapped in the face. At once he seemed completely sober.

"Chance, what are you fucking inferring here?"

His voice was a low growl. CC stuttered before Freethy did the decent thing.

"Nothing... nothing, guv. It just all seems a little, you know, action-packed and headline heavy. You know her, she hates the fucking paperwork that goes with this kind of run. Overtime or not."

Collinson snuffed down his nose like a horse who didn't want to wait any longer for its feed. "I can assure you both that all of that intel was fucking legit. If you must know it came from a very credible source."

CC and Freethy shot each other a look. They both knew what that meant.

"I need to break the seal... 'scuse me." Collinson lumbered off in the direction of the gent's toilets.

When he was far enough away, CC stepped closer to Freethy. "He's talking some Masons shit, isn't he? It's the only time he feels so certain about any info we're handed."

"Only one way to find out."

"He'll never tell us that."

"Watch and learn, young Chance..."

When Collinson re-joined them, his cheeks were a darker red than before he had broken away from them.

"So, guv. All these recent hits, they've all been lodge leg-ups, tip offs from the Masons?"

Christine might have gasped at Freethy's blunt question, but she was too desperate to hear the answer.

"Yes, it was, Mr. Freeth. And I am more than happy to admit it. Listen, you fucking babes-in-arms, we got the intel. We did the jobs. The criminals are off the streets. What difference does it make? You'll get your commendations. I get my stats and the public don't have to worry about another load of dangerous fucking criminals messing with their home insurance cost."

CC glanced at the clock on the wall. She would have to go soon if she were to make the consultation with the professor.

Collinson gave her a break. "Right, next round's on me." Collinson wandered off toward the bar.

CC turned to her best friend. "You can cajole him to talk a little more now. He's broken his own ice."

"And you are going where, exactly? This is your wild goose chase here, Christine. You are the suspicious one."

CC spread her hands in front of herself, pleading innocence

and playing her ultimate card all at the same time. "Consultant wants to meet. I can't miss it. It sounded all a bit... you know. And, anyway, Collinson's old school. He'll tell a bloke more than a bird."

Freethy relented as soon as the word "consultant" was mentioned.

"All right mate. I will text you if I can make him spill anything more. And listen, keep me posted on... you know."

CC waved him off, trying again not to let her mind run riot, certainly not now, not in the pub in front of her partner or even her boss if he came back.

"I just need to listen to what they have to say. I've been putting off even thinking about this kind of chat for ages. Right, I need to go."

"No worries, CC. I'll tell the guvnor what's happening. Go on."

It took twenty-five minutes to drive to St Michael's Hospice. Christine was taking her time leaving the car, gathering herself before the meeting. She felt like she was about to put some kind of final piece of the jigsaw of her daughter's health into place. She didn't want to be the person responsible for doing that but knew that no one else was around to take it on for her.

As she finally stood up, she felt her pocket vibrate. The mobile.

She pulled it out and tilted it to see the screen. A text message from Freethy. It simply read: I have a name.

So, another piece of that puzzle has fallen into place. If only the one before me right now wasn't one that might break my heart.

CHAPTER 23
YOU'LL DO FOR ME

THE ESTATE AGENT COULDN'T HELP BUT FEEL A LITTLE NERVOUS. SHE was on her mobile to her boss.

"Look, Tristram. I'm not happy about being here on my own. This ginger chap is a strange one. He's walked round the outside of the unit about five times already. He's not looking at the building itself. He is spending rather a lot of time along the street. And he just keeps staring at my boobs, without so much as an attempt to disguise it. Oh, he's coming back in. Call me in five minutes if you haven't heard from me."

She hastily hung up as Ciaran came back in through the side door.

"Are you one of those Sloany Ponies? You're right an' posh now."

"Ehh, I don't know what you mean. Anyway, Mr....?"

"Aye, so right enough. How long has this been lying useless?"

Her eyes scanned the empty warehouse space. There was nothing unusual about the unit. Prefab, low level, two garage type roller doors on the front, plenty of square footage inside, strip lighting and a little cornered off office area in the back right-hand corner. It, like the rest of the units nearby, had stood empty for many months. But she wasn't about to let a potential customer know that.

"Mr...."

Ciaran just looked at her.

"The recession has hit this kind of space. These units were normally leased by small retail businesses for storage or distribution purposes, to cater for the boom in online shopping and so on. But I am sure you will agree it is well connected to all the major roads from in and out of London. Park Royal is very sought after."

"Is that right, now? It's been lying empty for at least a year, like?"

"Not that long... I..."

Just as she was about to lie, Ciaran flicked his shoe at a pile of rubbish on the floor. He revealed a yellowing copy of The Sun newspaper, one with a whole page headline bemoaning the performance of the England football team at last year's World Cup.

If she had noticed it, fair play to her, she didn't bat an eyelid, thought Ciaran. Not that he was looking at her face.

What she was actually thinking at that moment was, *what if my mother was right? What if this was just too risky a job for a young, attractive female?*

"So, tell me, girl. The rest of these here units are empty now?"

He had a sing-song accent, talking at a million miles an hour, the sound of his voice reedy through his nose.

"Pardon, sorry, I couldn't..."

"Them ones, the rest of 'em, empty ya say?"

"Oh, yes..."

"And been a quare while?"

"A what? Sorry..."

"Stop apologising, love. You sound like a Catholic priest to an altar boy. How long have they been lying idle?"

"Oh. Does that really matter? I'm not sure."

"Jaysus. Let's just say your boy, the client, needs the few sheckles then."

Before she could say it, Ciaran interpreted for her. *Fuck me*, he thought, *these Brits are thick as pig's shite.* "The landlord must be desperate for a few quid."

"I suppose so. On this occasion I can speak reliably for the landlord because we actually own the units ourselves. You would be leasing directly from us."

The three things that happened next would form the basis of a story she would tell over and over again for the rest of her agent days.

Number one: The man with the shock of ginger hair produced a wad of cash, licking his fingers as he counted, all fifties. He made a sheaf of money that, as he separated it out, formed £10,000. It took a minute or two.

"Right girl, here's ten grand. You said it was twenty a year, so here is the first six months."

Secondly, he seemed to spit into the palm of his hand and then offered it to her. She was so shocked, she actually took it, albeit very slowly.

And last, but not at all the very least, after shaking her hand, he stepped past her into the centre of the storage area. As he did so he gently patted her on the arse.

"Pleasure doing business with you. Sure, you're a lovely girl. If I wasn't so busy, I'd buy ya a pint. You'd do for me, ya would."

He started toward the entrance, while she just stood there open-mouthed.

"Are ya coming or not, girl? I'm sure you'll have a shite load of paper for me to sign..."

Ciaran had just found Danny his HQ.

~

Later that same day, an ad was posted on Craigslist London. Its headline read simply... *Wanted: Ruby Red Slippers, Perfect for the Ball.*

And once you clicked on the ad, it opened to reveal...
Bring lots of money.

~

Ciaran wasn't surprised that the bicycle shop was packed. It was late afternoon, and just off Oxford Street in the heart of the West End. He liked the weird mix of customers: tattooed and pierced bike couriers waiting for replacement saddles, rubbing shoulders with be-suited office workers in to pick up a new helmet camera.

What he liked even more was the music playing over the shop speakers. The Waterboys were declaring that they'd seen the whole of the moon. Ciaran wouldn't have minded seeing all of that estate agent girl's moon, but sadly there was no time for play today.

He moved through the racks of hi-vis jackets, reflectors, and waterproofs, stopping to admire a bike that looked like it was an arrow. It was obviously built for speed and city cycling, the kind of bike that a courier would favour. A saddle on it that looked like a blade, tires that were thinner than the width of a good cigar. Ciaran couldn't resist running his hand over the centre bar of the frame. He then picked the bike up with one arm, surprised at how light the whole thing was.

"It's a fab machine, isn't it?"

Ciaran turned to look over his shoulder. One of the assistants was standing there, wearing the orange T-shirt with the shop logo on. But any sense of uniform ended there. He was wearing long shorts, with chains hanging from the belt loops to the pockets. His head was shaved on both sides, leaving the top of his head Mohican-style that led, improbably, to a ponytail. Completing the look, he had one arm and one leg festooned with tattoos. Ciaran thought the snarling wolf on his forearm was particularly good. It made it easy for him to throw the lad off guard with his next words.

"Howya, Howler? Sure, it was you I wanted to see."

Howler returned Ciaran's grin with a frown. He stepped closer in order that he might not be overheard as he spoke through gritted teeth. "Not just anyone gets to call me that... Who the fuck are you?"

"Jaysus, no need to get your gander up, lad."

"Who. Are. You?"

Ciaran's grin widened even further. He liked this one. "I'm the boy who is going to make you rich."

"Fred's Coffee Shop. Round the corner. In fifteen minutes. I drink flat white."

"Aww, Jaysus... d'ya not have a pub nearby?"

Howler sighed.

"The Half Moon, two doors down from the café. I still want a coffee... you can get me a takeaway."

And for the second time that day Ciaran found himself saying. "You'll do for me."

The pint was gloriously cold, both in his hand and as it flowed down his throat. He knew it would be thirsty work talking to all these people.

The most important thing however was that as soon as he had mentioned Danny's name, he grabbed this Howler's attention. And it was even more focused once he slipped the envelope under the table. It had 5,000 quid in it. Danny said to tell Howler it was a good faith down payment.

"I can't see any reason why I wouldn't be able to handle that."

He was quiet for a few seconds, staring into the surface of his girly, useless coffee. Flat white. For fuck's sake, what kind of a drink was that for a grown man?

"As long as the numbers don't concern ya, I can get the rest of the detail to you. Let's see... thirty-six hours' notice."

"That will be fine. Do you want my mobile number?"

For the first time since they met, the smile slipped from Ciaran's face. He reached across the table and put his hand firmly onto the boy's. "Now listen to me, fella. We don't do it like that. We don't use those things. Ever. For anything. Do we understand each other? That is one of our absolute conditions."

Howler could suddenly see that this Ginger Paddy was not to be messed with. His diddly-dee, Riverdance demeanour only served to cover determination and ruthlessness. Howler knew that Ciaran would gut him like a fish if it served the overall success of his plan.

"Uhh yeah, sorry. I forgot how Danny feels about mobiles."

Smiling again now. "There's my man..." Ciaran drained his pint... "Right, your round."

"Er, I have to get back to the shop, mate..."

The non-grinning Ciaran was back again. "You can get me one before you nip off now, can't ya?"

It had been as horrible as she imagined it would be. Gut-wrenching.

It made her feel enraged and broken all at the same time. A great wave of frustration crashed over her as the consultant, who looked young enough to be her kid brother, talked. He sat there and detailed the oncoming developments that amounted to nothing more than a timetable for pain.

Shauna Chance, over the next few weeks or a month at the most, would go through hell.

The young doctor was only doing his job. He was only trying to brace Christine for what was to come. The last of her daughter's days would be a catalogue of increased medication, long periods of unconsciousness, only waking when the pain managed to cut through the fog of her assorted drugs.

"Towards the end, with the amount of pain control Shauna will require, she may not be able to recognise you, Ms. Chance. But you must know that it is all we can do."

Christine could have punched him in the face.

A familiar voice broke into the painful reverie of the conversation she'd been replaying over and over in her head since she'd had it.

"CC. We're here. Are you all right? Are you sure you want to go in?"

Freethy's words brought Christine back to the here and now.

Feeling awkward, she ran her fingers through her hair trying to look tired instead of distraught.

"Yeah, I'm okay. You got the name, and then you found out where he is, so let's follow the rabbit down the hole."

Freethy paused, looking at his colleague, his friend.

"Christine, you don't have to be here. Not now, not with what is going on for you."

She looked over at him, her face hardening.

"My dad was a great copper. He always wanted me to be one, too. I'm right about this hunch. And good coppers listen to their guts. That fucker is in that bar now. My dad would tell us to shift our arses in there."

"Yeah, CC. But come on, give yourself a break. Shauna needs you. You need to be with her. This is just work."

"It's what I do. We do."

"CC..."

"Just shut the fuck up, Freethy. I'm here now. Doing this." She had to battle to keep tears from flooding her eyes.

"Okay, okay. Jesus. I just... I don't get it."

"I'll tell you, shall I? It's this simple. It's work. I know how to *be* here. It's easy. With Shauna? I don't know how to be... I can't...begin to process any of it, never mind handle it like a mother should be able to. So, I work...I can do that. I can *be* here."

Christine reached for the car door handle, letting herself out into the air of the street. As she stood up, facing the doors to the shitty pub they were about to enter, she felt her face set and her breath come easier.

Freethy was up and out too. "CC?"

"Time to ask some awkward questions."

So, they did.

CHAPTER 24

DIRECTIONS

As soon as she entered the pub, CC thought it was horrible. The carpet stuck to her feet, the smell of stale beer seemed to surround her like a fog, and the atmosphere was laden with desperation.

It wasn't so much a pub, as a refuge. A sinking ship filled with people who only came really to do one thing: drink. And this wasn't a 'meet you for a pint and a catch up'. This was drinking for the sake of it.

In one high corner of the long thin bar room hung a very old bulky TV, horse-racing flickering weakly on the greasy screen.

A selection of hunched patrons sat before a long galley bar. All nursed various drinks, all studiously avoiding each other's gaze, not wanting to lend anyone a misapprehension that they wanted to chat.

Opposite the bar was a series of small booths. All were cracked faux leather with yellowed stuffing bursting through the gaps. In the one furthest from the door, two men were in conversation. Whispering, faces close, drinks in front of them, one hardly touched his, while the other was half-quaffed and outnumbered by empties, both pint pots and shot glasses. CC nudged Freethy, gesturing with her chin towards them.

They were different ages. The one looking towards the door was younger, a big man, confident in his size and stature. He surveyed the room as Christine and Freethy

approached. The other man was older, going to seed, thickening around the middle, broken veins blooming across his eyes and cheekbones. Dandruff decorated the shoulders of his old-fashioned tweed jacket. The conversation between the two-seated men halted.

"We'd like a word, mate," said CC letting them see her Met Police badge.

The two drinkers looked up at their visitors. They simply stared at them as though they were aliens just landed on the planet preparing to invade.

"Always happy to help fellow serving officers," the older man replied. He was the one who fitted the description Freethy gave her, the one Collinson told them was the man behind the tip offs.

"Detective Inspector Christine Chance, Flying Squad. This is my colleague, Detective Constable Mark Freeth."

Freethy joined in the badge-flashing party now, just to underline his legitimacy.

The younger, bigger man spread his hands in front of him, before shuffling out of his side of the booth.

"Looks like you want some privacy. I'll leave you to it."

CC took a close look at him: big, broad shouldered, dark hair swept back, and eyes that looked like they could cut glass. He wasn't the one they wanted to talk to but for some reason it crossed her mind to stop him leaving. This thought was interrupted by their main target.

"I'll catch up with you later, Harkness. You can tell me the rest of that story another time."

The Tall Man waved over his shoulder as he left the bar, not even bothering to look back.

"Now, how can I assist you? I don't want my evening taken up with too much chitchat. I have some drinking to do."

CC sat down where the Harkness bloke had been. Freethy pulled up a low bar stool, sitting perpendicular to the table, so that their man would realise this was done in case he should decide to try to make an early exit. Once seated, Freethy took a second to send a text from his mobile phone while Christine started the ball rolling.

"I'm speaking with Detective Inspector Murray of SO15, aren't I?" she began, getting a nod as an answer.

"The very same. Has my fame reached all the way to Flying Squad then?"

"I wouldn't call it fame. I'd call it a sneaking suspicion."

"Suspicion? Officer, you're sounding less than professionally courteous. Need me to clear something up for you?"

"Yes, please. Why am I running around London picking up your shitty work for you?"

Murray lifted his pint glass, swallowing the remains of his beer, suds sliding down his chin as he set the empty back on the table.

"Well now, love. You know the expression... why have a dog and then bark your-fucking-self?"

This chat wasn't going to be friendly.

If Harkness was troubled that two detectives were in a bar bracing one of his little helpers, he didn't show it as he boarded the Tube train at Green Park. Murray had made a mistake, saying his name in front of them.

What of it? We're just two cops having a beer. No sweat.

And there, on the train, was Danny Felix. Right where he was supposed to be. Another special little helper. He was the only other person in the carriage... just the way they both liked it.

As the train pulled out, Harkness lowered himself into the seat next to his pet robber, passing him a heavy padded envelope as he did so. "There's your pin money, Felix. Don't go spending it all in the same sweetie shop."

"We're getting off at the next station, Bond Street. You'll walk across Oxford Street and into the car park at the back of Selfridges. Level three, silver BMW 5 series. Get in the passenger side. You're going to show me the route."

"I do like it when you get bossy, Danny. If by the route you mean the route that the money will take, then yes, that's no problem. We can follow that now. But I'll want to hear your plan in full as we drive."

Danny looked at the big cop, making sure his eyes stayed as dead and flat as he could muster. "I'll tell you fuck all until I am ready. Tonight, your only job is to be my guide."

The squealing grind of the Tube train's brakes drowned out whatever it was that Harkness said in response, but Danny didn't need to hear the voice to recognise the word "cunt" when it was levelled at him.

As they exited the pub, Christine felt like she wanted to stand under a hot shower for a very long time.

The interview had been as antagonistic as it could have possibly been. Murray sweated through his shirt while evading any version of truth. He neither confirmed nor denied CC's suspicions that the previous month's work had been nothing more than the bidding of someone much higher up. The bit that really rankled her was the thought that the jobs might have been rotten to the core. The thought that she and her colleagues had been put in harm's way for some dirty cop's plan was just about as heinous a crime as any straight-thinking law enforcement professional could envisage.

"If being an obstructive, obtuse, drunken fuck was proof of anything illegal, that wanker just gave us enough to send him down for life."

Freethy followed this by pulling fresh air into his lungs, trying to shake the toxicity of the bar from himself.

"What did you make of the big man? The one who left just as the party started?"

Freethy was smiling now. "Ha! We had exactly the same instinct, didn't we? The same urge to slap the big fucker in the face and tell him to sit the fuck down and join our friendly chat. I didn't like him one bit..."

"Me neither. Something not right there... confident but too cocky."

"Which is why I had him followed as soon as he left."

CC turned to look at her partner, a smile spreading on her face. "That was the text you were sending. And I just thought you were being rude in front of our new friend."

Christine was laughing as she said it. She should have known that Freethy would have been on the same page, at the same time as she.

"That's why I asked Little Colin to come with us and hang out in the background. We thought something else might catch our eye – and it did. Listen, it's obvious isn't it? Murray is a pisshead. Too drunk to be anything other than a man counting the days until he pensions out. If he was feeding jobs for a reason, you can near as damn it be sure..."

Christine finished the sentence for Freethy. "...that he's only the messenger boy. The monkey, not the organ grinder."

"Let's see what Little Colin comes back with. I asked him to get photos too... see if we can get an idea who the big man is."

"He said a name, didn't he? Clarken or Harken?"

"It was Harkness and I think he was police, mate. I'd put money on it."

"Yeah, right! You don't have any money."

"Oh, shit yeah, that makes it your round ..."

"Only a cheeky one. Then we'll see if Little Col has anything to report. Then I have to go, you know, to the hospice."

"Deal. But let's go to a nice pub, shall we?"

Once they were in the car, Danny in the driver seat, Harkness beside him, Danny felt much more at ease. He felt in control. To him, Harkness was like a wild animal, given to bursts of unpredictable, almost feral behaviour. He suspected that this is what it was like to try to rodeo ride on the back of a raging bull.

Danny glanced at the man sitting next to him, taking stock of him. His intense eyes that could seemingly burn into your brain. The way he would tilt his head to one side when in conversation, doglike and childlike in equal measure. Added to that the casual current of violence that never seemed too far from his surface. Danny couldn't shake the memory of how he had jammed the sharpened key into his hand, nor the vicious nature of how he had finished off his opponent in the cage fight, blows raining down so fast they were a blur. Danny had no doubt, this was one fucked up individual.

"Did you have a happy childhood, Harkness?"

The detective shifted in his seat to regard Danny not quite computing the question, but then responded in the only way he knew how.

191

"Stop talking shit and drive. Take us to New Scotland Yard. It's closer to us from here. We can drive the route in reverse."

"You'll never guess who I had in the back of my cab the other day..." And Danny swung the car out into traffic, snaking down from Oxford Street towards Victoria, passing Buckingham Palace.

Soon they were by the headquarters of the Metropolitan Police at New Scotland Yard. The iconic building that had been the base for countless landmark investigations.

"I've seen this place so many times on TV. All those journalists and their pieces to camera for the ten o'clock news in front of that stupid spinning sign. Makes it look like they sell vacuum cleaners instead of policing the nation. Can't believe they are going to sell it."

Harkness huffed his agreement.

"I can't think of anywhere near here that you would want to pull the hit off. Too close to the Yard. No point in making it easy for them to get to you once it's done."

"You said the transfer will happen early morning. How early? What time are we looking at?"

"That kind of shift can be carried out at any time of day. But because this one's such a big amount, they want to go during early morning rush hour. It makes it more difficult for anyone who might want to have a go at them, too hard to make a clear break for it if they did."

Danny was nodding, thinking it made sense. London traffic could cripple a job.

"So, aren't you going to ask me then? Or are you playing the hard man?"

Danny wasn't sure if Harkness was referring to Dexy or his sister's suddenly bulging bank account. He knew that his strategy of keeping any emotion out of this deal had been pointless. Still, Harkness was right. He didn't want to give him even a millisecond of satisfaction.

"I reckon you're the one with the problem. Anything happens to Dexy; it won't just be this job that goes wrong. And that doesn't take into account that she is more likely to kill you than I am, given half the chance." Danny didn't look at Harkness as he said it. He just kept his eyes on the traffic.

Harkness responded with a chuckle. He shifted in his seat. Reaching into his jacket pocket, he produced a flashy mobile phone. A few seconds of tapping and he was then holding it up to Danny. Moving pictures. Dexy, blindfolded. That day's news on a TV beside the chair she was tied to. No way of telling where this room was, but the news on the TV certainly dated it as that day. The Dexy on the screen then seemed to realize that she was not alone. Starting to kick and struggle against her bindings, fabulous blue language came out of her mouth, including threats, swearing and oaths of revenge. The whole thing made Danny's guts twist.

"I'm a good film director, don't you think? She's a hard bitch, I'll give you that. But your bravado doesn't fit, Danny. I like the version of you that stays focused. That's why I wanted the leverage."

Danny stayed quiet.

They were down by the river. The Thames flowed gently in the late evening glow. Industrial units sat cheek by jowl with new executive apartment blocks, built during the boom, trying to tempt people with a view of the river.

Harkness guided them through a few double back routes. He knew that despite the need for the rush hour traffic, the cops would still take these short cuts to ease some of the traffic pain. It was in one of these that Danny suddenly pulled the car over to a little side road that led down to the banks of the Thames itself. They were in Battersea Church Road. The water shimmered as it smoothed its own path out to sea, the reflection of the redeveloped Lots Road Studios dominating the water surface and the skyline itself.

To their right was a big ornate church, St. Mary's, which sat on the corner of a tight dogleg in the narrow road. Down one side was a gap to the river. Opposite was a high brick wall, bordering the residential properties that had stood for years. Georgian probably, Danny thought.

On the same side of the road as the church, forming the other side of the gap to the river, was a new apartment block. Danny parked the car just above the boat ramp between the church and the new block.

"Let's take a look."

Both men exited the car. Danny checking the view of the CCTV on the edge of the new apartment building, realised straight away that they were angled in order to cover only the perimeter fence.

"Those cameras probably don't cover too much of this area. Good stuff."

"This all looks a little tight to me." Danny could tell Harkness was still desperate to know what he had in mind. Danny didn't answer. But he liked the spot a lot.

The slipway emerged onto the road right in the middle of the dogleg turn. It was by no means a wide road, making it easy to block off if necessary. Danny turned and walked down towards the water's edge.

To his right was a smattering of houseboats. They were moored up, right on the edge of the river at the back of the church. The route to the water was unguarded.

Crossing now towards the church, Danny was further encouraged. In the church's courtyard, he could see a pathway that led onto a riverside path, obviously meant to afford walkers and cyclists a safe passage away from the narrow road. The path seemed to go all the way to Battersea Bridge.

"Is this your spot then, Danny?"

"Harkness, you teed up the job. You forced my hand, and my mind, with Dexy, so now you can fuck off out of the way. This is my bit of the game. I will not share with you. Like you said, you don't play well with others."

"If you don't share with me, Felix, this will not end well."

"Listen, I'm not some chump in a charity cage fight, ok? I didn't just float up the Thames in a bubble yesterday. I'm a pro. I don't scare easy. You want me here because you know I'm fucking good. Get the hell out of my way. Let me do what I do best. Anyway... you're not as good as you think you are."

Harkness just returned Danny's stare, doing his tilting head act.

"Because if you are all that, how come you didn't spot the geezer who followed you out of the Tube and over to the car park at Selfridges earlier?"

Danny walked back to the car, leaving Harkness to deal with that juicy little one.

CHAPTER 25
FAIL TO PREPARE

CIARAN KNEW HIS RED HAIR COULD BE A PROBLEM. IT WAS, AFTER ALL, fucking bright.

This meant that whenever he was engaged in any questionable pursuit, he always had to make sure that he was fully hatted up. Witnesses had an irritating way of remembering his fiery beacon at the scene of a crime. This wouldn't normally be such a big deal except that Ciaran had a tendency to sweat like a pig when under any degree of pressure. Not that he didn't behave coolly under fire. But he did sweat. A lot. To the point that it would leak from under his chosen headgear and at various points would render him almost blind.

And here he was, in one of those situations. Middle of the summer. North London. The dead of night in a knitted ski mask, wiping his eyes like crazy as he tried to hotwire the heavy-duty dumper truck.

Enda had given him all the information he needed. Where the storage yard was. How many security guards, and what time they were likely to be either asleep or busy streaming porn to notice that someone was about to fuck off with one of their biggest vehicles. The storage yard was huge. About the size of five full-size football pitches, and just off the M1 motorway. There were three exits, which included the security hut at the main gate. Ciaran fully intended to leave by the gate furthest from that point... if only he could keep the sweat from running into his eyes long enough to see the ignition wires.

"Holy Mary, mother of God, it's fucking hot," he whispered to himself in the truck's cab. Ciaran had to pause every thirty seconds to stop from drowning in his own gravy.

When the huge German Shepherd dog came sniffing, Ciaran was neither surprised nor frightened. Enda had warned him about the massive dog which the night man let run wild all evening round the yard, chasing cats, urban foxes and, when it was really lucky, flame-haired Irish truck thieves. The lump of minced beef with veterinary-grade tranquilizer crushed into it sorted the animal out in about ten minutes. This delay, however, only served to sour Ciaran's mood and make him sweat even further.

Eventually he thought, *fuck it*, and dumped the balaclava on the passenger seat in the cab of the dumper. If anyone clocked him, he'd rather just kill them than have himself melt down to a puddle on the truck floor. Witnesses were a pain in his hole.

Finally, after about twenty minutes, he managed to start the huge truck. Enda's exhortations to him to be careful beamed into his mind as the diesel engine growled into life and coaxed the young Irishman into a moment of caution. He pulled the woolly hood over his head again before easing the truck out of the line of vehicles it had been parked in. No point in tearing off at fifty miles an hour and making too much noise. Downloading porn or not, the security guards would only be alerted by the noise of the big engine. Why make life more difficult? And, anyway, if it came to a chase, should the paid-for-guards discover his theft quickly, there was no way he would be able to outrun a police patrol car in something like this.

And that was the bit Ciaran didn't understand. Who needed a big rumbling truck for a robbery? Surely you needed to escape quick? I mean, for fuck's sake, the getaway drive was always the best bit as far as he was concerned. But he didn't have the first clue what it was that Danny was planning. All he knew was that it was a robbery. That they needed Enda and his skill set. They needed Howler and a load of his mates. They needed an industrial unit and they needed to steal a dump truck.

The rest of it was all in Danny's head. At least, it was going to be that way until they were to meet at the unit later that evening. Excitement was already building in Ciaran. Jobs always did this for him. Especially since Danny hinted to him that it was a job that would make the headlines.

Ciaran had always fancied being a bit famous... or better still, infamous.

This made him gun the truck's engine a bit too much, and for a second he considered just barrelling through the gate at the rear of the storage yard. But then he saw Enda's face again in his mind. Not yet, young Ciaran... save the excitement for the big day. He stopped and cut the gate open with his huge bolt cutters instead.

Best of all, nobody was around to see him or his ginger nut when he did it.

~

Christine had a problem.

"Here he is leaving the pub. Another one of him going into the Tube. Crystal clear, as good as any I've taken." Little Colin had done a cracking job and he was proud of it. His compact five-foot-six frame, clean-shaven head with a somewhat everyman face allowed him to disappear in a crowd. He was someone you would look at once but never twice, and barely recall having seen him at all. And this was why he was so good at following suspects and better at getting surreptitious photos of them.

"You'll like this one even more," replied Little Colin, his nasally whine of a voice peaking as he got more excited about his handiwork. He flicked through to another of the many pictures he had just loaded onto CC's laptop.

Christine was now looking at a photo of two men. It showed the big bloke who had left the pub earlier with another man, this time exiting the Tube.

"Top work, Col. Thanks for all this." She blew out her cheeks as Freethy rose from the café table, pointing at Colin's cup.

"Another, mate?"

"Nah, nah, I have to do one. The Mrs.... waiting for me at home. We're into that new Scandinavian crime series on Netflix. She can't get enough of it, so we watch one every Wednesday, no matter what time I roll in at. So, I'm off. Anything else, just shout, lads."

And with that he was gone, melting into the crowds like a pro.

These photos would of course be invaluable in getting Christine closer to whatever it was that was going on, but they also presented her with a huge hurdle.

Freethy came back with two more coffees for them.

"Jesus, Freethy. We're going to have to tread lightly here."

"You thinking what I am?"

"My instinct is screaming at me. The big man is on the force, too...The way he carried himself...Old Bill"

"Yep...I thought that too."

She kept flicking through the photos, stopping at one where

the big man's coat was partly flapping open. They both saw it at the same time. CC pointed at what they had spotted. The fragment of a Metropolitan Police badge on his belt. They looked at each other, Freethy taking a deep breath.

"Where's this going to take us, Freethy?"

He shrugged. "We can't share info with anyone now. We don't know where the rot starts and stops... unless we're jumping to conclusions."

"Our friendly chat with Murray was too antagonistic to be just brushed off as professional rivalry. We just need to confirm who this Harkness geezer is, and now, who this other one is too, coming out of the Tube with him."

"But who the fuck do we ask?"

"Computers are out... electronic trail and all that...

"Even pressuring Collinson may have been a risk."

"No, Collinson's old school. He may be a lot of things but he's not dirty. Jesus, why am I the suspicious type?"

"Bit late for wishful thinking, CC."

Her coffee tasted particularly bitter.

"You look tired, Mum."

"I look tired?" Christine rolled her eyes at the irony.

She was sat at Shauna's bedside. The machines bleeped softly. Technology was telling them, and whoever else was interested, that all was still okay with the world.

"It's just work stuff. I think I've stumbled into something a bit... messy."

Shauna's eyes took a beat to focus. "What's going on?" She tried to shuffle up in bed. CC eventually helped pull her up, once again heartbroken at how light her girl's frame had become.

"I think I may have rumbled some cops who are playing both sides... corrupt."

"Oh... sounds tricky."

"Pretty much..."

And suddenly she was laying the whole picture out for Shauna, knowing that her little girl was probably only taking in about sixty percent of it. Also knowing she was retelling it for herself. Feeling her gut as she stepped through what she thought she knew of the conundrum, gauging where her instincts were triggered the most.

By the end of it, Shauna was dozing, and CC felt just as drained. The hypnotic thrum and beep of the ward took her off, into sleep. A deep sleep, the likes of which CC had not allowed herself for some time.

She didn't know what time it was when Shauna's voice woke her.

"This could be dangerous for you, Mum... Mum?"

It took a second for CC to compute, but Shauna was continuing the conversation from where both had let it trail off.

"Umm, yes, I suppose. In fact, no suppose about it. It will be. I feel so stupid. Stupid for being nosey, letting my suspicions lead me and Freethy to here. I've put both of us at risk."

"Yeah, but... it's what you do, Mum. And you're not stupid. Never have been."

They looked at each other, silence settling between them.

CC broke it. "I don't know, Shauna. I don't know how to do this."

"You'd be a pretty weird mum if you did... you mean me, now, don't you? All this crap."

She lifted her arms in the air, gesturing at the paraphernalia of illness. "It's just dying, Mum."

"Don't..."

"No, it is. If you think about it. That's what I'm doing. It's something we all get to, but I'm just ahead of schedule. The reason you don't know how to be is that we didn't expect it. You only do this a few times, so we aren't supposed to be used to it."

CC sighed, nodding.

"The important thing is, just because I'm stopping, it doesn't mean that you have to as well. If anything..."

She didn't need to finish the sentence. She could see her mum understood. And she felt better for having said it.

"I was always a better cop than a mum. And now I'm not even doing that right."

"You are just good at being Christine Chance..."

CC felt a flutter in her chest, her shoulders relaxing.

"Mum...?"

"Yeah..."

"Are there any Haribo left in my locker?"

"Let me look..."

CC stood. As she opened the drawers of the white bedside cupboard looking for the sweets her daughter loved so much, she rummaged passed countless magazines covered in boy bands and young, bare-chested actors.

At the bottom of the drawer, she came across a newspaper and a bag of the sweets. It was the newspaper Shauna had shown her a week earlier, the one that covered the Heathrow job where this had started. The page was still folded over at the article. CC once again recognized herself at the scene in the photo.

"Bingo, one bag of Haribo."

"Cool..."

"You kept this from the other week."

"It's not every day your mum makes the papers."

"Shame it's not a nice photo of me. Mind you, every time I have had my photo taken for The Job, it's been a bad one."

"Yeah. The one you showed me that time, of you graduating from the cadet school... your hair... you look like something from Monsters Inc." Laughter passed between them.

"That was a long time ago. And my hair was very trendy. I must look that out, see what Freethy looks like as well."

And then she went silent.

"Mum? You okay?" The question was asked through a mouthful of gummy cola bottles.

"Yeah... The Job."

"What about it?"

"No, The Job... The Job magazine."

"Now you're not making sense, Mum."

"No... no, I am. The Tall Man, I told you about... if he's a cop... a senior cop, his picture might be in The Job, our internal magazine at work."

Shauna thought she understood, but she knew her mum's brain was off and racing, and soon so would she be.

"Before you disappear, Mum... I'm going to need more Haribo next time you come."

CC was already grabbing her mobile phone and car keys.

It was the fifth time Danny had walked that part of the route. The impact site. Checking, re-checking all the details that had first excited him about this spot when he had driven it with Harkness.

He paced out the distance from the boat ramp to the edge of the road. Then again from the ramp to the opposite side of the road, making mental notes, assessments for timing. He spent five minutes jamming a huge, sharp-ended stone into the metal automated bollard set in the ground that was installed to prevent access to the horseshoe drive in front of the church. It didn't look like it had been operational for a long time, but there was no sense in leaving that to chance. Soon, he had ringed the whole outer tube of the metal post with a series of stones, wedging them down with his boot heel repeatedly, hoping that it would stop the mechanism grinding into life any time soon... or in the next few days at least.

Once he was satisfied with his survey, he climbed into a car that he had stolen for the night and drove the few short miles back out to west London and to the industrial unit that Ciaran had leased for them. After spotting Harkness's shadow earlier, he took a circuitous route to make sure he didn't have any unwanted hangers-on.

That was one major concern. Two actually. Firstly, Harkness hadn't spotted the tail. Admittedly Danny did not doubt the short man who was following was good, but still, Harkness should have been better, should have had 'eyes about.' Secondly, if Harkness was under scrutiny, was Danny also attracting attention? Ordinarily, under such circumstances, Danny would have postponed the job. But this was not an option for him now. Not with the Dexy factor and the ticking clock on the movement of the money. It was Hobson's choice... and Danny didn't like it one bit.

The next conundrum for him was whether to share the presence of the tail with the rest of his team. Common sense almost certainly dictated a 'yes', but Danny was hesitant. What if the tail was the result of a leak? A leak from within his team, not at Harkness's end? Also, he didn't know the team really well, so didn't know how they would react to the news. Enda was Danny's biggest concern. He was a new face to Danny's band of merry men. And for this job, he was also the most vital.

If Enda didn't weave his magic, the rest of the gig was as good as fucked.

Danny's jumble of thoughts was still bouncing around in his head as he finally turned down the potholed lane towards the industrial unit, satisfied that he didn't have any company behind him.

As he pulled the BMW up to the garage style doors, they opened, clattering as they went. Ciaran was grinning like a mad man behind them. Danny eased the car in. He parked it next to the huge dump truck that would prove invaluable in the coming days. The rest of the team was there already, all waiting to hear what was what, when and how... all waiting to be clued in. They were all waiting to hear Danny tell them they were going to change London forever. Harkness was right... cities don't stand still.

~

'The Job' was a typical internal communications magazine. Sterile. On-message. It was not widely read. By producing it, the Met Police could always say we told you about this or that change months ago... it was in 'The Job'.

CC used a large pile as a doorstop—a marker of the high esteem the publication generated amongst the entire staff of the Met. Each month, when the new edition came out, she placed it on the top of the pile, until the stack was too big and she tossed half into recycling.

Now, here in the wee small hours, Christine sat at her desk leafing through the issues in the pile. She examined every group photograph she came across — all PR opportunities announcing new initiatives... or charity functions.

She had already gone through thirty with no luck. No photo of the man, Harkness, in any of them. In fact, she was beginning to think that her gut reaction was wrong. That he wasn't law enforcement. And if that were the case then Christine needed to enjoy more of that sleep she had had earlier.

She finished flicking through the last magazine. Nothing. Fuck it. Time to sleep.

She stood up and carried the pile over to the doorway, allowing it to return to what she figured was a much more useful application than the one they were actually published for.

She made her way to the locker room, realising she needed the toilet. Pushing her way into the ladies, she picked the cubicle closest to the door. It was in a filthy state so, pulling a face, she went to the next one, pushing the door and stepping in.

She caught herself laughing out loud as she locked the cubicle door behind her. There sat on the top of the toilet tank was a new copy of 'The Job'.

Might as well, she thought, scanning it for photos again. *No. No. No. No, then... hold on.*

She went back a page. A big group photo. A load of police officers in suits. Among them were some men, kitted out for what looked like boxing. They were bare-chested with shorts on. And one of them, to the extreme right of the picture, was beaming at the camera. Blood all over his big wide-boned face. His nose obviously smashed. But he must have come off better, as he was holding a trophy in one hand.

The by-line beneath the photo read: Congratulations to the Mixed Martial Arts Fundraisers! Freemasons Grand Trust make Charity Thousands in One Night.

And then a list of names, from right to left. But the name Christine was most interested in was the last one listed: Detective Inspector James Harkness.

"Fuck me, I've got him."

CHAPTER 26
LISTEN UP

Danny looked at them. All their faces were turned to him. He enjoyed this part of the game. He liked having people to work with, to rely on. His job, as leader, was to enable them to do their best, albeit illegal, work.

He talked for about sixty minutes in front of a large wall map of London. Red rings were littered across the face of the map, times noted beside them. A green line traced the route from the Barnes Flying Squad all the way to New Scotland Yard in Central London. Drawn at the point where this green line met Battersea Church Road was an even bigger yellow circle.

Danny felt sure he was pretty clear with the instructions. Some of his points were greeted with looks of incredulity, the odd intake of breath. But, by the time he expanded and expounded, understanding and acceptance seemed to bloom on the faces in front of him. Insight was followed closely by nervous excitement as the men began to realise that this plan could... might... just work.

A question-and-answer session followed, clarifications delivered, adjustments suggested. Some were taken up, some rejected.

And now all that was left was to make sure they were ready to put their backsides on the line, to take the risks and see them out to the end, bitter or sweet.

"Gentlemen, all I can say now is I am ready," announced Danny. "If any of you feel you can't execute your part in this plan now is the time to speak up. If that is the case, we walk away. The job doesn't get done, and we get to lie on our death beds thinking what if…"

Ciaran, Big Enda, and Howler all sat, staring back at him, knowing, in reality, they had no choice. Coming this far in a job of this size and potential, they would be mad to back out now. Plus, they would probably spend the next few months hunting each other down if they did. Loose ends were never an attractive proposition.

"Enda. You and your men, do you feel you can achieve what we need you to?"

Big Enda took a deep breath, his gaze never leaving Danny's face.

"Ye have some fucking *out there* ideas, Danny, but I'm clear. Me and my boys will deliver."

"Howler. You feel the same?"

His answer was straightforward and confident: "Ready to rock, ready to roll, Danny."

Finally, Danny looked at Ciaran.

"Danny, I'm in, fella. Can't wait," was the response, accompanied by a wink.

Danny weighed up what he was about to say next, deciding then that it was right that he shared.

"Okay, we are a go. One last word, gents, though. Eyes about. I don't trust our friend, Mr. Harkness. Neither should any of you. He has been attracting some unwanted company of late, but I don't believe that has spread to us. I have one more meet with him, later today. After that, it is our gig until divvy up time. But keep your wits about you. Fuck knows what he might be planning or thinking. Last but not least, here are the remaining payments for your boys and don't forget to pick up your transistor radios and earphones on the way out."

Ciaran spoke up.

"Harkness is being followed?"

"I think he might be, yes."

"If that's the case, what do we do with him?"

"You mean after?"

Ciaran nodded.

"Don't worry. I have a special treat planned for the Detective Inspector."

That brought a grim chuckle from Ciaran, but silently Danny wondered if they would ever get that far.

~

It wasn't what you would call a comfortable night's sleep.

The cot was lumpy, the locker room draughty, and as Christine tossed and turned crazy dreams added to her suffering.

It was about five forty in the morning. She decided she'd had enough lying around.

Routine. Habit would help about now, so she indulged in one of her own. She changed into her gym gear and grabbed her jump rope from her locker. Once in the courtyard, with the early morning sun creeping across the concrete towards her, she started to skip.

It felt good to her. The rhythm of the rope. The flexing of her arms. Her muscle memory kicking in. She varied her tempo and steps. The sweat breaking on her forehead. Feeling it run between her shoulder blades. As she tightened her core muscles, she whipped the rope over her head and down to her feet. She enjoyed the rush of blood through her veins. It was hypnotic to her: meditation at 200 skips a minute.

She used the time to run the facts about the conspiracy once more through her mind.

The ease of the jobs. The large amounts of money recouped at each one. The boss ignoring her suspicions.

Harkness. Murray. With each slap of the rope at her feet she counted off each factor.

What should she do next? She needed some kind of indicator, a signpost that showed her the way to concrete proof or a fact that would burst the bubble.

Shower.

Trying to wash away some of her anxiety.

As she dried herself, feeling a little more human as she did so, CC began to feel foolish. Was she on a wild goose chase? Was this notion of a grand conspiracy of cops tipping off criminals and in turn directing informants so that other cops would intervene just the stuff of Hollywood movies? After all, the recovered money was safe. It was under lock and key and, she believed, due to be moved to Scotland Yard any day now. Where was the benefit?

Doubt crept into her mind, then her bones, then her theories.

As she dressed, she realised she was hungry. When had she last eaten?

By six forty-five she had bought a paper and was settling into a seat in her favourite local café. She knew the bacon, sausage, beans, fried egg and toast was not 'good' for her, but they tasted more delicious than any food she had eaten in months. She abandoned notions of dietary guilt in favour of sheer indulgence.

At seven thirty, she was enjoying a third cup of piping hot

tea and was most of the way through 'The Times' when her mobile buzzed.

Text message. Freethy.

"Where U?"

"Caff," was her simple reply. He'd know which one.

Five minutes later, Freethy walked in. He looked down at the damage CC had done to her plate.

"Bleedin' hell, Christine, there's a Third World out there, you know!"

She laughed. She was pleased to see her mate. He ordered his own breakfast and coffee. But when he sat down in the seat in front of her, Freethy put on his serious face; CC waited for it.

"Have you heard?"

"Heard what?"

Just at that moment, CC's phone chimed out again. This time her ringtone gave out some ridiculous pop song programmed in for her by Shauna. She held a hand up and took the call, leaving Freethy to pour sugar into the coffee the waitress, with all the grace of a wrestler, had set in front of him.

"Detective Inspector Chance here."

"It's Ayoade. I've just come in and found Mr. Fisty's final test results from the post-mortem in my in-box."

"And...?". She held her breath.

"Toxicology levels show he overdosed, by a lot. My examinations show no sign of any force majeure or coercion. Plus... he was a ticking clock."

"What does that mean?"

"He had advanced cancer of the liver. Untreatable. They say only a few weeks to live. There's no way he could not have known. His pain levels must have been off the chart. But considering the amount of drugs he was using... and the amount of evidence of sexual activity on him, he was determined to go out in a blaze of debauched glory."

"And that is what your report will say?"

"Absolutely."

"Right, okay, thanks. I owe you one." CC was deflated. It sounded like her doubts had just all come home to roost in one, fuck off, fell swoop. She ended the call.

It was Freethy's turn to look puzzled.

"Fisty had advanced liver cancer and he OD'd."

Freethy looked even more confused. "What?"

CC took a swig of tea before she replied. "Isn't that what you meant when you asked me had I heard?"

"No, mate. But what was that about Fisty?"

She told him how foolish her mad conspiracy theories made her feel. She questioned a gut instinct so far off it was on another planet.

But Freethy shook his head. "No, CC, no. The news I was referring to is about Iggy Adesina. He was found late last night in his cell. He'd hung himself using pillowcases and the end of his bunk bed."

"Dead?"

"As a big fat dodo. And now I am beginning to go as crazy as you. This is adding up."

"But Fisty..."

"Our killer wouldn't know Fisty was sick. Even if he did, he couldn't leave that loose end to take its natural course."

"But Ayoade said no signs of coercion or force majeure."

"Yeah, but, as you and I both know, where there is a will, a criminal will... there is always a way."

Danny looked across the table at his sister. She was fidgeting. That only ever meant one thing. She was worried.

"This has got to be something to do with you, Danny. I

mean for fuck's sake. First trouble, then guns, now a shitload of money in *my* bank account that isn't *mine*!"

"You have to be the only person I know who is pissed off because they found an extra eighty grand in their bank account."

"If you don't tell me what you're up to right now, I'm going straight to the police. This is all too much for me, Danny. I'm not joking... my career and therefore my family are at risk."

"Listen up, Celeste."

Using her name with such a stern tone she sat up and sat still.

"Where did the bank say the money came from? What account?"

She shrugged her shoulders and spread a page of paper in front of him, her bank statement, printed off at home.

She had run a highlighter pen over the deposit that was causing her to lose sleep.

"Have you told your husband?"

Celeste shook her head.

"Anybody?"

Another shake of the head. She knew Danny was in his no nonsense mode. This was exactly when she was a little bit scared of him. She could never tell him that. Nor could she ever say to him that in these moments he reminded her most of their father.

Danny laid his hand on hers.

"Okay, Celeste. The truth is the bank will already be investigating this and they will flag it all the way up their chain until it reaches the police."

"The pol–"

Danny cut her off. Her shrill voice was starting to attract attention. "Shush. Yes. And I already know who in the police will be handling it. So, don't worry. Don't tell anyone. Don't go into your bank unless they summon you. If they do, talk to me first."

"I... I... I don't want the money. Whoever owns it can have it back. Jesus, Danny. I just want to be left alone. They must know this is nothing to do with me."

She was unravelling. He grabbed her hands and without anyone being able to tell, he squeezed them. Hard. Celeste didn't shut up until she registered the pain. She tried to pull her hands from him, but Danny didn't let go.

"Listen. To. Me. Celeste," he snapped.

She finally focused on him.

"What if I was to tell you that there is a way that this can all go away?"

She looked at him. Distrust flashed in her eyes, but only for an instant.

"I know you don't trust me, sis. That's okay, because I love you. I know, in your world at least, I'm not easy to trust."

"Danny..."

"But I will make this go away. And... you will get to keep the money too."

A puzzled look crossed her face. Danny let go of her hands and nonchalantly took a sip of his coffee.

CHAPTER 27
CAT AND MOUSE

LITTLE COLIN WAS FAIRLY SURE HE'D BEEN SPOTTED BY THE BLOKE walking with the tall man. He followed them from the Bond Street Tube over to the car park at the rear of Selfridges. It was time to change tactics... and for a bit of ingenuity. So, today, he donned his long-haired heavy metal wig, put on the boots with the lifts in them and applied a beard where one had never been before.

What interested Colin the most was Harkness. He didn't seem to be behaving in an over-cautious or deviant way. He hadn't tried to evade Little Colin. There were no extra double-backs or wariness in his movements as he travelled.

The tall bloke arrived at the Finchley Road police station. Little Colin had been with him since before dawn. He was careful not to be too obvious, calling on all of his surveillance experience to avoid being spotted the second day in a row. Not easy when you are on the follow on your own, but he couldn't change that right now.

Little Colin was able to put his feet up in a Costa Coffee right opposite the front entrance to the station.

He didn't like this very much. The thought that he was on

the trail of a fellow cop made him uneasy. However, he knew Christine and Freethy well, and as far as he was concerned, they were good police. If they wanted someone shadowed, there had to be a very good reason. He trusted them, having had to rely on them to get him out of a few tricky scrapes in the past. Now, if they needed his help, he gave them it. And here he was.

Waiting... watching.

⁓

Harkness had spotted his tail too. He didn't think it was the same one as the day before, but nonetheless, he was there.

And that angered him.

How could he have been so lazy? How had he not seen him before Danny Felix had?

And who the fuck was following him in the first place? He could think of only one possibility. Who were the cops who had confronted Murray in that shithole bar of his? He needed to find out.

A quick phone call to Murray furnished him with a name. Two names in fact. Chance and Freeth. Out of Barnes. Close. Too close for comfort. Murray was dispatched to do a little more digging... with orders to text over anything else he might find out.

Harkness looked at the names he had written on the post-it note on his desk. He sighed and then muttered to no one in particular: "Ms. Chance and Mr. Freeth, you do know what happens when you try to corner a rat? It gets very aggressive."

⁓

Little Colin was given the run around all day. New Scotland Yard. A café off Wigmore Street in the Marylebone area that looked like it still inhabited the 1950s. The British Museum in Holborn, and finally an apartment block in South Kensington. Harkness liked to travel. But now Colin had a problem. He knew the apartments. He had been to them before a few years back on a previous follow, tracking a team known for 'home invasions.' He remembered this particular building had more than one main entrance. It straddled the entire block, with roads bordering both the eastern and western sides. And despite how good he was, even Colin couldn't be in two places at once. There was only one thing he could do. He called Christine.

Harkness liked her. Not that he would ever tell her, but he liked her all the same. The defined Eastern European cheekbones, slender frame, long legs, and the fact that she knew when to speak and when to shut up. And today, he most definitely didn't want to talk. He was tense. It was all knitting together now; he could feel that the endgame was in sight. He knew what the next steps needed to be, what he had to do, but he was still on edge. Not nervous. Not worried. No, he was just... edgy. He was buzzing, waiting for the bell to ring. For his opponent to come out of his corner, face him for the first time, to throw the first swing of his fist, then calm down and go about his work. That's what it was... an overwhelming desire to start, an itch to start scratching.

And right now, this young lady could help him ease the tension. She could help scratch the itch until such times as he really started, which would be the next day. And anyway, he liked the idea of making the wanker following him cool his heels for an hour or so; see if he could work out that this place had two doors.

And at that, she walked into the bedroom, a vision in very

217

little... Harkness felt his mouth go dry. My... he did like her. More than he wanted to admit.

It took CC just forty-five minutes to reach South Kensington. It took her a bit longer to find Little Colin, especially as she wasn't used to looking for him in his disguise... the bearded heavy metal look.

Once that barrier was overcome, Colin gave her a full rundown of the follow. She was always impressed by his work. He was the best cat-and-mouse man she had ever worked with.

"I've been circling the block every ten minutes, but can't be one hundred percent that he's still in there, CC. It takes more than three minutes to do the block and if I go too many times, I begin to stick out like a sore thumb."

"Yeah, no worries. So, you backed off how long ago?"

"Twenty minutes? But he'd gone in about twenty to twenty-five before that."

"Okay, I'll take the east side. You the west? Is that how you want to go?"

"Easy by me. There's a Carluccio's restaurant on the east side, so you can enjoy the better coffee."

"Shame, that," grinned Christine, and off she went.

CC had just ordered her second coffee when she saw The Tall Man. Harkness emerged from the double doors on the eastern side of the apartments. Shit... she'd been enjoying her drink. They were off and running.

Harkness took them to the one place they hated. The London Underground.

CC cursed him. She knew a follow was fucking difficult on the Tube. She couldn't get too up close and personal, especially because they had met.

They sandwiched him. Christine in the carriage down from Harkness. Colin was one up.

District line. Going eastbound. Until they got as far as Westminster, then Harkness looked to change lines. Before now, CC always liked the look of Westminster Tube station. It was all metal struts and shiny surfaces, like something from a science fiction film. The walkways and escalators snaked around the interior, linking the District, Circle and Jubilee lines. They made for a labyrinth of grey steel. But today, she hated it. It was a maze and trying to keep track of Harkness without getting discovered was a fucking nightmare. At first it looked like he was heading street-wards. Maybe to join the tourists as they "oohed" and "aahed" at Big Ben and the Houses of Parliament, but at the last second, he switched direction. He went back into the bowels of the station.

He was dry cleaning. Christine could spot it a mile off. Which was weird, as Little Colin had earlier told her he hadn't bothered. She felt her stomach tighten. He didn't care earlier. But now he was going somewhere that he did care. Or going to meet someone he wanted to keep under wraps...

She hung back. Looking around carefully, she finally spotted Little Col, leaning against the station wall, trying to look nonchalant. As if he was waiting for a friend to catch up. So, she acted like his friend.

"He's dry cleaning..."

"I think so too," agreed Colin. "It means he wants to be alone. He's looking for me more than you. I'll leave you to take the lead. He won't be expecting to see your face. Then when we see who or what he is trying to protect, we might need to split again."

Christine nodded. It made sense. So that was exactly what they did.

Harkness boarded the rear carriage of the northbound Jubilee line train at Westminster, this being his turn to wait to see if Danny Felix joined him at Green Park. He thought he had shaken off his 'new friend' at the Tube station. Westminster was excellent for that sort of thing, lots of escalators and big open landings. Contact could be lost easily. He suspected it had.

All he had to do now was keep a lookout and wait to speak to Felix. At the next station, Danny appeared. However, they weren't alone in the carriage, causing a delay to the start of their conversation. Harkness didn't mind, it gave him more of a chance to be cautious. He needed to make sure he was clean before starting to talk.

CC's breathing was shallow. She was tense as she fought to keep her eyes on Harkness. He had taken her all the way to the Jubilee north platform. She had to time her last-minute hop onto the train carefully to avoid being spotted. She could only hope that Little Colin had managed to keep up. At least she still had her eyes on the prize.

The carriage didn't empty until they were quite far north, in fact as far as where the train left the tunnels and came out above ground at Finchley Road. Once they were alone, the two men sat opposite one another.

～

Emerging into daylight, Christine felt her pocket vibrate a couple of times. Text messages. The first was one from a friend, asking about Shauna and a drink later. The second was far more interesting. From Little Colin:

Harkness joined by guy. I spotted him other night at Bond St.

Christine edged forward in her seat slightly, snatching a glance down into the next carriage. Harkness was sat opposite the man. They were talking.

CC quickly tapped out a message back to Colin.

Col u take new guy I take Hark if poss. Might be tricky as stations quiet from here out.

She pressed send... at least they had a plan.

～

Danny was staring blankly at the adverts on the inside of the Tube carriage until the two of them were alone. That took a while. Finally, as the train pulled out of Finchley Road, they had the carriage to themselves. Harkness made the first move.

"Are you ready?"

"Yes, we are."

"Tell me..."

"No. Be at the unit. Tomorrow night. Ten o'clock. Have her with you."

"Or?"

"I pulled a job once, poured petrol all over the van guard

before he even knew it was happening. He didn't see me coming. You won't see me coming either."

He paused while the train stopped at West Hampstead, making sure no one joined them. The train pulled away again.

"You know I'm capable, Harkness. From now on, every time you smell a car getting filled up, you'll think of me. Want to wake up to a damp bed and the sound of a match being struck? If Dexy is not there safe and sound tomorrow night..." added Danny, letting the words hang.

The train squealed. Metal wheels screeched against metal rails. The sparks threw splashes of light onto Danny's face, creating shadows around his eyes. They made him look, for an instant, cadaverous.

"You bring the money. I bring your precious redhead."

Harkness then reached inside his jacket, Danny tensing as he did, but the hand emerged holding a sheaf of papers.

"These, Danny boy, are the investigation orders for Mrs. Celeste Winslow. A financial matter, possible proceeds of crime. It says I am to be the investigating officer."

Danny gave him nothing back.

"Of course, if this paper was to disappear, or I was to report that I had found nothing untoward... I just thought you might need another little incentive. Keep you between the lines, Danny. Now I want to know. How exactly are you going to pull this off?"

Danny managed to keep the hatred he felt for Harkness from his face, the jolt of the train helping.

The train pulled into Kilburn station. Danny stood up.

"Watch the news, Harkness. Watch the news... oh and by the way, does my sister get to keep your money?"

Danny got off the train.

∾

They split up, just as CC's text had suggested. But Christine's end of the deal was a short one. At the next stop Harkness simply switched platforms. He took the train south again, alighting at Finchley Road. From there it was straight to the police station where he entered and stayed put for at least an hour.

Little Colin, on the other hand, had a far trickier time of it. His lead took him on a merry dance, doubling back, ducking in and out of dead ends, retracing steps then deviating from them a third time around. All the while though, Colin managed to keep the target in his sights... but only just. Almost an hour and a half after exiting Kilburn Tube station, Col gave in and texted CC. Seconds later his own mobile rang. It was her.

"I need your help now," said Colin. "I'm getting tired and this guy isn't dry cleaning, he is positively fucking with me. It's like he knows I'm here and he's almost willing me to be bold and front him."

"My boy's been inside Finchley Road Station for a while now," explained CC. "Where are you?"

"He's got me all the way down in Holborn. About fifteen minutes ago he went into the Chancery Lane Hotel. There is only one main door in and out, but no sign of him yet. I need to eat, I need to pee, and I need you to come now or I will break off."

"I'll come down."

It took her twenty minutes to get there. A coffee shop, a little way along from the grand frontage of the hotel. Little Colin look wrecked, dead on his feet with fatigue. Nothing CC could do but let him go and take over herself.

Half an hour later, it all started again. Christine was in pursuit of the new man, snaking her way down, on foot, through Covent Garden. Over to Leicester Square, which was a nightmare as the summer funfair was in residence. There were huge crowds, the noise and light of the rides adding to the confusion and then, after a wander through China Town, it was back up to Covent Garden.

In the piazza, a street performer had a large crowd applauding his fire-eating karaoke act. Any other time, CC would have found it funny but that evening it was all just more irritation, watching the back of her target's head appearing then disappearing, until finally she'd lost him.

After all this time. Christine felt gutted. Both she and Colin had been on the go for hours and had learned next to nothing about their targets. Fucking pointless!

Fatigue then hit her too, like a sideswipe from a giant's fist, making her head feel too heavy for her neck. Exhaustion dragged her shoulders down, and her spirit with them. She took her mobile out, she was going to call Freethy, update him on the days wasted efforts as she headed to the Tube station and home. She was fishing in her pocket, the phone not co-operating with her, snagging on the lining of her jeans, when she walked right into someone. Christine looked up. It was the man she and Colin had been following for most of the afternoon and evening.

"If you want to talk to me, all you have to do is ask."

Christine was lost for words; all she could do was gawp. And as she finally put her brain in gear and was about to speak, her phone rang in her hand. Dumbly she looked down at it, expecting to bounce the call, until he saw it was the hospice.

Shauna.

She held a finger up in her quarry's face, gesturing the phone with her other hand.

"One second, please."

Her target just shrugged.

"Christine Chance here..."

"Ms. Chance, it's your daughter. Can you get here as soon as possible? Her condition has deteriorated considerably over the course of the last two hours."

CC felt like she'd been kicked in the gut, not this. Not now. Not right now. Fuck, fuck, fuck.

"I... I'm on my way."

She ended the call.

"I suppose this means you don't want to talk to me."

CC stuffed a business card into the man's hand.

"I have to be somewhere else. Now. But if you are involved with the man we saw you with earlier today, you need to think again. Call me. Tomorrow. Whatever trouble you're in, I can help get you out of it."

"Who said I'm in trouble?"

"I... I don't... just call me tomorrow. The man..."

Christine just stopped. She'd blown it. Everything that could have gone wrong with this follow just had... and then some. All she could do was step aside and run. Run. Run to the Tube, run to the hospice. Run to the one thing she wanted to run away from.

For his part, Danny stood still for a second. He looked around, trying to see if he had missed another follower. Where was the one who had been on him earlier? After a while he was fairly sure he'd been left alone. He had knackered the first one and then freaked out the second one. But no, he wasn't stupid. Something in the phone call had spooked her... not just his own bold-faced cheek.

He looked at the card. Metropolitan Police. Barnes.

Flying Squad. Det Insp Christine Chance.

Well, well, well. If they did suspect that their money van was going to get burned the next day, there was no way that Danny would be stood right here right now.

Fuck me... they're fishing. They have no idea. Fuck me. This might just work.

It's amazing what you don't see, even when you are looking.

You could stand on a Tube platform, looking at a huge poster of a beautiful young couple walking on a beautiful beach having a beautiful holiday somewhere— beautiful. But as soon as Freethy's train clattered into the station, he wouldn't have been able to tell you where the advert was imploring him to go. He had been looking, but not seeing.

Not surprising really. He was exhausted. The events of the past few weeks were enough to make anyone's head swim.

The carriage was one of the new Metropolitan Line trains, open plan, flip seats and brightly lit.

The passengers all looked as miserable as sin, jostling against each other as the train sped out of London, out towards the leafy Hertfordshire countryside.

A young Asian man, furiously tapping on his smart phone, was battling some electronic monster. A businesswoman had obviously had a wine or two, her suit skirt showing a little too much leg as she gently dozed through her journey home. Three blokes in army fatigues and rugby shirts, looking like they were on their way to meet mates, passing a can of cider between them. Countless other commuters, all with varying degrees of urban numb plastered across their faces, enduring the Tube train and the proximity of strangers. A means to a destination end.

But even with all that looking. Freethy didn't see it.

Didn't spot the threat.

He needed to piss. So, at his stop he didn't go straight to the exit gates. He went to the loo. He didn't look over his shoulder to see the three lads in combat trousers and rugby shirts delay their exit from the train until the last possible second. He didn't see them quicken their pace to come through the door of the gents after him.

But he did feel the first boot square in his back that propelled him into the wall over the urinals. He did feel the thrashing of six fists and boots as their blows rained down on him from behind. What he did see was himself, in his mind, disappearing down a long, black hole, with the taste of blood in his mouth and the sensation of his own urine flowing down his legs. They decorated the walls with him and his blood.

They left him for dead. Or they assumed he was. The paramedic certainly thought so when he first arrived.

CHAPTER 28
A MOMENT OF QUIET

BURSTING THROUGH THE DOORS OF THE HOSPICE LIKE A HURRICANE, Christine almost took out a nurse. She caught herself, embarrassed by her haste in a place where speed is the last priority.

Apologising profusely to anyone in her path, she finally reached Shauna's room.

This was it.

She knew it. Instinct was telling her. She could feel it, like a heavy cloak that wrapped itself around her, smothering her. She stood still, her thoughts thrashing around inside her head. She felt like she was walking out onto a frozen lake, knowing the ice was only thickest and strongest at the edges, but still striding out to the middle anyway, just waiting for the crack and the give, waiting to plunge into icy blackness.

But from somewhere, Christ knows where, she found the strength to reach out and push the door open.

She caught her breath. If it was possible, Shauna seemed even smaller in her hospital bed. Her breathing rattled unevenly in the silence of the room. The usual barrage of monitors had all been silenced. It was as if they knew, with all their technological wizardry, that there was nothing left to do.

Christine stepped up to the bed. She took her daughter's hand and just held it. She sat like that for a very long time. Shauna's breathing was sporadic at best, long gaps forming between each draw. At some points CC wondered if the moment had finally arrived, only for another gasp to emerge and take her back from the brink.

They sat together.

"I love you, Baby Boo."

Christine whispered it, barely out loud.

It was strange to her. She had feared this moment for so long. From a distance it had always looked insurmountable to her. But, with the advantage of time and love, it simply was a moment of quiet and pure acceptance of how things were.

She had been dreading a tempest. But she found herself, now, in a space of calm, feeling respect and love.

It was all right, it really was. They had both done all they could. Shauna had to go, and Christine knew she had to let her.

And that is exactly what they both did.

Danny sat on the grass in the park at the very top of Primrose Hill. It was, many believed, one of the best views of London. He agreed with them. The city spread out in front of this little patch of green, like an apology to nature. It was simply a small reminder of what London would have looked like had man not excavated, built, concreted, and developed.

Danny just sat, creating a space within himself. Finding a moment of quiet before the upheaval to come. He was not nervous or doubtful. He knew he could pull the job off. He also knew that Harkness would try to kill him once it was done. Danny had thought about that too. He had thought about it many times over the last few weeks.

Was he afraid to die?

What unnerved Danny most was his answer; not really.

What angered him most was the thought that he might not shuffle off on his own terms. No, that was very different. He had never viewed death as a finality, rather just as a fact of life, a development. He wasn't religious, unlike his parents. He didn't think there was a bearded man in the sky waiting for us all to clean up our acts. But he did like to think that there might be another space, another form of consciousness that you could morph into after this collection of atoms, chemicals and biology had taken you as far as it could. It was a process, and like all processes it moved forward, whether you liked it or not. Like a job. The moment you pulled out your shotgun or grabbed the security guard, you were in a process, and even if you started it, it would finish with or without you.

Just like London would, as with any big city. Whether you rolled out of bed, the city still cranked up, still went about its state business, still moved forward with its own processes. Like Harkness had said, a constant state of forward flux.

Except, Danny knew that the following day would be different. He might indeed die. Maybe not on his terms and perhaps even because of them.

Who knew?

He sat there taking the city in. He could feel its rhythms, its heartbeat. He could predict how it would react to almost any given situation. He was able to spot its patterns and behaviours.

He smiled to himself. He imagined he could feel every cross word, every orgasm, every act of kindness, each and every moment coming to life in the city before him right there and then. He took a deep breath, feeling his lungs expand, his chest rise, and his heart and mind fill with even more of London.

It had always been this way for him since his childhood. A basic distrust of his family life, and his disappointment in that system meant that he could now look at certain situations or scenarios and in an instant map how they might play out. From figuring out his own origins, he gained an innate sense of how all systems behaved. How they resolved within their own internal logic.

And a city, London, any city was a huge lumbering system. That is why he knew he would succeed with the robbery.

London would be his. His process would crash into this city's. Interrupt it. De-stabilise it. It would be a day London would never forget. What was it the villain in the film Highlander said? "I have something to say. It's better to burn out than to fade away..."

Danny agreed. He nodded gently to himself as he sat still, feeling the late evening breeze on his face. Atop Primrose Hill, he enjoyed the moment, enjoyed the anticipation. Soon, Danny would bring a stillness to the whole of London.

CHAPTER 29
A MOMENT OF DISQUIET

ONCE THE DOCTORS HAD OFFICIALLY PRONOUNCED SHAUNA'S DEATH, there was the inevitable flurry of activity.

The questions about arrangements and information about the process now kicked in. The death certificates, funeral directors, and a myriad other things seemed to pass Christine in a blur.

One of the nurses could tell CC couldn't hold it together for much longer. In a quiet moment she came and found her, bringing with her a cup of tea, an act of kindness.

"Your daughter was a lovely girl. I'm so sorry for your loss."

Christine took the cup from her, smiling vaguely at her words. It took her a little longer than she normally would have. She looked at the clock on the wall for the first time since she had arrived there. It was almost five in the morning.

"We see a lot of loss here, but also a lot of hope. Your daughter was so proud of you. She always talked about you and the work you do. She wanted to be a detective, she told me, just like her mum."

"Eh... did she?... she never told..."

"It was nice that one of your colleagues came to see her too.

Very late, last night. Your colleagues obviously think a lot of you."

It took a second to understand what the nurse had just said. But when she did, it made Christine sit up.

"What? Sorry, what did you just say?"

"The other policeman, who came to see Shauna. Last night. In fact, I think he left an envelope for you."

She beetled off to the nurses' station. She returned with the envelope, handing it to Christine.

"Such a big, handsome man. I know police have to be able to handle themselves, but he was very tall. Once he showed me his badge, I knew it was okay to let him visit."

CC was now practically clawing at the envelope, pulling it open, taking the small card out from inside. It was a Metropolitan Police business card, standard issue, with the name and contact details printed on the front. On the back, a handwritten note that simply said...

Just so you know I was here.

"What was the policeman's name again?" The nurse's question broke into the blizzard of her thoughts.

CC looked up at the nurse's query. She held the card in mid-air as though that was the answer. Her blood ran cold and her guts turned weak as water. The nurse took the card from her, not registering the look of panic that was now growing across CC's face. She read aloud.

"That's right... Inspector Harkness."

CHAPTER 30

SURPRISE

For Enda, it had been relatively easy to acquire the explosives.

All his life he had been able to sense where to look, which palm to grease, which favour to call in, and which threat to dole out.

Even now he could hear his da's mantra, ringing in his ears as it had done during his childhood. "Ye can get a howl of most anything so long as ye know where ye shud be lukking."

It was advice he had taken to heart ever since.

The years of service in the everyday world of construction and demolition gave him the right kind of connections to stock up on his favourite fireworks in no time at all. And given his years of service in the not so everyday world of Irish insurgency, he was an expert at putting them to use.

Danny was very specific in his instructions. Enda was to produce two actual live devices. The rest were to be nothing more than a good old-fashioned 'flash, bang, wallop'. Enough to cause havoc and panic, but no actual harm.

Standing over them now, he felt satisfied with his handi-work. Each separate device clearly marked up in his own code. At a glance, he knew which was which, each for a different destination. No one else would know the difference. No one dispatcher would know where the others were bound.

He had spent the last few days visiting the places where each of these dark parcels would be deployed. All those car journeys in different, often stolen, vehicles. Pretend breakdowns while wearing a variety of outfits and head gear.

Then there were the walks around the train stations and, most unnerving of all, Heathrow. Looking without seeming to be looking, trying to spot likely locations, trying to make it easy, trying to make it possible even.

Using a flashy camera with a sizeable lens, he took a series of photographs that went from wide shots to slightly closer, then closer still, until the last pictures were extreme closeups of the spots he wanted the packages placed. Each of his dispatch boys would be left in no doubt as to exactly where they were to make their drops.

All was going according to plan. Danny's plan. Thus far.

But it didn't have to stay that way now, did it? Sitting in his Willesden Green storage unit, Enda eyed the little packets of mayhem in front of him. A dryness was developing in his throat with a familiar tightness in his chest. His tongue clicked in his mouth as he reached for the hip flask in his coat pocket hanging on the back of his chair. The familiar smoky slide of the 'Green Spot' down his throat was a welcome distraction from his thoughts. But as he lowered the flask from his lips, he was strangely unsurprised to hear the three sharp knocks on the metal door.

Opening the heavy door with one hand on the gun tucked into the back of his waistband, Enda didn't recognize the big man standing there, but he was pretty sure he could guess.

"You're a polite one for a fuckin' copper."

"And you are casual for a man who is about to participate in the job of the century…"

Enda let his hand drop loosely at his hip, to reveal his handgun.

"You won't be needing that this evening, I'm here under a white flag."

"When did rules ever stop a fucking British cop from doing what he wants?"

"Ah, Enda... a life of bitterness is so unbecoming... I'm James..."

"Harkness. I know who ye are."

By way of acknowledging Enda's perception, Harkness reached slowly into a black bag he was carrying, his hand emerging with a bottle of Jameson 12 Year Old. The amber glint in the dim room was enough to make Enda involuntarily run his tongue over his bottom lip.

"Can we play nice, Enda? Even for just a little while?"

Enda answered by stepping to one side, allowing Harkness to enter the room.

Two dirty mugs were briefly run under a tap at the back wall of the workspace. Enda set them on his table. Harkness broke the seal on the bottle as he pushed a wooden box in front of it to sit down. The pair didn't clink glasses or even make eye contact as they shot-gunned the first measure. Harkness instantly poured more into the mugs. He surveyed the array of devices on the table and the floor around him.

"Quite some night's work... but then you are Enda Crilley. Or should I call you Big Man Boom...?"

Enda didn't react.

"Omagh... Enniskillen. Rumoured to be involved in the bombing of Horse Guards Parade in 1982... you have quite a CV for a man who builds motorways."

"Am I supposed to feel scunnered that you know so much about me?"

"Feel what?"

"Scunnered. Embarrassed. Off kilter. Because, right now, I couldn't give a shite."

Harkness chuckled softly. "Not at all. I just wanted to meet the man, the legend. Wanted to see whose hands were getting ready to do my work for me."

"Your work, is it? I think you'll find I only answer to me. The money will be my reason for being sat here."

"Ah, filthy lucre. The root of all evil, or so they would have us believe. But surely a man like you has more than just a few quid to motivate him."

Enda raised the mug to his lips, giving Harkness a look as he did so. "If you're so fucking smart, how come you are being followed?"

The attempt to throw Harkness didn't have the desired effect. A smile spread across his wide-boned face.

"I am the one who walked into your lock up unannounced, Enda. Being Anti-Terrorist Squad has its advantages."

"But will ye get out alive?" asked Enda, nudging the gun in front of him for emphasis.

"Oh, Enda. I come in peace."

"Brits don't know the meaning of that word."

"I am the exception... I brought you some gifts, besides decent whiskey." Harkness hoisted the black satchel onto the only free corner of the worktable, setting it down carefully. Enda reached out to pull the mouth of the bag wider, peering in.

"Semtex. Now what would I need Czech Semtex for?"

"Very good, Enda. I'm impressed." Harkness leant forward, a conspiratorial look on his face.

"You see, our boy Danny may not have shared his plan with me, he may not have shared it all with you, but it doesn't take Stephen Hawking to work out that if you are involved, which I know you are, then something is going to go bang. And if that is the case then I just wanted to lend a helping hand. Make sure you have enough... supplies."

"D'ya think I'm completely stupid? You're fishing. I don't have a fucking clue why but... you're fishing."

"Not at all. Call it more like insurance. Danny strikes me as a cautious type. He wants or needs a distraction for London tomorrow, and I am more than sure you will be the one to provide it for him. I want to make sure the job gets done... properly, not cautiously. He'll need all the time he can get. I want the job to come off. I am just giving you this bag of supplies to make sure that the distraction is as eye-catching as possible."

"And what makes you think I might choose your orders over Danny's? I don't know you from Johnny Fucking Ga-ga."

Harkness stood slowly, his full height blocking out most of the light from the strip neon above his head, casting his shadow across Enda and his handiwork.

"Because you are Big Man Boom, Enda. An artist with a trip-wire. Because you aren't done with whatever version of the Irish Troubles that gnaws away at your heart. How many times was your house raided in Belfast? Was it the Paras or the SAS who shot your brother coming out of that betting shop on the Falls?"

Enda was up out of his seat, faster than Harkness would have believed a man his size could move. A smash reverberated as the mug of half-drunk Jameson's shattered against the far wall.

"You don't fuckin talk about my brother, you English bastard... every last one of you has blood on their hands, your own people and mine."

"Which is exactly why you will take that bag and make every last one of these go off with a proper bang. Give London what you always felt it deserved, Enda. Do it for me, do it for the success of the job or do it for your brother. Whatever your reason, just fucking do it. I want this city distracted. I want this job to play out just like Danny's imagined it... and then some."

Harkness turned, walking towards the door. "Enda, do you know who Robert E. Lee was? He once said that you should always try to mystify, mislead, and surprise the enemy, if at all possible. You have your chance to do that tomorrow."

Enda mumbled something in return. Harkness was stood in the doorway, not quite catching it.

"Something to tell me, Big Man?"

"Ay... it wasn't General Lee said that... it was Stonewall Jackson. Now fuck off, ye cocky bastard."

Christine was reeling. She'd often heard the expression but never expected to ever feel it herself.

But there was no doubt. Christine was reeling. Driving like a woman possessed, she was desperate to get to Collinson, to Freethy, and quiz them about this Harkness bastard and to tell them what had happened and where she had been.

What she didn't realise was that she was actually in shock. She had been from the moment Shauna died, a state that was only deepened by the note from Harkness and hammered home by her blind rage and panic.

She reached for her mobile for the third time, trying to ring Freethy. Voicemail again. She needed to tell someone. Needed to talk it out.

She punched the 'on button' of her car stereo. Perhaps music might help. Some human babble, some background mindless noise might steady her.

The first station to appear was a news talk one, some idiot blathering on about what the government was or wasn't doing for the taxpayer. She hit 'seek', watching the frequency change at a rate of knots until it settled on what sounded like a seventies rock song. That would do, but almost immediately as the station locked on the DJ's voice kicked in.

"Great tune there, a little blast from all our pasts. 'Touch of Grey' by the Grateful Dead."

Christine felt liked she'd been slapped. Dead... grateful? Fucking grateful? Dead? Fucking Dead? Dead... my Shauna dead.

And that was when it truly hit her. Crashed through the shock, crashed into her consciousness, and wrenched her heart.

She could feel the wind being knocked out of her, the bile rising in her stomach. She didn't know it, but she was letting the car coast. Taking her foot off the accelerator, thankfully somehow remembering to knock the car into neutral, she let it drift until it came to a halt of its own accord. She opened the driver's door and leant out, vomiting onto the road, her chest and stomach heaving, salt tears wringing from her eyes.

And then she sat upright. Just sat there. Gradually one emotion battled to the fore, rising up in her as surely as the bile and cups of tea just had.

Rage. Pure white, hot rage.

Rage at Harkness.

Harkness, who had inserted himself into one of the most private moments of her life. He had come between her and Shauna's passing. He had put himself into a memory that she should have been able to look back on as some sort of relief, a release from the suffering her little one had endured. And now, here was this fucker Harkness making Christine think that her child's death was not just her own experience but was maybe hastened on someone else's terms. Played out according to their agenda, not God's or love's or nature's.

"You cunt." She actually said it out loud. "You fucking cunt." Screaming it now. Starting the car again.

But before she pulled away, her mobile phone rang. She snatched it up, expecting to see Freethy's name, her friend returning her many calls. But the screen showed a number she didn't recognise. She hesitated, until the earliness of the hour made her realise that this might be no ordinary call. Clearing her throat, she hit the receive button on the handset.

"Hello, is this Chance?"

The voice wasn't one she recognise but what it said made her sit up.

"Detective Chance, can I talk to you about a very bad man? His name is Harkness."

CHAPTER 31
PICK OF THE POPS

It was obscenely early. The birds had no right to be so fucking cheerful. His missus had snored so loudly the previous night that even the dog had left the bedroom. But Collinson was still walking into his office at precisely the time he wanted to. He was a stickler for never being late to work. Ever since he had joined as a cadet, aged sixteen, and now at fifty-five was still clocking in before most of his team had woken up.

Frankly, Collinson would be glad when the day was over. He wanted the pile of around twenty-two million pounds gone... and gone today. All that money gathered in a short, six-week span had been stored in his evidence room, all under plain packaging after the counting team had come in and checked it, wrapping it in bundles of fifty grand each. More money than he had ever seen in his life.

The sheer amount made him feel dizzy and nervous. Ever since Christine Chance and her mate Freethy had whined about the intelligence which had led to its gathering, Collinson had had a dull ache at the back of his old copper's brain.

He sighed to himself, peering out of his glassed-in office as the first few bodies appeared in the squad room.

He looked over one job sheet in front of him, the fingers of his left hand playing along the roughened edge of the leather wallet containing his police I.D., a habit he developed when he first received his badge. The once-black leather now looked almost silver, his fingers had passed over the smooth surface so many times, burnishing it with years of nervous energy. That wallet had seen almost forty years of service. Now he was so close to the end of it all.

He hoped his fellow police would recall him as a "cop's cop." He loved the job, but there was no doubt it was changing. Everything was changing. One second you were a fresh-faced cadet. The next you were old, labelled a dinosaur and being investigated for 'improprieties', even though in the intervening blink of your eye you had given your entire life to the job.

Time.

Collinson looked at his watch. 5:05 a.m. He wanted that load of money on the road before six. He would feel better then. He wanted to watch the three junior detective constables, Young, Sharp and Imbeki, drive that money out the gate. He could see them now, preparing to load up the white unmarked Luton van they hired for the job.

It was a joke really. Shifting all that money with no protocol in place to handle such an event, no way to use an armoured vehicle or a secure alternative. Cutbacks, rare event, the usual blah blah blah explanations. Just restrict the order to those who needed to know and use unmarked... it'd all be fine.

The bigwigs... they didn't give a shit beyond what box they could tick and how many corners they could cut to make their budget look tight. And that included doing everything they could to remove the experienced, and therefore more expensive, old boys off the books. By hook or by making them all feel like crooks.

If you were going to be made to feel like a wrong 'un...

Collinson swept his fingers over his badge holder once more.

A copper's cop.

And yet as soon as he watched those boys pull out of the gate, he made a call the likes of which he never thought he would make. He even had a throwaway mobile to make it on. Time and circumstance had caught up with another old school copper.

Time. It marched on, and sometimes it took you places you never saw yourself going.

DJ Johnny Dearie had never even received so much as a speeding ticket in his whole life. That was at the heart of his appeal. He was the whiter-than-white housewives' choice.

His boundless optimism and enthusiasm went a long way towards making him the most popular radio host in Great Britain. His breakfast drive time show was a ratings juggernaut. Nine million people chose to tune their radio to his station every morning between 5 and 9. He filled the airwaves with genial music, positive musings on everything good about the world and had a stubborn resistance to anything that might be seen as even slightly controversial.

This, of course, won Dearie as many trolling haters as it did doting fans. Once, on Facebook, a page had been set up calling for the extradition of Johnny Dreary (sic), for crimes against entertainment. It went viral and within twenty-four hours it had over 30,000 members and twice as many 'likes.'

Not that Dearie could give a damn. He knew exactly why his audience liked him. He knew exactly what it was he liked about himself and his show and he never swerved from that course. After all, he had one and a half million reasons a year to stay true to that formula and every single one of them had the King's head on it.

He always knew he wanted to be a disc jockey. To be the man who would fill the airwaves with the right song at exactly the right time, bringing little slices of musical joy to a commute or a moment of isolation for even just one listener. That's what drove D.J. Johnny Dearie on.

He pursued his dream, starting at hospital radio, then moving to local, local to network, late night to lunchtime and finally the Holy Grail: the breakfast show.

He was a radio genius. He knew what people wanted to hear and when they wanted to hear it. It was why they kept listening. It was as if he were a radio Pied Piper. This laced with his sunny attitude and willingness to avoid becoming cynical, made him a star.

Which made that morning, that day, even more ironic.

Not that Dearie would ever know. Nor would anyone.

"Ahhh, good morning, Great Britain. Another faaaabulous day on our planet earth."

An imaginary crowd cheered for him at the touch of a sound effects button.

"What time is it, D.J. Johnny?" his Greek chorus of sidekicks all yelled in unison.

"Glad you asked, gang. It's that time, the time where we cheer up Chingford, smile down on Solihull, tickle Tewkesbury and give Glasgow a giggle..."

More sound effects. A giggling little boy with a bicycle bulb horn on the end.

"It's time for our regular sunny song, the music that makes your commute that little bit easier. And today, just like every Thursday, it's my all-time fave..."

'Mr. Blue Sky'!!!

"That's right, gang... If this song doesn't make you smile,

you need to see a doctor!!! Who doesn't like to hear The Electric Light Orchestra singing about Mr. Blue Sky?"

Johnny Dearie started the track.

The drums. The throbbing bass line. The opening strains of Mr. Blue Sky filled the ears of every single one of Danny's team.

Today, as the song poured out of the little portable transistor radios he'd handed out, Danny Felix and his team used it as their joint cue to swing into choreographed action...

At approximately 5:50 a.m., it was their synchronized signal to rip London's head off and shit down its neck.

"The sun is shining in the sky..."

And their dark work began

CHAPTER 32
BOOM BANG A BANG

As soon as he heard Jeff Lynne's opening lyrics, Big Enda knew it was game on. Party time. All of his planning and work was about to be put to the test.

Enda both loved and hated this bit. He hated the thought that he might have missed a detail, missed a crucial connection, or misjudged a position. But once the chain of events kicked in, he was always... Enda didn't have the words to express it other than a rush of blood to his head and other parts that left him feeling a little dizzy and more than a little thirsty. If he had the words, they would have been ones like 'elated', 'euphoric', 'orgasmic', or perhaps 'deific'.

In the end, it all came down to what Big Enda knew best. Danny told him: "Play to your strengths, Big Man Boom. This is your moment in the sun... so make it work, make it count... play to your strengths and play them fucking sure."

So, he did. All of Enda's devices were packaged up in very traditional ways. Fairly dated technology that still worked. Old school knowledge that still packed a punch. A hell of a punch, and for London, that day, it needed to be a straight knockout. And the impact would be so much heftier with the help of the extra Semtex that Harkness had given him. Now he could give the Brits the kicking he had always dreamed of delivering. Danny Felix may have wanted to cause a modicum of real damage and then use misdirection and natural panic to do the rest. But there was room for doubt, happenstance, and failure in that plan.

After Harkness had intervened with his wishes, Enda had thought about it all. Why not be sure? And why not be brutal while you were at it? Two birds, one big fucking stone.

And so, as Enda listened while the radio asked why Mr. Blue Sky had to hide away for so long, he was busy pushing a series of buttons on some low-frequency transmitters arranged in a very particular order in front of him.

As the rush engulfed him, he could only begin to imagine the chaos those little commands were unleashing, but he would savour every second as his revenge rocked London.

Enda had done what was asked of him... and then some.

Enda's explosions tore into London in a brutally choreographed manner.

The first took the M1 and M25 motorways out of the equation. A 2010 Mercedes family estate that appeared broken down had been parked up on the southbound side of the M1 at 4.45am, the hazard lights left blinking. A shop dummy dressed in a waterproof jacket and jeans had been left in a seated position with its back to the safety fence about twenty feet behind the car itself. The car sat right on the hard shoulder just at the start of the bridge that took the M1 over the M25. When the bomb loaded into the back seat received the radio-signalled green light, the blast was hot, loud, and almighty.

Luck can play its part in absolutely anything, and

depending upon your point of view, luck, of a kind, showed up here. As the blast radiated heat, energy, and debris up, out, and away from its core, a heavy goods vehicle approached the site. One of the Mercedes' alloy wheels ejected sideways at about a hundred feet per second, punching into the base of the driver's cab, just where the wheel arch and the chassis of the truck meet, causing its own wheels to skew and lock. Covered in glass and debris, the driver of the forty-footer suddenly realised his huge transport was jack-knifing. The giant vehicle was folding in on itself, the smell of burning rubber, squealing of air brakes filling the void around him.

The massive juggernaut took out two more alongside it. First, a car containing three Eastern European lads on their way to a day's labour in London. Their tiny, relatively unprotected 1990 Skoda got swiped to the side as if it were made of nothing more than paper. It eventually flipped onto its roof in a shower of sparks, glass, and screams as it slid for at least another fifty yards, actually going under the fuselage of another vehicle. This one was the second casualty of the jack knife.

The next, a fuel tanker, was far more deadly. Freshly loaded and barrelling on its way to refill a north London garage. The jack-knifing forty-footer swung out in front of it. The tanker driver watched as if he was in a weird, slow-motion dream. He felt his calves cramping as he stomped on the brake pedal. All to no avail. The back end of the forty-footer smashed into the front of his cab. Their joint momentum created what was essentially a ten-ton, out-of-control bomb. Both vehicles careened down the carriageway at an angle that brought them to and then through the safety barrier. The sound of metal squealing and shearing, giving way, bombarded the forty-footer's driver. Flinging his door open, he tried to avoid being pulled over the edge with his truck and the tanker. He made a vain attempt to leap to safety only to be swatted over the edge by his own vehicle as it pitched over the freshly broken barrier. The only consolation was that he didn't have time to feel anything as his truck landed on him as he hit the M25 below.

Less than half a second later, the fuel tanker crashed into the ground too. The resulting blast could be heard up to twelve miles away. Not that it mattered, for all over London the sounds of exploding fireballs were drowning out everything.

There were other M25 explosions, the worst of which happened on the eastern side of the circular roadway, where it met the M20. The car bomb took out a minibus full of French exchange students. Their van disintegrated in the hot slam of the blast, casting metal and bodies into the air like burning feathers in a whirlwind. A total of seventeen cars cannoned into each other as a result.

Passengers were thrown about like rag dolls. Twisted metal and debris scattered across the highway. Everywhere was filled with the funk of gunpowder and charring rubber. Each blast sucked the air away from the immediate surroundings as oxygen fed the flames. The resulting plume reached thirty feet in the air.

The M4 was blocked off in a similar fashion. Except here the bomb was not in a car, but a metal trunk left just over the verge of the road. As it went off, roads and routes into the capital city were being shut down faster than you could say "boom".

The metal trunk packed an impressive thump augmented as it was with Harkness's extra ordinance. The explosive was packed around a firing pin normally used to excavate pathways for new roads through hills and mountainsides. It created a firestorm that melted most of the facing road surface in a bright instant.

The human toll was less there. A brief respite in traffic was caused by an accident two miles farther down the motorway and doubtless saved lives. As it was, only one car felt the full smack of the explosive. A pensioner in a little Nissan Micra, on her way to London for an art exhibition. She had been gently singing along to a song she remembered from the 1970s on her radio, a record her son had liked if she recalled correctly, about the sunshine. It was a nice song. Then a hot white blaze in front of her car and she knew nothing else.

CHAPTER 33
LONDON INTERRUPTED

THE FIRST THOUGHT THAT CROSSED THE BUSINESSMAN'S MIND WHEN HE first saw the mangled fingers flying through the air in front of him was, *Oh my God, some poor devil's hand*. It was only afterwards, much later, when he came round, that he was informed that they had been his fingers. He was the poor devil in question.

He had been reaching up into the luggage rack for his bag as he travelled on his 5:35 train into London's Waterloo. At precisely 6:01 the bomb packaged tightly in a rucksack next to his briefcase went off, causing the train carriage to lurch to one side, throwing him back onto the seats and the aforementioned fingers to break free from their knuckles and into the smoked-filled air. His was double bad luck really, as this was one of the devices Danny wanted to be nothing more than a flash bang rather than an actual bomb.

At just about the same time a coach arriving at London's Victoria Bus Station was lifted four feet into the air by what should have been another dummy package. A bomb in a suit-case jammed in amongst the luggage was the cause. The crack reverberated around the coach station and up into the adjacent train station, like some kind of cri-de-couer telling the early commuters to get the hell out.

Panic soon set in among the early morning rush hour crowds. Word spread quickly, across email, radio, TV, social networks, and frantic phone calls from loved ones. London was under attack; London was under siege. London was the one place on earth that no one wanted to be that deadly morning.

Similar scenes played out in other stations across the city. Most notably in Cannon Street Station and Clapham Junction, where the devices that brought fire and death were both hidden among deliveries to newsagents on their respective concourses. Here the victims and casualties were showered with burning paper and debris.

And as if all this wasn't enough chaos and carnage, Enda had reserved his best until last. The knockout punch. At 06:08.

Heathrow Airport. The short-term car park lit up like a firework display.

A new Ducato van was parked on the top level of the Terminal One structure. The rear of the van was packed with enough roofing tar and petrol to blow away a whole building. Which is exactly what it did, firing the surrounding parked cars out onto the adjacent road as though a giant had decided to upend a box of toys. The worst was a rental car coach carrying fourteen passengers... in the wrong place at the wrong time. A Range Rover Sport landed on their transport just as it was smashed by the secondary blast wave from the explosion rumbling out of the parking garage.

Destruction.

Death.

Mutilation.

Shock and shockwaves.

All accomplished within a space of exactly ten minutes to one of the world's most important cities.

Emergency services were dashing into action across the entire length and breadth of London, the system immediately overwhelmed and swept up into a panic that had not been experienced since the Tube and bus bombings of July 2005.

And now the city would go into spasm. No one would be let in... or out. It would contract in on itself in fear and desperation. The police would be pulled in all directions. Suspicious packages would be identified on practically every street corner by frightened members of the public. The city's heart would be crippled.

That is exactly what Danny Felix had asked Big Man Boom to do. It had been his final, whispered words to him when he first told him what his plan was to be. "I want this city to be interrupted. Enda. Shockingly, violently interrupted. You know how to. You are Big Man Boom."

As Big Enda took the cap off the first of his one-litre bottles of super strength cider after locking himself into a storage room at his construction company workplace, he re-tuned his little transistor radio, away from the fucking droning shite music played by that wanker Johnny Dearie and onto the news radio station he liked best, BBC Radio 5 Live.

An interruption, on an unprecedented scale.

What a thing of beauty. London streets ground to a halt. A smattering of traffic where there were usually hordes. A concerto of emergency sirens echoing off the concrete canyons of the financial district and beyond.

What a shame that he couldn't just go and walk for a while to enjoy the pause that he had created. What a crying shame that he couldn't take pleasure in his own vengeful masterpiece. But never mind, he hoped that Danny Felix would make the most of it.

At that, Enda took a big, long drink and sat on the concrete floor with his back to the wall. Soon the tears of joy came, running down his face. Just like the tears of pain his planning and expertise had caused his myriad victims in that ten-minute spell of destructive misdirection.

CHAPTER 34
THE STEAL

IMBEKI HAD BEEN PRATTLING ON FOR AT LEAST FIVE MINUTES NOW. THE only reason that Collinson had put three of them on this job was because there were so many packages to be lugged around. Loads of them... and if the office gossip was to be believed every single one of them was full of dirty, cold cash.

"Boi, this is not what I got into the fucking force for, playing at being a glorified removal man."

Greg Young just kept driving the Ford Mondeo estate through the sparse, early morning traffic in west London.

Young wished that Imbeki would shut the fuck up. He didn't much like his fellow recent recruit. He was pissy about almost everything and didn't mind telling you about it either. To drown him out, Young reached for the radio, flicking it on just as The Electric Light Orchestra's 'Mr. Blue Sky' was starting. Just as Young was thinking he liked that song, that it made him smile, the car was flooded with the sound of some godawful hip-hop crap.

"Sorry, mate, had to change it. I can't stand that wanker Johnny Dearie on the radio."

"Bloody hell! You're even chippy about the radio."

Young glanced in his rear-view mirror to make sure that their colleague Graham Sharp was still behind them, driving the Luton van with its unbelievable load in the back.

"What would you do with all that cash?"

Imbeki sat forward in the passenger seat, twisting to look at Young.

"It *is* cash! A shitload!"

"Yes, mate. That, I believe, is the official job term. M'lud, we entered the premises and found what can only be described a suspicious shitload of cash. The prosecution rests."

Imbeki let out a soft whistle, followed by a sucking of air in through his teeth.

"What now, you twat?"

"Boi, who says crime don't pay?"

"I've been daydreaming about what I'd do with even one of the millions I helped pack into the van. I fancy a trip round the world but would do it in style, like, take in the sights, go to some of the big events. Real Madrid against Barcelona at the Bernabeu. Or that mad horse race they have in Italy, round the courtyard of that ancient building. What's it called? The Palio? In Siena?"

"The one James Bond fucked up in that film?"

"Yeah, that's it..."

"All I would want, blood, is a suite at the Dorchester, champagne and that booty off of the dancing show... the judge... Darcy thingummy... lock the fucking doors... sweet as..."

"She'd only end up giving you no points."

The car filled with laughter.

Meanwhile in the Luton van, Sharpy was chuckling, congratulating himself for his speed at picking up the van keys and suggesting that Imbeki hop in with Young. He couldn't bear the thought of that whinger going on and on in the van with him. He could see them now, in the car in front. It looked like

Young was mainly silent while Imbeki's head was bobbing and weaving, doubtless bitching about this, that, and the fucking other. He had been in the office barely a month and already everyone had him down as a tricky dickhead. It wouldn't surprise Sharpy if he thought that the fact that the Luton van was white was some kind of coded racial slur.

Sharp turned the radio up, enjoying Johnny Dearie's music choice that morning, just like he always did. He couldn't remember what that day's *smiley song* was, until he heard the opening notes of 'Mr. Blue Sky'... Not bad, not bad at all...

Sharp sang along at the top of his voice and had they all not been so intent on other things, one of the three of them might have noticed that, since leaving the office, they had been accompanied by a variety of cyclists. Nothing unusual in seeing commuters on their bicycles in London, but if they had looked closely, they would have noticed a pattern to how the bikes were keeping pace with the van.

Like some kind of mad peloton, a mix of about five cyclists were swapping the lead as they either rode just behind, between, and in front of the two vehicles making their way from Barnes to Scotland Yard.

And in case they were taking notice, the riders would occasionally break away, into a side street, change a top or bag or helmet. They kept their sunglasses on though, pulling their cycling bandanas up round their noses, as if they were in place to filter out the car fumes and not just obscure their faces.

The riders jockeyed for position in the light traffic next to the Mondeo and the Luton van, measuring their progress across the city, swapping, rotating, tracking.

Following.

Ciaran and Danny had been parked since five a.m. The lumbering dump truck proved to be surprisingly comfortable, the big sprung seats bouncing the pair of them as they meandered their way down towards the Thames, over Vauxhall Bridge and along to Battersea.

Once in place, the first order of the day was to neutralise the one and only closed-circuit camera that overlooked where they wanted to execute the hit. Watching Ciaran shimmy up the balcony to where the camera was fixed, Danny thought of Cheetah from the old black-and-white Tarzan movies, with Johnny Weissmuller yodelling the Tarzan call while the mischievous monkey was up to no good. Probably best not to share that thought with his ginger-haired mate.

Once Ciaran had spray-painted the glass fascia of the hanging security camera, a feat that took no less than a minute and a half from start to finish, the pair settled into their respective seats, waiting for the big show.

This was the part that Danny hated the most. A pause just before the game began. The tick of the clock, the space between him and the job, a gap filled with unknown circumstance, happenstance, and endless permutations of what might or might not go right. Once he had started, he always itched to begin, to start for real. It didn't matter to him if he was about to rob a cash in transit van or rob a flat to retrieve a mobile phone clip. As soon as the job was moving, he wanted, no, needed, to keep moving it along.

He also realised that this type of wait, one that came immediately in the teeth of a job, was the kind of pause that made him sharpen up. It put him in a heightened state of awareness. He could feel the root of every single hair on his body. He could detect the flutter of birds' wings from a hundred feet. He could sense subtle atmospheric changes. For instance, right now he knew that Ciaran was gagging for a cigarette, but he wouldn't want to risk anything drawing attention to them. Not even the flare of a matchhead struck, or a plume of sweet smoke carried on the wind to one of the residential balconies directly to their right.

Their dumper truck was parked on a small service ramp that led directly from Battersea Church Road down to the river, the one that he had scoped out with Harkness just days earlier. All was as before when he and Harkness had pulled in from the road. He had come back a few times, and he had sat watching the road, the apartments, the river houseboats. He particularly liked the quiet, almost anonymous feel, to this little slice of London. The longer he stayed the more he knew that he could pull the job here, and maybe, just maybe get away with it, too. Of course, a lot of that would be down to how well Belfast Enda fulfilled his part of the process.

Danny was sat with an earbud stuck in one of his ears, listening to the Johnny Dearie show, waiting to hear the signal that they had all agreed was the one to start the festivities. And when it came, Danny felt the rush of heat into his face as he looked sideways at Ciaran.

"Mr. Blue Sky," is all Danny said.

"I hope the sun shines on the not so fucking righteous today, Danny." A smile as wide as the river Thames split Ciaran's face. He clapped his hands together gently and then rubbed them together.

Danny retuned his transistor radio to 5 Live, just as he knew Enda would, and listened for word of their little symphony of chaos, not suspecting it would be so much more chaotic and deadly than asked for.

∼

At just about the time that Sharpy had yelled his last ear-splitting note as he sang along with the radio, his own rover walkie-talkie went mad with emergency calls. Sharpy turned down his van radio and his rover up; almost rear-ending the Mondeo carrying Imbeki and Young because of a sharp stop. They pulled to a halt at the lights beside Smugglers Way in Wandsworth. At that, his mobile went. He answered to hear Imbeki's voice crackle from the handset at him.

"You hearing this, Sharpy?"

In the distance a boom rumbled across the sky towards them.

"Yep, sounds like something's kicking off."

"Something? A lot of things, mate... Young reckons we should check in."

Sharp thought about that for a second. Check in and do what? They were on a specific duty, one that the guvnor had been very clear about in his briefing, right down to specifying what route they should take to Scotland Yard. He had looked like he'd meant business when he talked to them that morning, and Sharp didn't fancy crossing swords with his new guv so early in his stay at Barnes.

His move to the unit had been one of convenience given that he had fallen out so dramatically with his last guvnor just weeks before the transfer. He had visions of spending a life investigating domestics when the new orders had come in, and Sharp just wanted his grace period to go as smooth as possible. And anyway, if the rumours about their cargo were true, he wanted to deliver it as safely and as quickly as possible and return to base, no dramas, no worries, no possibilities of a fuck-up.

"Check in and do fucking what exactly?" snapped Sharp. The rover, his hand-held radio sitting on the seat next to him was going proper nuts now. Dispatch traffic was going back and forth at a furious pace. What the fuck was going on out there?

Holding the phone away from his lips, he could hear Imbeki share his opinion with Young. Some kind of reply, a little muffled to-and-fro.

"Listen, Sharpy. This sounds like it is escalating, bruv. Have you actually got your rover turned up?"

"If something is blowing up, all the more reason for us to get this drop finished and jump back onto the radio when we are proper done and dusted. That way we can help, whatever mess is developing."

He could hear sirens across the city, faintly but definitely there, and he could feel a dull ache starting in the pit of his stomach. He didn't like this.

"Good enough. Lights changing. Let's get to the Yard, then see what's occurring."

Imbeki cut the line dead, and Sharp tossed the phone next to his rover on the seat beside him. But he now couldn't ignore the increasingly urgent chatter that was emanating from the handheld radio. What the fucking hell was going on? It sounded like war had broken out or something.

Just as he was about to pull away, he had to slam his brakes on again for a second time, blowing his horn hard and heavy at the cause of the latest disruption to what should have been a straightforward drop and return job.

"Fucking cyclists!"

It sounded to Danny's ears that Big Man Boom Enda had done his damnedest. The radio was flooded with breaking news, travel alerts and instructions for all commuters to stay home and not try to enter London. It was exactly as they had envisaged, or rather as Danny had hoped.

But his first feelings of satisfaction darkened as more reports emerged. How many casualties? How many explosions? He'd insisted on only two real ones.

The way Danny saw it, if you were going to steal from The Met Police you had to keep them occupied. Plus, if you were feeling like making doubly sure, shut the city down to keep the streets relatively clear. Danny had never forgotten how quiet the city had been in the immediate aftermath of the July bombings in 2005. London had emptied like a chamber pot down a sewer. The rush to put distance between the city workers and the terrorist threat was instant and dramatic. And here was just such a panic again. There wouldn't be a cop for at least a twenty-mile radius who wouldn't be either shitting himself at every empty paper bag discarded on a street corner or trying to marshal panicking punters away from the centre of the city. By his estimation, Danny reckoned he had at least a good thirty to forty minutes of wriggle room once the actual hit had gone down... now if only the wriggling could fucking start. He shook his head slowly, bringing his focus back to the here and now. Rolling news always got the details wrong at the start of a major incident. Concentrate on the job.

~

Young and Imbeki could feel an urgent panic rising between them. They had been debating putting a call back into their Barnes HQ. They were starting to imagine the trouble they might be in professionally if they stuck to their course and ignored what appeared to be the outbreak of a major terrorist incident in the city around them.

Just at that, Imbeki's mobile chirped into life, the screen telling him it was Sharp calling.

"Just had the guvnor on the line. He says we make the drop and await our next move once we are clear of the load."

"What the fuck is going on out there?"

"He says we aren't heading directly for any of it at this point, but we have to listen up to the rovers. If that changes then he will call us or if we get caught up in anything, we are to call him."

"Yeah but, seriously, what the fuck–"

Sharp cut him off. "Listen Imbeki, Old Man Collinson was very fucking clear. Keep our wits about us. We are less than fifteen minutes from the Yard. Once there, we can start into it, whatever it is. And watch out for those frigging cyclists, they seem to be the only ones who don't know what's going on. I've nearly killed two of them this morning already."

Imbeki saw Sharp was right. They were about two buses away from a set of lights just before a dog-leg bend on the road ahead them just where Vicarage Walk joins and turns into Battersea Bridge Road. As the light changed, a cyclist ahead of them, one of those crazy, courier types put his body and his bike between the two buses, then up the side of the lead bus. He cleared the front of it as the light changed again from green to amber, like a man possessed. Imbeki didn't care what anyone thought or said. If you were mad enough to cycle in central London you deserved every near-death experience you got... which, judging by the guy ahead of them, added up to a lot.

"Okay, we'll stay the course. Ring us if the guvnor comes back."

The line went dead, and Young looked sideways at his companion.

"We have to make like Curtis Mayfield," offered Imbeki by way of reply.

"What?"

"Guv says, 'Keep on keepin' on'."

Young put the car in gear and followed behind the bus, which made it through the lights, but they changed too quickly to red and he didn't want to hop the junction. It would have meant leaving Sharpy and the Luton van behind.

He glanced into his mirror and had a reflexive thought that he immediately forgot as soon as he had it: *no cyclist there now*.

Danny's inspiration had come from the words of Harkness. An uncomfortable thought, but still the truth. He had told Danny that he would be his "chaos".

Chaos.

Despite all his bullshit philosophical warbling, Danny wondered if Harkness knew where the word had come from; the Greeks used it to describe a gaping void, or more precisely, the gaping void before the creation of the universe. What Danny suspected was a better word for Harkness was crisis, which the Greeks used firstly to describe the turning point in a medical condition or disease.

Danny had needed to create a turning point, one that would turn this situation in his favour, or at least the circumstance and context within which he could steal this money. And as for Harkness, disease was a fitting word to describe him in Danny's mind.

Radio 5 Live was now feverishly spewing out the rolling news' version of the chain of unfolding events. They were simultaneously offering conjecture with the odd scrap of fact and dressing them up as both.

In his ear, Danny was hearing tales of fireballs over the M25, commuters caught in panicked crushes and emergency services struggling to keep up. There were flying flaming cars at Heathrow and a train derailing just as it reached its destination of Waterloo.

So far, Danny had tried to sequester any thoughts of the human casualties that would result from his plan, but even he could see now the collateral damage was unavoidable. But as he listened to the radio, he became sure that there had been way more live devices than he had ordered.

"Big Man Boom..."

Ciaran looked at him.

"Wha?"

"How crazy is your man, Enda?"

"When you say crazy, what do you mean? He's spent a life hating the Brits and thinking up ways to blow them the fuck up..."

"I think he may have taken up his role this morning with more gusto than I required."

"Huh? I thought we were only going to mean business with one or two. The rest were for show and panic."

Danny handed the radio earpiece to his wing man.

After a moment's intent listening, Ciaran turned, wide eyed, his face paling.

"Jesus, Mary, and Joseph. What has that fucker done?

Danny wanted to disappear. Withdraw from this fame obsessed, unjust and unbalanced, so-called society. And one big job, one like this, could make that happen for him. A sum of money that could magic him away to somewhere warm and balmy, where Amazon delivered movies by Wi-Fi and the drinks were funky colours and always came with little umbrellas. That would do for Danny. And all he had to do to get there was to pull this job and put Harkness back in his place. Not such a small picture to paint, but one worth attempting.

His biggest job ever. His masterpiece. And if you are going to paint on a canvas as huge and dramatic as London, then he realised his primary colour would have to be red. But not anywhere near as much as seemed to be splashed all over the streets this morning. He felt sick.

And at that thought, in a burst of yellow hi-vis jacket and speed that would have been more appropriate from a moped than a pushbike, a courier cyclist came around the bend of the dog leg corner. He raised his arm above his head, pumping it in the air once, twice, three times and then he was gone as quickly as he appeared.

"Three waves. The target is three vehicles behind whatever comes 'round that corner next."

No time to think about anything else. They were about to move forward. The job was on. Ciaran pulled his mask down over his face. Danny tightened the bandana he was wearing around his nose, mouth, and chin. He reached down between his feet in the cab of the truck and grabbed a cowboy hat, screwing it firmly onto his head. Lastly, he double-checked that his seat belt was securely fastened. Were the pair of sawn-off shotguns safely wedged into the adapted carpenter's tool belt cinched around his waist? The answers to both were "yes". A bus was coming into view, followed by a second. Ciaran and Danny didn't realise it, but they were both holding their breath.

Harkness was being a good boy. He was doing what he was told. He stood in his apartment, naked and newly awake, overlooking what was once Highbury Stadium. But he wasn't ruminating on the footballing glory of Arsenal Football Club. Harkness was listening intently. He had put his television on as soon as he had the call on his mobile, and now he was taking in the stream of consciousness that twenty-four-hour news traded as reportage. He always marvelled at how minutiae and speculation was presented as crucial fact. The ever-hungry monster of airtime to fill and not a lot of truth to fill it made for a strange mistress within an industry that once prided itself on reporting the truth at all costs. To his mind, journalism was now nothing more than entertainment. A sport just as much as the one that used to be played out on the grass below. Who could get the next nugget of possible fact first? Which channel could find an eyewitness that no one else has? Eye-witless was more like it most of the time, though.

And so, it was now. A delivery driver who had narrowly avoided a fireball on the M4 was repeatedly answering the staccato questions of a reporter with the mantra that comprised of nothing more than "I thought I would die" and "It was like something from a film. I can't get my bruvver on the phone." The line of investigation was quickly becoming circular but that didn't deter the reporter or her bosses from their persistence.

What was most definitely true though was that Big Man Boom had put his gifts to devastating use. Action? Christ, there was plenty of action.

Harkness turned to face the television. The graphic scrolling at the foot of the screen carried the all-important bullet point headlines. Multiple explosions across London. At least thirty-three dead and hundreds injured. The city in lockdown, and the mobile phone signal suspended across the central parts of the city. Emergency services were at full stretch. The public were advised not to travel into or around London. Other cities of the UK and indeed Europe had been placed on high alert. It was a suspected major terrorist event.

The ticker then started to repeat itself and Harkness tuned it out.

"Terrorist event."

Misdirection more like. Sleight of hand.

Harkness laughed. A chuckle at first, growing to a giggle, ending in a gale of his own laughter. He had to set his coffee cup down for fear of spilling it or burning his own privates if he wasn't careful.

He had challenged Danny Felix to write his own moment in London history. If he could pull off this robbery, he would be etching his name big among the capital's criminal elite. But with his intervention, this job wouldn't write Danny's name in the history books, more like it would tear it up and piss on it. All to nick a few quid.

What a legend. What a fucking legend.

Harkness laughed again. Gently this time as he approached the low-set bed in the middle of the room. Watching the form under the duvet stir at the sound of his amusement, a whisper of red hair on the pillow, the slender calf protruding from one corner.

Harkness grasped the ankle, firmly at first, but then more tenderly, running his hand slowly up under the covers, finding what he was looking for, achieving the response he wanted.

"Wakey, wakey, love. It's another beautiful day in the big city. We ought to start it as we mean to go on..."

~

It's fucking agony when you bite your own tongue practically in two.

Charles Imbeki regrettably knew this to be a fact, because that is exactly what he did when the huge dumper truck struck the front side of the Mondeo.

The force of the vicious jolt caused Imbeki to be flung forward, his seatbelt arresting his progress felt like hitting a brick wall, his tongue involuntarily pushed between his teeth as the wind was knocked out of him, only for his jaw to be

269

wrenched firmly shut as his body slammed back into the seat. An airbag added insult and further injury to an already nasty turn of events. It was at that point that his tongue gave way to the force, his blood exploding in his mouth with a coppery taste just as his nerve ends did their duty and communicated the pain signals to his brain at highspeed.

Young didn't fare much better, but the fact that his seatbelt was fastened more snugly across his solar plexus meant it winded him. His fight to inhale sent his tongue backward, not forward. Needless to say, he didn't come away unscathed. The impact whipped the steering wheel all the way to the right, dislocating his left thumb and breaking his right index finger. The next gift was the shower of windscreen shatter that found his face before his airbag could go off. Like a volley of buckshot to his eyes, he caught multiple fragments in both, the world turning an excruciating watery red as the car settled back onto its suspension after the initial brutal, sideswipe, a wrecking ball of a blow. Finally, the popping noise that he had heard go off in his head wasn't actually the airbag but the music of his own body, as his right shoulder tore free from its ligaments, dislocating like a lid being flicked off a tube of Pringles. A red-hot knife of pain shot through his body as he crashed back into his driving seat, pressing the shoulder joint into the socket where it should have been but couldn't actually fit into anymore.

They hadn't seen the truck until it was on them. A hurtling metal weapon, swatting them as efficiently as one might stop a fly from hitting one's face.

Ciaran had judged his take-off perfectly. As soon as the cyclist had ridden past them, he held the big truck on the bite of its clutch. He could feel the power of the big fuck off vehicle beneath his touch like a wild horse trying to break free. All he had to do was release that clutch at precisely the right moment. Then they would be up over the brow of the little boat ramp that led down to the Thames. Up over into the narrow road, stopping anyone and anything that might be there... an unmarked police convoy perhaps.

Ciaran screamed as they took off. "JesusMotherFucking-HolyShitFuck!"

He had executed the collision perfectly. The crunching impact with the Ford Mondeo felt as satisfying as landing a punch on the point of a jaw at the moment of maximum effect. When you struck that kind of blow, you instantly knew that this part of the fight was won. He had a hard-on the size of Westminster Cathedral and a snarling smile plastered across his face to match. Not that anyone could see that beneath his mask (or trousers), but he knew they were both there.

"Jaysus, but I love my fucking job," was his cry, for anyone who could hear.

Danny was out of the door of the truck as soon as the smash-tinkle-tinkle had stopped. He had to jump away from the massive vehicle as Ciaran had already thrown it into reverse, pulling it away from the wrecked car. Danny knew he was making sure they could still drive it. They would need to be out of here in the next three minutes. If they were too entangled, the job would be simply fucked. However, the motion of the big dumper reassured him that the stolen juggernaut had been well chosen and more than fit for purpose.

Danny made straight for the Luton Van. It was directly behind the Mondeo with its brakes slamming on hard, tires sending the dark delicious smell of burnt rubber in the air. Too little, too late. It rear-ended the Ford. Poor bastard Imbeki coughed a lump of his tongue onto his own chest at this point.

Danny was sprinting.

The act of braking had sent Sharp's mobile phone and rover radio into the footwell of his cab. He was thrown forward, the seatbelt doing its job, but his impact was much less than the car in front meeting the truck. His airbag didn't go off, a blessing to his nose, and also to Danny. It would be easier to get this done if he could pull the driver and snatch the keys out of the van as fast as fuck.

By the time Danny had leapt over the roof of the Mondeo using the rear tire to leg him up to reach the driver's side of the van, Sharp was coming to terms with what was happening. Although it all looked more than a little surreal, a construction truck had just stopped his colleagues dead. He had then smacked into the back of them and suddenly someone who looked like 'Jesse frigging James', complete with Stetson, was coming at him, from the driver's side. As the cowboy yanked the door open, he pulled a pair of sawn-offs out of what looked like holsters. Sharpy suddenly had a lot of gun in his face.

Did this fucking nutcase just scream: "Stick 'em up, pardner!"

CHAPTER 35
SAVING THE PLANET

WITHIN HALF AN HOUR OF THE FIRST EXPLOSION TWO DIFFERENT militant Islamist groups had claimed responsibility for the whole damn show. Not that they were responsible... or Islamist. It suited their own insane misanthropic agendas.

This was exactly as Danny had planned. There was nothing like the vanity of a bunch of madmen to help misdirect investigations even if it was only for a few hours. But those few hours were all he and his crew needed. They were more than enough to get the show on the road.

And the show was going like clockwork.

The cop in the Luton van was wise enough to play ball. He allowed Danny to plant him face down across the seats of the cab while he wound insulation tape around his hands at his own back, then his ankles and finally around his eyes. Danny then picked up the police rover and the mobile phone off the floor of the van.

Three men leapt out of the back of the huge dump truck and lined up in formation, making up the middle and end of a human chain. It was completed by Ciaran and Danny after they had finished with their tape and the coppers in both vehicles.

They formed the chain running from the Luton to the back of the dump truck. They then played the world's richest game of pass the parcel, taking the packets filled with money out of the van and ferrying them into the rear of the dumper. The whole operation took less than five minutes, by which time a few pedestrians and a smattering of cars had come upon the scene. Everyone acted sensibly though, the sawn offs at Danny's waist enough to inspire timidity. Danny could see them reaching for their mobiles to dial 999 for the police, but again his foresight proved correct. The bombs had forced a shutdown of the mobile signal, hadn't they? Even if they wanted to report the crime, they couldn't and those in the flats adjacent found that when they tried their landlines, the emergency number was constantly engaged. Not that it mattered. Even if the reports got through, there simply weren't enough police available to respond.

Once the transfer was complete, they jumped back into the dumper truck.

Ciaran could feel the heat of excitement rising in his chest. It was a result of the huge adrenalin rush he felt as soon as he had put the truck into gear for the initial impact. He also knew that when the job was done that adrenalin rush would be replaced by an almost inescapable exhaustion. But for now, fuck, he felt good.

Danny was in the same mindset, elated that they were climbing back into the truck having not had to put anyone, cop or bystander, down with the sawn offs. And while he could hear siren after siren in the distance, he was fairly sure they weren't coming for them.

Ciaran, still wearing his mask, put the great truck into gear and pulled away from the wreckage of the Mondeo. He drove up on the little sliver of pavement on the right-hand side to navigate their way past the small knot of cars that arrived on the scene. Danny couldn't resist a tip of his cowboy hat at the staring public, about twelve people in all, as they passed them on the dog-leg corner. He reckoned that if he had been chewing tobacco, he could have spat on one of them like Eastwood in The Outlaw Josey Wales... but no sense in leaving unnecessary DNA at the scene of a crime.

They were retracing the route the money van had already taken, driving back towards Wandsworth. As they did so, with their precious cargo on board, the peloton of cyclists appeared alongside them. This time their numbers were a little larger. Danny watched them materialise behind the truck, telling Ciaran they were all there, present, and correct. And among them was Howler. Even with his disguise on, his helmet pulled low, Danny recognised him. He saw the slight wave of the hand, the acknowledgement that the next part of the process was about to kick in.

At that point, London was treated to another surreal sight. The bike team now formed an orderly line across the rear of the truck, maintaining speed along with the lumbering workhorse. One by one, each cyclist went forward, gripping onto the back of the truck, using its momentum to pull them forward. This allowed them to sit upright in their saddles for an instant, taking their other hand off the handlebars long enough to receive a backpack stuffed full of cash from inside the rear of the dumper.

Then it was a super-fast sling over the shoulder and a let go, some of them pulling away and going left, some right and others doubling back, returning from where the truck had come.

Dispersing.

Two of them had to take a couple of goes at the tricky manoeuvre, but they managed it. Danny was watching all this from the side mirror, breathing out as the last rider pulled away from the rear. Another part of Danny's plan was completed. No sense, he thought, in rocking up to the industrial unit with the entire twenty-two million for Harkness to drool over. And anyway... why would you expect a master thief to do as he was told?

"Done and dusted?" Ciaran said, now looking at Danny.

"Yep... at least some of the cash is safely away. Now, let's rendezvous."

Smugglers Way. A perfect place for the last act. First, it actually served their purpose well, a side street in Wandsworth right off the main road. Blink and you could miss any vehicle turning into it. Second, it was populated by some drab industrial units and a huge council-run domestic waste site. And third? Smugglers Way, for fuck's sake. It was too delicious. The clue was in the name.

Ciaran guided the truck into the dead-end street, marvelling again at how light the traffic was, and how Danny's huge gambit had paid off. As he made the turn, he couldn't help but look at the McDonald's drive thru. Wouldn't that have been the ultimate 'fuck you' to the Met?

Nodding to the fast-food joint. "Jaysus, I could murder one of those now. Can you imagine? 'Yes, Officer, they pulled in at about half six. There were five of them. I knew they were desperate men, they all ordered black coffee with their sausage McMuffins. That and one of them was dressed like Woody from Toy Story, cowboy hat and all.' Funny, what you think about as you're committing the crime of the century."

But Danny's face was grim.

"How many has he killed, Ciaran? What have we done here?"

They drove down Smugglers Way just far enough to be hidden from the main junction, but also not so far that they would be seen on the CCTV cameras around the waste site.

Waiting there were two parked vehicles. One a car, the other a small white van. The five of them leapt out, repeating the unloading and loading job they had just executed earlier. Only this time they were even quicker because there was less, and also as they were desperate to get the job done now. The remaining money went into the white van. The three who had ridden in the back of the truck stripped to their underpants, flinging their clothes into the back of the dumper, reaching into the waiting car and fishing out new clothes. Once dressed in what made them look like painters and decorators in overalls, they climbed into the car, each of them now carrying a money packet.

"Don't spend it all in the one shop now, lads... or should I say the one strip club, ya dirty hoo'ers." Ciaran laughed at them through the driver's window as they prepped to drive off. Danny just nodded at the driver.

"Thanks, lads."

A broad Belfast accent replied: "Sure it was wee buns. A pleasure doing bizness with ya, mucker. Hope you get the rest to your piggy bank safe now, like." And they drove off.

Ciaran and Danny did the strip, staying close to the dumper as they did so, pulling on a change of clothes from the white van.

"Are you good to go?"

Ciaran nodded back, smiling eagerly at his fellow thief.

"Aye, now, ready to fucking rock. I'll just move this into the recycling centre, flick the switch on Big Enda's bit of gear... sure, Danny, did ya not realise we were saving the planet? I'm going to recycle this here rig and then later I'm going to help you recycle that money we just nicked."

"Saving the planet... but what about Enda? We'll have to deal with that."

Ciaran's expression turned grim. "Leave that to me..."

"Just let me know where he is when you find him."

"No Danny, I recommended him. I brought him in. I feel like he's mine."

A look of understanding passed between them.

"Okay, Ciaran. See you as planned. Keep your head down until then."

Danny finished by throwing the police rover and mobile into the dump truck.

Ciaran checked that the bicycle was where he had left it, chained to the fence farther down the street on Smugglers Way. It was. He jumped up into the cab of the dump truck and started up the huge engine. He then positioned the truck so that once he jumped out of the cab, he would be mostly shielded from the centre's CCTV cameras by its bulk. Just before he jumped out, he reached under the driver's seat, between his own legs, flicking the switch on the timer.

He vaguely wondered if he should have been concerned that he had spent the whole drive sitting on top of enough industrial Semtex to take out a whole street.

As he rode away on his bike, Ciaran heard the blast clearly enough. He imagined it as he pushed himself away from the scene. All those tin cans, reams of newspaper and wine bottles flying through the air, along with the charred remains of their clothes and the truck they had so profitably used to stop a Ford Mondeo.

I tell ya. We're saving the world, he thought...

CHAPTER 36
SETTLING DUST

Danny was satisfied with the way London's systems had reacted to his plan.

To say that the city had been "thrown for a loop" was equivalent to suggesting that the marriage of Prince Charles and Lady Diana had been a tad unsettled. The chain of events that Danny had foreseen in his mind all came to pass. Like dominoes, each development had knocked the next one into place.

There were instantaneous raids. Specialist police units crashed hostels, flats, and flophouses in every corner of London and its outskirts. Every suspected nutjob preacher, acolyte, internet militia man, bedroom blogger and blind follower was on the end of the policeman's knock. It began to resemble some kind of bizarre pilgrimage to London's holding cells, with every stripe of militant religious mad dog all being slung in together until such times as alibis could be checked, questions asked, and flats and laptops searched to within an inch of their very existence. The process of bagging their hands while awaiting forensic swabbing for traces of explosive, gunshot residue or even so much as a smidgen of fertilizer under the fingernails slowed the process the most.

There was a huge influx of journalists and commentators from all over the world, all piling in to cover the 'Shutdown of London'.

In the following days it seemed that the streets carried more TV crews and international news correspondents than actual inhabitants. The populace seemed reluctant to trust that the authorities really had the situation back under control.

In the midst of all the clamour, Danny's team managed to reach their respective hideouts easily. This had been another facet of Danny's thinking. With the exception of himself in the white van and the three loading boys, everyone else had departed the scene of their deeds on push bikes.

To say that the police would not be looking for modern day highwaymen on bicycles would be an understatement. They were simply too busy.

But Danny knew this hiatus was very much a temporary one. The forensic geeks would soon do their work. The explosives used by Big Enda would, ultimately, be traceable. And it wouldn't take forever to see that most of the part-time terrorists had solid alibis.

The clock was still ticking. Danny's escape route was part of the plan. He knew where he would go, and how he would get there.

Except there was Enda, first, and then Harkness to deal with, plus the small matters of Dexy, the money and some payback.

As he made his way to his own refuge, Danny also carried out a few minor chores. A few little bits of preparation. Ciaran may have thought that the morning had been the 'big show', but Danny had always felt it was only the ticket to the 'big show.' That evening would bring the 'main event'. Anyone in their right mind wouldn't want to miss it.

∼

Barnes Police Station was like a ghost ship when Christine arrived. Her shock compounded as she heard the reports of what was taking place around the city. Almost all personnel had been summoned to other duties, like rodeo cowboys gathered to throw a rope around every wild horse in the land. She worked her way through the empty locker room and ground floor offices.

It took a few minutes of wandering around until she was beckoned up into the back of the squad room, to Collinson's office. It was the sweet caress of cigarette smoke that drew her upstairs, like a beacon from another time. The heady aroma at first seemed entirely normal, like background noise, until Christine finally computed that it was her boss, despite the fact that it had been forbidden to smoke indoors anywhere in Britain since 2007.

The boss was asleep. Feet on the desk, a cigarette burning between his fingers, an open bottle of Bell's whisky on his desk, a good eight inches missing from it.

"Guv?"

She said it gently at first, like she was waking a sleeping child. She then realised that she wasn't waking a kid. Her boss was blind drunk while London burned.

Another "Guv", then a kick of the table to accompany the greeting awakened Collinson. Startled he sat bolt upright, instinctively flicked the cigarette away from himself, a glowing ember still managing to singe a perfect circular hole in his tie.

"What the... Chance? Fucking Chance."

"Guv, what are you doing? Do you know what's happening out there?"

It took Collinson a few seconds to meet her gaze. His eyes

looked like they needed rounding up and pointing in the right direction and it wasn't an easy job.

"Of course, I fucking know," spat back Collinson. Literally, flecks of saliva hitting his desk.

"Guv, you were asleep...or fucks know what. Have you heard about Freeth?"

"It's all a fucking mess. The whole thing, burning down round me. Just burning."

"Do you know that Freethy is in hospital? He's in intensive care! I need to ask you a few things. Do you think you can sit up to answer?"

"The world has just gone mad, luv, just fucking mad. Who would blame anyone? Eh? Who would?"

"Who would blame anyone for blowing up the city? Sir, is that what you are saying?"

"What? No, no, no, I'm talking about the rest of it. The other fucking shite that is going to land right here." Collinson pounded the top of his own desk and then reached for the bottle, but CC got there first, sliding it a few inches away from him.

"What did you do? Is this to do with Harkness? Guv?"

Collinson's head snapped up at the mention of that name. His rheumy eyes tried their best to harden. He started to cough, then he managed to stifle it.

"I knew you would work it out. Part... part of me hoped you would."

The rapid truth now, tumbling out in Collinson's drink-laced words.

"He had me. That fucking bastard had me. You have to know that. They have to know it. He had me. What could I do? They were going to do me over. No pension. No fucking life after I gave them mine. How could I tell my Mrs. that? What would my girls think of their dad then? But he said he could make it go away. All I had to do was help him..."

Christine couldn't believe what she heard, but at the same time she could. All the pieces -- the letter handed to her by the nurse, Freethy, Fisty, Iggy, and now Collinson. And worst of all herself.

What a fucking joke. She had run round London as a bag carrier for Harkness. She had been gathering the money into one handy place. Harkness had a finger in every bit of this, even to the extent of manipulating Collinson... possibly even hastening her daughter's end.

"Guv, the money?"

Collinson just shook his head. "Gone already." Collinson reached the bottle this time, not bothering with the glass, tilting it straight to his mouth. Then he started to cry, babbling in between the sobs about his life and career. How he was a good copper, bending the odd rule, kicking the odd arse, but never anything like this.

"In for a fucking penny, in for a pound. They make you feel like a fucking criminal. You might as well act like one."

"We'll get him. We'll get this cleared up. You just need to tell me a few things, that's all. A few details and we can get this settled."

Collinson looked at her, sat back, and really looked at her.

"Settled? Are you fucking mad, luv? After today, it'll take a long time for the dust to settle in London... a long fucking time."

CC hadn't seen the gun. It was wedged under Collinson's crotch, but by the time it was swung up and under her old guvnor's chin, it was too late to do anything. It was too late to try to launch herself across the desk, knock the pistol out of his hand, stop him in any way she could.

The shot went off and CC's ears went dead. The bullet caught Collinson under the soft part of his throat, travelling up through his mouth into his brain, laying waste to tissue, veins, arteries, and all in its path. It finally exited through the top of his skull, punching a flap the size of a fist in the top of the old cop's head. A vivid splash of blood, flesh and brain coated the wall behind, like a rotten tomato crushed under foot.

Ciaran had little trouble locating Big Man Boom. Having been discovered pissed in a storeroom at work, he was driven home by one of his fellow workers, except he had insisted on being dropped off at The Spotted Dog pub.

All Ciaran had to do was wait. As the bomb expert emerged from the pub into the afternoon light, he carried a bottle-shaped brown paper package under his arm. It was a short walk to the storage unit, although it did take the Big Man a few goes to unlock the heavy door. Ciaran was close enough to hear the swearing, Enda's hangover causing him more than a little grief.

As he finally managed to open the door and went to step through, Ciaran strode quickly up behind Enda, using his momentum to push them both through the metal door.

Ciaran shut the door behind him, Enda staring at and then recognising the small ginger lad instantly.

"It's you, is it?"

"Ay, Big Man, tis."

Enda turned, walked over to his work bench, and plopped himself down into the battered old seat he kept behind it. He put his elbows on the bench, his face in his hands, running his fingers through his hair. "I couldn't pass up the opportunity."

"And why would that be, Enda?" asked Ciaran softly, the musical lilt to his Cork accent stronger than usual.

"All those times. All those jobs. We never really stuck it to them. And then, those fuckers, those slimy politician fuckers, they just gave in so that they could become respectable and fill their own bellies. Suddenly, none of it mattered. The Hunger Strikers, Bloody Sunday, the torture, the history. All fucking forgotten. Brushed under the carpet."

Ciaran slipped his hands into his pockets.

"But when they work it all out...when they realise that a Paddy finally made them pay, that there was at least still one Irishman willing to fight them, it will all be worth it."

"You're dead right, Enda. Chucky Ar La an' all that."

Enda nodded at this. "Our day will come... our day just did come. What made it even sweeter was that the extra explosives came from that fucking copper, Harkness."

"Is that right now? How'd that happen?"

"He just showed up. Where you're standing. Called me an artist, he did. I called him a bastard. But I took his Semtex, and I did what I do best."

"Went a bit further than we were expecting, Enda."

The Big Man looked up at Ciaran, reaching for the brown paper bag. He took the bottle of Jameson out of it, opened it, and took a long swallow.

"Ciaran."

"Yes?"

"Would you ever just get the fuck on with it and kill me. My work here is fucking done."

Ciaran did exactly as he was asked.

CHAPTER 37
A DOG HAVING HIS DAY

IT WAS GROWING DARK, THE LATE JUNE SUN FINALLY GIVING UP AND beginning to shrink in the inky city sky. The warehouse in west London was practically empty. Every shred of the crew's presence there had been carefully, meticulously disposed of. Ciaran put so much drain cleaner down the toilet that Danny suspected that there wouldn't be a rat left alive in Acton.

But now, the big space was exactly that, just a big, low-lit space except for a single chair right in the middle. Danny sat here. At his feet were piles and piles of packets.

Glancing at his watch, he was unsurprised to see the door in front of him open, just as the second hand brought itself and the others into line at twelve o'clock exactly. Midnight. Danny noted the lack of vehicle noise preceding this. Had they been parked for ages?

Harkness entered. Tall, imposing, almost swaggering, but seemingly alone. Danny knew that would definitely not be the case, watching as the big cop spread his arms expansively in front of him, a grin slicing across his face, the hands coming back together now. Harkness clapped.

"Fuck me, Danny Boy. You are the king of misdirection. I

mean, I knew you were good. I had high hopes and ambition for your endeavours, but you even made me feel... how would I describe it? Proud? Yes, that would be it, proud. Like a doting, fucking father."

Danny sat stone still. He watched Harkness move like a cat stalking a mouse, moving slowly towards the stacks of packages he so coveted.

"You knew that the crazies would jump in, claim your fine work as their own, give you the time and a little bit of room, didn't you? Fucking genius, Danny. I have to applaud that kind of chutzpah. Harry Truman once said that it's amazing what you can accomplish—"

Danny cut him off with the rest of the quote "If you don't care who gets the credit."

Harkness was stood opposite him now, ten feet away, smiling.

"Always full of the surprises, Danny. I am sure you have one cooked up for me right now. But first, business. I take it this is the fruit of our labours?"

Danny nodded, straining to hear beyond Harkness, listening for clues as to who was with him without looking like he was doing it.

"If you don't mind me saying so, Danny, that doesn't look much like twenty-two-point-four million to me. Have you had some tucked away?"

"I'm a thief, Harkness. Shake my hand and be sure to count your fingers after."

Danny's breathing was shallow. He could feel the heat rising in his body. The tension notched up in the space between the two of them. He could tell that Harkness was feeling it, too. He had shifted his standing position, ever so imperceptibly. Danny knew that Harkness was on his mettle, bracing, feeling ready, ready for... what?

"I'm offended, Danny. Did you think I would try to keep it all for myself? Cut you out? Are you suggesting I am not a gentleman of principle?"

"We're about to find out, I feel. When's Dexy going to show up? This is her game after all, isn't it?"

"Ahhh, Danny, Danny, Danny. People are not always what they seem. Are they? Bravo for working it out."

And at that, Danny heard the unmistakably expensive click-clack of high heels. His eyes snapped to the doorway as a vision of cascading, red hair sat atop a beautifully tailored double-breasted dark suit stepped into the big room.

"Hello, gorgeous. Did you miss me?"

Her lipstick was blood red and flawless, her hands deep in the pockets of the jacket, making the neckline plunge a little further than it should, giving just an extra hint of her outrageous sense of style and glamour. Especially as she wasn't wearing a blouse underneath the jacket.

"I want to thank you, Danny Darling. You have exceeded even my expectations. When James first came to me with his... little plan, I knew you would be the only man who could pull it off."

It had all started to stack up for him a few days earlier. How else could Harkness have come into his life? Who else could have talked about Danny, pointed him out for this kind of work, given so much detail so as to gain just exactly the right amount of leverage? It could only have been the one person he would never have suspected. Dexy.

"So, this is what it feels like to be the set-up-to-fall guy, then?"

"New experiences make us better men, Danny," chuckled Harkness.

Dexy joined in. "Oh, darling, that's not the way to look at it. After all, every great musician needs to play on an equally fabulous instrument... and you made London yours. It was a virtuoso performance. But now, for your encore darling, where's the rest of my money?"

Dexy took her hands out of her pockets, revealing a beautifully crafted one-shot Derringer handgun, pointing it squarely at Danny's head. This was Harkness's cue, which he took gleefully. He closed the space between him and Danny smartly, one big hand encircling Danny's throat with an axe man's grip, the other giving his balls the same, unwelcome treatment. Harkness pulled Danny up out of the chair, up off his feet, dangling him in mid-air as though he were nothing more than bothersome child.

"Darling, I have gone to a lot of trouble in my life," Dexy continued. "I have built up my club from nothing to what it is today, the venue of choice for the most respectable and unrespectable people of their generations. I have made sacrifices and I have made compromises. But this job is my cherry on top. It may have been your finest work, Danny, but it is my job. You want to live. I know you do. You like fine bourbon, expensive and beautiful women, and most of all you love the thrill of the steal. You want to live, so I know you will tell me where the rest of the money is."

Harkness loosened his grip a touch on Danny's throat, allowing him to take in some much-needed air. It allowed him to speak, even as he felt that his balls were about to be ripped off.

"It's mine. I designed the job. My team pulled it. Our balls were on the line...This is the only way I could guarantee our share. As for the rest...Go fuck yourselves. You screwed with the job; you pushed the IRA man over the edge. You have painted this city in unnecessary blood."

Harkness rearranged his grip on Danny's neck, hissing into his ear as he did so.

"Fuck this city. It's all about the money, Danny. What do you think I spent my time doing in the Sandbox, eh? I wasn't making tea for the ragheads. I was squeezing their deepest fucking secrets out of them. I will afford you the benefit of that experience and it will not go easy for you. I will know where the money is. You. Will. Tell."

The last three words were each underlined with a twist of his lower hand, sending shards of hot pain up into Danny's guts.

At that moment Ciaran came crashing through the unit's suspended ceiling.

The plan had been a simple one. Ciaran was to secrete himself up there, in a section which they had reinforced to take his weight. When the time was right, he was to put a bullet squarely in the middle of the forehead of whoever deserved it first, which hopefully would have been Harkness.

Sadly, when Ciaran fell through the ceiling, he was not alone. One of the Harkness crew came with him. In a bit of luck, Ciaran landed on top of Harkness's man, using him as a gym mat, protecting himself from the concrete below. The heavy didn't move after landing, given that his head had taken most of the brunt of the impact.

At the same time, Ciaran's chunky desert eagle pistol went off, the impact of the fall triggering the shot accidentally. The bullet ricocheted around the warehouse, filling the air with the bittersweet smell of gunpowder.

Instinctively, Harkness dropped to one knee. He let Danny go as he did so, giving Danny the time to barrel-roll back up onto his feet. Before Harkness could stand upright, Danny's right boot connected with the side of his face, laying him flat out. Danny leapt onto the big cop's barrel of a chest, gripping his hands around Harkness's head, thrusting his thumbs into the eye sockets, and pushing down with full force, trying to make a path to the back of the bastard's skull. Harkness was bucking like a wild stallion, fighting to shift Danny's weight off him, struggling to loosen the grip tightening around his head.

Ciaran, meanwhile, had recovered his gun and his balance, firing twice beyond Dexy to take out the two heavies who were bundling into the warehouse. Thinking he was firing at her, Dexy flung herself to the side to avoid the shots.

Harkness was now bellowing like an injured animal. Danny could feel the big man gathering his strength for one last almighty push back into the fight. Danny knew he couldn't allow that to happen, so he changed tack. He shifted his weight, smacking Harkness's head on the concrete as he did so, enjoying the crack as it hit the floor. He then stood to a sideways position and brought the full weight of his body, knees first, down onto Harkness's throat. He felt the windpipe crush as he did so, most of the fight going out of the man in that instant.

Suddenly Danny was pitched forward by a blow to the back of his skull, delivered by another of Harkness's crew, summoned into the room by the sound of Ciaran's gunshots.

There followed an eerie moment of stillness in the room. Danny managed to climb to his feet, despite the hot sticky flow of blood that crept down his neck and the dizziness that went with it. The only sound in the room was that of Harkness, dry clicks emitting from his mouth as he struggled to get air into his lungs, his boy trying to roll him onto his side in the recovery position.

Danny saw that he and Dexy had been joined by two other heavies, both holding Ciaran, plus the one attending to the big cop.

"Are you quite finished with the macho nonsense, darling?"

Dexy was looking at him like one might look at an errant

child who had just delivered his parents a school report that was less than glowing.

"Danny, the money was never yours, my love. The job wasn't even yours. If letting you live is not reward enough, I don't know what is. We have disposed of every major stumbling block in our way, especially the ones that might have stopped you from doing such a fine job across this city of ours."

"Dexy, you're just like Harkness. You both think you glide on a cushion of free air. Your arrogance is your weakness."

"Darling, being able to do the things we do is not arrogance, it's merely talent. Force of will, vision some people call it. You either have it or you don't."

"Yes, Dexy, but you have to factor in uncertainty, happenstance, even Harkness's favourite: chaos. They all play a role. You have to think of it all as a system. You know the expression; every dog has its day?"

Dexy looked at him, curiosity brewing in her eyes.

"Today, that's what I am. A dog having his day."

And with that, the room exploded into noise and movement. About twenty cops came into the space. Through the doors. Through a section of the prefab wall that Danny and Ciaran loosened earlier. Loads of the fuckers, the leads carrying automatic rifles, shouting for everyone to get down on their knees, hands behind their heads. They were followed by plainclothes men in little police caps, checked strips down the side of them. Some had their warrant badges strung round their necks, some of them armed with handguns and some not.

Dexy roared like a banshee. For a second, she actually considered firing off her one-shot Derringer in Danny's direction. However, as she raised the deadly little gun one of the cops calmly put a shot squarely through her clavicle. The bullet went 'through and through', clanging off a steel girder in the opposite wall. She screamed, crumpling to the floor, and commencing a tantrum fit of pure rage and frustration. Her whole body thrashed as she beat the floor with her feet and one good hand, snarling, screaming, bitching like a thing possessed.

Christine Chance entered the room just behind the armed officers. She made a beeline for Harkness, rolling him onto his back, frantically checking for a pulse as the others busied themselves with the heavies. It was obvious that the thugs were professionals, no resistance was given once the cops entered the equation. They were resigned to the awful knowledge that they were well and truly fucked.

Finally, CC crossed over to where Danny was standing, watching it all. She had to usher away one of the plainclothes men preparing to cuff the thief.

"I'll look after this one."

Danny exhaled, long and low. Breathing normally for the first time in what seemed like a lifetime, but in reality, had only been a few short weeks.

"What's your name?" CC looked into his eyes, thinking the man in front of her looked like he'd done ten rounds with Tyson.

"No, sorry, Detective Chance. That is not how this is going to work."

"It will eventually. Is the money all there?"

Again, Danny shook his head, looking almost sorrowful about it.

"Jesus, not you as well. Everyone seems to be obsessed with the fucking cash. Like I said, Detective, that is not how this is going to end."

"And why would that be?"

"What time is it?"

Christine was puzzled but she felt that she was indebted to this guy. She knew he had made the call. He had invited them here. He had given her the opportunity to get Harkness in a room. She could find the answers she needed about this whole fucking mess. And once she had those answers? Who knew?

CC looked at her watch.

"12:25."

"Okay. You and your colleagues have, I think, three minutes to leave."

"What?"

Danny brought the small switch out of his pocket; it looked like something you would open an automatic garage door with. He purposefully pressed the button at the centre of it and the room was filled with a hissing noise and the sudden smell of butane.

CC's eyes widened and she yelled for the cops to fall back. The others clocked the smell of the gas as she did so. There was a scramble for the exits.

Christine tried to keep hold of Danny as they exited, but it was a tall order in the confusion. That, plus the deft elbow to the side of the head that Danny adroitly delivered to her.

And suddenly, in the road leading to the unit, there was Ciaran. He was on a big Triumph Daytona, screeching to a halt by Danny, gathering him onto the bike. He gunned the engine and they took off like a firework. The big bike wobbled beneath them as he almost over-throttled it. He just managed to get it back under control as they shot out onto the A40 West Way and off into the night.

Instantly an explosion filled the night sky. It was exactly what Danny asked Big Enda to supply... all heat and flames, perfectly contained, pushing force, prefab, and roofing sheets up into the night air. The blast wave knocked a few of the cops off their feet, one taking a piece of sheet metal in his leg, but otherwise, it was all noise and light. Enough to scare the shit out of anyone, but not enough to wipe them out.

CC stood open-mouthed. Her amazement deepened when

she realised that the bits of paper floating in the air all around her weren't all twenty-pound notes. Only some were. The majority were blank pieces of paper. She blew air out of her cheeks and said the only thing that she could manage.

"Fuck me, you're good."

And as he and Ciaran raced up the divided highway, wind rushing past his ears and through his hair, Danny couldn't resist the urge, screaming as they flew past the light traffic around them. "Harkness, you fucker... I'm alive!!!!!"

CHAPTER 38
TWENTY-EIGHT DAYS LATER

THE CAT! THE CAT! THE FUCKING CAT!

Barry Blount was awakened, yet again, by the fucking cat. It wasn't even his. It just showed up one day, about a year earlier, decided it liked the look of the place and moved in. It regularly terrorised him out of bed in the mornings with demands for food, water, or just the game of 'you try to ignore me and I excavate your forehead with my claws'.

Barry took a look at his bedside clock. It was nine a.m. He had already fed the frigging cat an hour earlier. What was its problem? Then Barry heard the buzzer go at his door, a long-held buzz, like it might not have been the first go.

Barry shuffled to the front of the flat, opening up to find another cycle courier. It was the third one this week. Barry accepted the packet, heavier than the last couple, signed for it and mumbled his thanks.

"Shit! Nine a.m."

He'd just remembered. Holy shit, he was due on location in the centre of London by eleven a.m. Today was a big day. The first day of filming on his new television series pilot. The show that was going to put Barry Blount back on the map, back up there on the Google pages and the covers of the magazines. *Barry's Brotherhood* was the show to do all that for him.

Okay, it was a self-funded pilot, but still, it was his big shot. You made your own luck in showbiz, and since he had come into a little money, he had to put it to the best use.

It had all been a blur since that day, that awful day in London a month earlier. The intruder he thought he dreamt up until he discovered his mobile was gone and then returned! The mystery man dumped a load of packages in Barry's flat. Gave him a load of printed labels and strict instructions of when to start sending them off, in the post. The address was some kind of P.O. box in America. Florida, by the looks of it. Barry had never been there. Didn't like the sound of it ever since he had watched re-runs of 'The Golden Girls'. It was a place Americans went to grow old and die. It must stink of pee and lavender.

He had started the process that week. And now, like the man had said, couriers were turning up with more packets and Barry was to use the extra labels to post those, too.

The man had given Barry an envelope, a big jiffy one, stuffed full of money. Told him there was more once he had sent on all the packages. All he had to do was post and promise not to look in the packets when they came. If he did, the man would know. He would come back again. And Barry didn't want that, did he? No, he didn't. People who could just come and go out of other people's homes as they pleased were not the type Barry wanted to see very often. It wasn't natural.

The money looked fabulous. He emptied the jiffy envelope onto his bed, and then rolled around on it. It made him feel dirty, in a good way.

And now, he was spending. Spending it wisely, or foolishly. A little ounce, or seven, wasn't so bad, was it?

"Right, better hit the shower... it's a big day, after all. Showbiz doesn't stand still for anyone..."

Celeste was puzzled. The police stopped by to ask her questions about her brother on five different occasions. They never once gave her an indication of where he might be or what they thought he might have done this time.

She was out of her mind with worry at first, but as the return visits mounted up, she resolved herself to being cross. *What has that useless brother roped us into now?*

Eventually her anger and worry subsided as the police questions stopped. She chilled out about it, especially as, despite all those visits and all those questions, not one of the investigators ever mentioned the money that showed up in her bank account. The money that Danny told her to not worry about and that she would be able to keep. The money that was going to pay for a sunroom on the back of her house. She felt sure Danny would show up when he wanted to...

Christine stood over Shauna's grave. The earth didn't look as fresh any longer, and the headstone had finally been ordered.

"Right, Little 'Un, time I was going. I think I will find out today. I hope to, anyway. I'm going to enjoy my time in a room with that bastard. They have finally finished all their top-level shit. Now I get my go. Don't worry, I'll be the officer you would want me to be, but I will get my answers, I promise. You try to rest now, Shauna. I'll see you at the weekend."

Christine stood, letting the breeze touch her face, breathing in the stillness of it all.

Stillness. Like the day London exploded and then, just as suddenly, fell silent. At a standstill. Just as CC's life came to a stop at the moment her daughter finally gave in. She would never forget the experience, the stillness as her only child breathed her last, as she took her leave and slipped away.

On reflection, it had been on her own terms, whether Harkness had intervened or not. Christine had been there. CC and her daughter, together, in the stillness. No one could ever rob either of them of that.

Her phone chirruped. It was Freethy's number. Hopefully his wife had news on her friend's progress.

"Hello, Agnes, give me the good news..."

She walked away.

~

It had been quite a journey but somehow, they managed it. Changing cars a couple of times, switching drivers, both of them shaving their hair off to put people off descriptions or CCTV footage.

At first, they laid low for a few days, both of them in a safe house Ciaran had arranged. Not going out, not taking any chances. After that they travelled to a remote part of Wales, where Ciaran had a fisherman friend. They took his boat overnight to Ireland, making land at the Ardglass Harbour.

From there they parted ways. Ciaran wanted to take his chances in the Old Country. There were places he knew in the southwest of Ireland where you could hide forever, no one ever asking awkward questions or wanting to know too much.

Danny kept going. He bribed his way onto a freighter headed to the Dominican Republic. Then after a few weeks' rest and a visit to a good passport man, he was off again. He made the short hop across to Florida, settling down in Islamorada in the Florida Keys.

Waiting for him there was a post box, stuffed full of packages. The postal worker behind the counter complained that there were so many he had begun to store them in a safe out back.

Danny apologized and made some excuse, being sure to let the old guy know that more were still to arrive. A healthy tip smoothed it all over.

Danny Felix's days were easy, long, and enjoyable. He got himself a little place right on the beach. He bought a modest boat and felt himself settle. He opened a quiet business of his own, taking tourists deep sea fishing off the Gulf coastline. The sun. He enjoyed the sun, sea and especially the sky at sundown. Danny liked to drink in the orange light of the evening sunset with an expensive bourbon in his hand, the smokey taste of it dancing on his tongue.

He could hide here. Secret himself away from the rest of the world. He could ignore what he loathed of his London life. Hide from prying eyes and uncomfortable questions, even the ones he was asking of himself. Yes, there was remorse. Too many lives were snuffed out after Big Man Boom went rogue. But Danny knew in his own heart that was as much a part of the chaotic system playing itself out as anything he might have inspired. He would have to deal with his own regret a little at a time.

He started growing his hair out, on both his head and his chin. He put on a little weight, formulating a backstory about himself that included a dotcom windfall and a desire to drop out. It wasn't such a big lie when you thought about it.

No doubt he was on all manner of wanted lists. Number one with a bullet on some of them. But he firmly believed that 'long runs the fox' and he was a fox with very long legs.

In the meantime?

Danny adored his solitude. But he began to take a strange enjoyment in meeting the people who turned up at his door wanting to catch some fish and drink a few beers out on the

Gulf of Mexico. Amazon delivered a decoder so he could stream movies and more, straight to his TV in his little bedroom, all paid for with a credit card he purloined from a particularly drunken, obnoxious businessman.

But what Danny loved most was the stillness. When he was alone on the boat, out on the Gulf, feeling the craft gently shift under him, the sound of water lapping against the sides, his face tilted to the heavens, he breathed in the stillness.

Danny had time.

His Time. Uninterrupted.

COMING SOON

COMING SUMMER 2023

BOOK 2 IN THE DANNY FELIX SERIES .

THE UNHOLY HOURS
*IF YOU'RE GOING TO STEAL FROM THE CARTEL
STEAL SMART....*

ACKNOWLEDGMENTS

As with every creative endeavour, this book has been helped by many hands and minds.

Firstly, let me thank the fabulous KT Forster, who knocked the myriad 'Irishisms' out of my prose when needed, and gave much encouragement.

My sister Josephine deserves credit for always inspiring me to write and Maggie at Chorleywood Bookshop, who was generous with both her time and comments after reading the early versions.

Gratitude also goes to my agent and dear friend, Liz Nealon, who encouraged me to scale the London Interrupted mountain one last time and for all the right reasons. It's worth losing a few games of 'Words with Friends' for that kind of wisdom and help!

There was some incredible help with authenticity, especially with the tricky business of making my coppers act and sound like Old Bill. My gratitude goes to Detective Chief Inspector Sarah Staff, Detective Inspector Caroline Clooney and Detective Inspector Keeley Smith. I now know what to do if I drop my bullets down a toilet...

But my most thorough cop collaborator was Detective Constable Mark Freeth (Ret'd) who bravely battled through every draft and kept me focused when my imagination was getting out of control! I owe him at least one tin of Lupaloid...

And last, but never least, a huge debt of gratitude and love to my wife, Helen Jane, who put up with four a.m. writing bursts. She kept my chin up when I couldn't face another re-write and always told me not to focus on how far I have to go, but rather on how far I had already come.

J.A. Marley

Printed in Great Britain
by Amazon

39500026R00179